Dick Francis

# RISK

PAN BOOKS

First published in Great Britain 1977 by Michael Joseph Ltd

This edition published 2011 by Pan Books
an imprint of Pan Macmillan, a division of Macmillan Publishers Limited
Pan Macmillan, 20 New Wharf Road, London N1 9RR
Basingstoke and Oxford
Associated companies throughout the world
www.panmacmillan.com

ISBN 978-1-4472-2832-5



1 3 5 7 9 8 6 4 2

A CIP catalogue record for this book is available from
the British Library.

Printed in the UK by CPI Group (UK) Ltd, Croydon, CR0 4YY

# RISK

DICK FRANCIS wrote more than forty international bestsellers and was widely acclaimed as one of the world's finest thriller writers. His awards included the Crime Writers' Association's Cartier Diamond Dagger for his outstanding contribution to the genre, and an honorary Doctorate of Humane Letters from Tufts University of Boston. In 1996 Dick Francis was made a Mystery Writers of America Grand Master for a lifetime's achievement and in 2000 he was awarded the CBE in the Queen's Birthday Honours list. Sadly he died in 2010.

***By Dick Francis and Felix Francis***

Dead Heat    Silks

***By Dick Francis***

Dead Cert    Nerve    For Kicks
Odds Against    Flying Finish    Blood Sport
Forfeit    Enquiry    Rat Race
Bonecrack    Smokescreen    Slay-Ride
Knock Down    High Stakes    Longshot
Decider    In the Frame    Risk    Trial Run
Whip Hand    Reflex    Twice Shy
Banker    The Danger    Proof
Break In    Bolt    Hot Money
The Edge    Straight    Comeback
Driving Force    Wild Horses    Come to Grief
To the Hilt    10lb Penalty    Field of 13
Second Wind    Shattered    Under Orders

*Autobiography*

The Sport of Queens

*Biography*

Lester: the Official Biography

To the memory of

Lionel Vick,

first a professional steeplechase jockey,
then a certified accountant;
always a brave man.

And my thanks to his associate,

Michael Foote.

# CHAPTER ONE

Thursday, March 17th, I spent the morning in anxiety, the afternoon in ecstasy, and the evening unconscious.

Thursday night, somewhere between dark and dawn, I slowly surfaced into a nightmare which would have been all right if I'd been asleep.

It took me a good long time to realize I was actually awake. Half awake, anyway.

There was no light. I thought my eyes were open, but the blackness was absolute.

There was a lot of noise. Different noises, loud and confusing. A heavy engine. Rattling noises. Creaks. Rushing noises. I lay in a muzzy state and felt battered by too much sound.

Lay . . . I was lying on some sort of mattress. On my back. Cold, sick and stiff. Aching. Shivering. Physically wretched and mentally bewildered.

I tried to move. Couldn't for some reason lift either hand to my face. They seemed to be stuck to my legs. Very odd.

An interminable time passed. I grew colder, sicker, stiffer, and wide awake.

Tried to sit up. Banged my head on something close above. Lay down again, fought a sudden spurt of panic, and made myself take it step by step.

Hands. Why couldn't I move my hands? Because my wrists seemed to be fastened to my trousers. It didn't make sense, but that was what it felt like.

Space. What of space? I stiffly moved my freezing feet, exploring. Found I had no shoes on. Only socks. On the immediate left, a wall. Close above, a ceiling. On the immediate right, a softer barrier. Possibly cloth.

I shifted my whole body a fraction to the right, and felt with my fingers. Not cloth, but netting. Like a tennis net. Pulled tight. Keeping me in. I pushed my fingers through the mesh, but could feel nothing at all on the far side.

Eyes. If I hadn't gone suddenly blind (and it didn't feel like it), I was lying somewhere where no light penetrated. Brilliant deduction. Most constructive. Ha bloody ha.

Ears. Almost the worst problem. Constant din assaulted them, shutting me close in the narrow black box, preventing me hearing any further than the powerful, nearby, racketing engine. I had a frightening feeling that even if I screamed no one would hear me. I had a sudden even more frightening feeling of *wanting* to scream. To make someone come. To make someone tell me where I was, and why I was there, and what on earth was happening.

I opened my mouth and yelled.

I yelled 'Hey' and 'Come here' and 'Bloody bastard, come and let me out', and thrashed about in useless rage, and all that happened was that my voice and fear bounded back in the confined space and made things worse. Chain reaction. One-way trip to exhaustion.

In the end I stopped shouting and lay still. Swallowed. Ground my teeth. Tried to force my mind into holding on to sense. Disorientation was the road to gibbering.

*Concentrate*, I told myself. *Think*.

That engine . . .

A big one. Doing a job of work. Situated somewhere close, but not where I was. The other side of a wall. Perhaps behind my head.

If it would only stop, I thought numbly, I would feel less sick, less pulverized, less panicky, less threatened.

The engine went right on hammering, its vibration reaching me through the walls. Not a turbine engine: not smooth enough, and no whine. A piston engine. Heavy duty, like a tractor . . . or a lorry. But I wasn't in a lorry. There was no feeling of movement; and the engine never altered its rate. No slowing or accelerating. No changes of gear. Not a lorry.

A generator. It's a generator, I thought. Making electricity.

I was lying tied up in the dark and on a sort of shelf near an electric generator. Cold, sick and frightened. And where?

As to how I'd got there . . . well, I knew that, up to a

point. I remembered the beginning, well enough. I would never forget Thursday, March 17th.

The most shattering questions were those to which I could think of no answer at all.

Why? What for? And *what next?*

# CHAPTER TWO

That Thursday morning a client with his life in ruins kept me in the office in Newbury long after I should have left for Cheltenham races, and it seemed churlish to say, 'Yes, Mr Wells, terribly sorry about your agony, but I can't stop to help you now because I want to nip off and enjoy myself.' Mr Wells, staring-eyed and suicidal, simply had to be hauled in from his quicksand.

It took three and a half hours of analysis, sympathy, brandy, discussion of ways and means, and general pep-talk, to restore the slightest hope to his horizon, and I wasn't his doctor, priest, solicitor or other assorted hand-holder, but only the accountant he'd engaged in a frenzy the night before.

Mr Wells had bitten the dust in the hands of a crooked financial adviser. Mr Wells, frantic, desperate, had heard that Roland Britten, although young, had done other salvage jobs. Mr Wells on the telephone had offered double fees, tears, and lifelong gratitude as inducements: and Mr Wells was a confounded nuisance.

For the first and probably the only time in my life I

was that day going to ride in the Cheltenham Gold Cup, the race which ranked next to the Grand National in the lives of British steeplechase riders. No matter that the tipsters gave my mount little chance or the bookies were offering ante-post odds of forty-to-one, the fact remained that for a part-time amateur like myself the offer of a ride in the Gold Cup was as high as one could go.

Thanks to Mr Wells I did not leave the office calmly and early after a quick shuffle through the day's mail. Not until a quarter to one did I begin to unstick his leech-like dependence and get him moving, and only then by promising another long session on the following Monday. Halfway through the door, he froze yet again. Was I sure we had covered every angle? Couldn't I give him the afternoon? Monday, I said firmly. Wasn't there anyone else he could see, then?

'Sorry,' I said. 'My senior partner is away on holiday.'

'Mr King?' he asked, pointing to the neat notice 'King and Britten' painted on the open door.

I nodded, reflecting gloomily that my senior partner, if he hadn't been touring somewhere in Spain, would have been most insistent that I got off to Cheltenham in good time. Trevor King, big, silver-haired, authoritative and worldly, had my priorities right.

We had worked together for six years, ever since he'd enticed me, from the city office where I'd been trained, with the one inducement I couldn't refuse: flexible working hours which allowed time to go racing. He already had five or six clients from the racing world,

Newbury being central for many of the racing stables strung out along the Berkshire Downs, and, needing a replacement for a departing assistant, he'd reckoned that if he engaged me he might acquire a good deal more business in that direction. Not that he'd ever actually said so, because he was not a man to use two words where one would do; but his open satisfaction as his plan had gradually worked made it obvious.

All he had apparently done towards checking my ability as an accountant, as opposed to amateur jockey, was to ask my former employers if they would offer me a substantial raise in salary in order to keep me. They said yes, and did so. Trevor, it seemed, had smiled like a gentle shark, and gone away. His subsequent offer to me had been for a full partnership and lots of racing time; the partnership would cost me ten thousand pounds and I could pay it to him over several years out of my earnings. What did I think?

I'd thought it might turn out just fine; and it had.

In some ways I knew Trevor no better than on that first day. Our real relationship began and ended at the office door, social contact outside being confined to one formal dinner party each year, to which I was invited by letter by his wife. His house was opulent: building and contents circa nineteen twenties, with heavy plate glass cut to fit the top surfaces of polished furniture, and an elaborate bar built into the room he called his 'snug'. Friends tended to be top management types or county councillors, worthy substantial citizens like Trevor himself.

On the professional level, I knew him well. Orthodox establishment outlook, sober and traditional. Patriarchal, but not pompous. Giving the sort of gilt-edged advice that still appeared sound even if in hindsight it turned out not to be.

Something punitive about him, perhaps. He seemed to me sometimes to get a positive pleasure from detailing the extent of a client's tax liabilities, and watching the client droop.

Precise in mind and method, discreetly ambitious, pleased to be a noted local personage, and at his charming best with rich old ladies. His favourite clients were prosperous companies; his least favourite, incompetent individuals with their affairs in a mess.

I finally got rid of the incompetent Mr Wells and took my tensions down to the office car park. It was sixty miles from Newbury to Cheltenham and on the way I chewed my fingernails through two lots of roadworks and an army convoy, knowing also that near the course the crawling racegoing jams would mean half an hour for the last mile. There had been enough said already about the risks of putting up an amateur ('however good' some kind columnist had written) against the top brass of the professionals on the country's best horses in the most important race of the season's most prestigious meeting. 'The best thing Roland Britten can do is to keep Tapestry out of everyone else's way' was the offering of a less kind writer, and although I more or less agreed with him I hadn't meant to do it by not arriving in time. Of all possible unprofessional behaviour, that would be the worst.

Lateness was the last and currently the most acute of a whole list of pressures. I had been riding as an amateur in jump races since my sixteenth birthday, but was now, with thirty-two in sight, finding it increasingly difficult to keep fit. Age and desk work were nibbling away at a stamina I'd always taken for granted: it now needed a lot of effort to do what I'd once done without thought. The hour and a half I spent early every morning riding exercise for a local trainer were no longer enough. Recently, in a couple of tight finishes, I'd felt the strength draining like bathwater from my creaking muscles, and had lost at least one race because of it. I couldn't swear to myself that I was tuned up tight for the Gold Cup.

Work in the office had multiplied to the point where doing it properly was a problem in itself. Half-days off for racing had begun to feel like treachery. Saturdays were fine, but impatient clients viewed Wednesdays at Ascot or Thursdays at Stratford-upon-Avon with irritation. That I worked at home in the evenings to make up for it satisfied Trevor, but no one else. And my case load, as jargon would put it, was swamping me.

Apart from Mr Wells, there had been other jobs I should have done that morning. I should have sent an appeal against a top jockey's tax assessment; I should have signed a certificate for a solicitor; and there had been two summonses for clients to appear before the Tax Commissioners, which needed instant action, even if only evasive.

'I'll apply for postponements,' I told Peter, one of our two assistants. 'Ring both of those clients, and tell them not to worry, I'll start on their cases at once. And check that we've all the papers we need. Ask them to send any that are missing.'

Peter nodded sullenly, unwillingly, implying that I was always giving him too much work. And maybe I was.

Trevor's plans to take on another assistant had been so far halted by an offer which was currently giving both of us headaches. A big London firm wanted to move in on us, merge, amalgamate, and establish a large branch of itself on our patch, with us inside. Materially, we would benefit, as at present the steeply rising cost of overheads like office rent, electricity and secretarial wages was coming straight out of our pockets. We would also be under less stress, as at present when one of us was ill or on holiday, the burden on the other was heavy. But Trevor agonized over the prospect of demotion from absolute boss, and I over the threat of loss of liberty. We had postponed a decision until Trevor's return from Spain in two weeks' time, but at that point bleak realities would have to be faced.

I drummed my fingers on the steering wheel of my Dolomite and waited impatiently for the roadworks' traffic lights to turn green. Looked at my watch for the hundredth time. 'Come on,' I said aloud. 'Come *on*.' Binny Tomkins would be absolutely furious.

Binny, Tapestry's trainer, didn't want me on the horse. 'Not in the Gold Cup,' he'd said positively, when the owner had proposed it. They'd faced each other belligerently outside the weighing room of Newbury racecourse, where Tapestry had just obliged in the three mile 'chase: Mrs Moira Longerman, small, blonde and bird-like, versus sixteen stone of frustrated male.

'. . . just because he's your *accountant*,' Binny was saying in exasperation when I rejoined them after weighing-in. 'It's bloody ridiculous.'

'Well, he won today, didn't he?' she said.

Binny threw his arms wide, breathing heavily. Mrs Longerman had offered me the Newbury ride on the spur of the moment when the stable jockey had broken his ankle in a fall in the previous race. Binny had accepted me as a temporary arrangement with fair grace, but Tapestry was the best horse in his yard, and for a middle-ranker like him a runner in the Gold Cup was an event. He wanted the best professional jockey he could get. He did not want Mrs Longerman's accountant who rode in thirty races in a year, if he was lucky. Mrs Longerman, however, had murmured something about removing Tapestry to a more accommodating trainer, and I had not been unselfish enough to decline the offer, and Binny had fumed in vain.

Mrs Longerman's previous accountant had for years let her pay to the Inland Revenue a lot more tax than she'd needed, and I'd got her a refund of thousands. It wasn't the best grounds for choosing a jockey to ride for you in the Gold Cup, but I understood she was thanking me by giving me something beyond price. I quite passionately did not want to let her down; and that, too, was a pressure.

I was worried about making a reasonable show, but not about falling. When one worried about falling, it was time to stop racing: it would happen to me one day, I supposed, but it hadn't yet. I worried about being unfit, unwanted, and late. Enough to be going on with.

Binny was spluttering like a lit fuse when I finally arrived, panting, in the weighing room.

'Where the hell have you been?' he demanded. 'Do you realize the first race is over already and in another five minutes you'd be fined for not turning up?'

'Sorry.'

I carried my saddle, helmet, and bag of gear through into the changing room, sat down thankfully on the bench, and tried to stop sweating. The usual bustle went on around me; jockeys dressing, undressing, swearing, laughing, accepting me from long acquaintance as a part of the scenery. I did the accounts for thirty-two jockeys and had unofficially filled in tax assessment forms for a dozen more. I was also to date employed as accountant by thirty-one trainers, fifteen stud farms, two Stewards of the Jockey Club, one racecourse, thirteen bookmakers, two horse-transport firms, one blacksmith, five forage merchants, and upwards of forty people who owned racehorses. I probably knew more about the private financial affairs of the racing world than any other single person on the racecourse.

In the parade ring Moira Longerman twittered with happy nerves, her button nose showing kittenishly just above a fluffy upstanding sable collar. Below the collar she snuggled into a coat to match, and on the blonde curls floated a fluffy sable hat. Her middle-aged blue eyes brimmed with excitement, and in the straightforward gaiety of her manner one could see why it was that so many thousands of people spent their hobby money on owning racehorses. Not just for the gambling, nor the display: more likely for the kick from extra adrenalin, and the feeling of being involved. She knew well enough that the fun could turn to disappointment, to tears. The lurking valleys made the mountaintops more precious.

'Doesn't Tapestry look *marvellous*?' she said, her small gloved hands fluttering in the horse's direction as he plodded round the ring under the gaze of the ten-deep banks of intent spectators.

'Great,' I said truthfully.

Binny scowled at the cold sunny sky. He had produced the horse with a gloss seldom achieved by his other runners: impeccably plaited mane and tail, oiled hooves, a new rug, gleamingly polished leather tack, and an intricate geometric pattern brushed into the well-groomed hairs of the hindquarters. Binny was busy telling the world that if his horse failed it would not be from lack of preparation. Binny was going to use me for evermore as his reason for not having won the Gold Cup.

I can't say that it disturbed me very much. Like Moira Longerman, I was feeling the throat-catching once-in-a-lifetime thrill of a profound experience waiting just ahead. Disaster might follow, but whatever happened I would have had my ride in the Gold Cup.

There were eight runners, including Tapestry. We mounted, walked out on to the course, paraded in front of the packed and noisy stands, cantered down to the start. I could feel myself trembling, and knew it was stupid. Only a cool head could produce a worthy result. Tell that to the adrenal glands.

I could pretend, anyway. Stifle the butterfly nerves and act as if races of this calibre came my way six times a season. None of the other seven riders looked anxious or strung up, yet I guessed that some of them must be. Even for the top pros, this was an occasion. I reckoned that their placid expressions were nearly as phoney as mine, and felt better.

We advanced to the tapes in a bouncing line, restraining the eager heads on short reins, and keeping the weight still back in the saddle. Then the starter pressed his lever and let the tapes fly up, and Tapestry took a great bite of air and practically yanked my arms out of their sockets.

Most three and a quarter mile 'chases started moderately, speeded up a mile from home, and maybe finished in a decelerating procession. The Gold Cup field that day set off as if to cover the whole distance in record Derby time, and Moira Longerman told me later that Binny used words she'd never heard before when I failed to keep Tapestry close in touch.

By the time we'd swept over the first two fences, by the stands, I was last by a good six lengths, a gap not much in itself but still an I-told-you-so sort of distance so early in the proceedings. I couldn't in fact make up my mind. Should I go faster? Stick closer to the tails in front? Tapestry had set off at a greater speed already than when he'd won with me at Newbury. If I let him zip along with the others he could be exhausted and tailed off at half-way. If I held him up, we might at least finish the race.

Over the third fence and over the water I saw the gap lengthening and still dithered about tactics. I hadn't expected the others to go off so fast. I didn't know if they hoped to maintain that speed throughout, or whether they would slow and come back to me later. I couldn't decide which was more likely.

But what would Binny say if I guessed wrong and was last the whole way? What wouldn't he say?

What was I doing in this race, out of my class?

Making an utter fool of myself.

Oh God, I thought, why did I try it?

Accountants are held to be cautious by nature but at that point I threw caution to the winds. Almost anything would be better than starting last and staying last.

Prudence would get me nowhere. I gave Tapestry a kick which he didn't expect and he shot forward like an arrow.

'Steady,' I gasped. 'Steady, dammit.'

Shorten the gap, I thought, but not too fast. Spurt too fast and I'd use the reserves we'd need for the last stretch uphill. If we ever got there. If I didn't fall off. If I didn't let Tapestry meet a fence wrong, or run out, or refuse to jump at all.

Only a mile done, and I'd lived a couple of lifetimes.

I was still last by the end of the first circuit, but no longer a disgrace. Once more round . . . and maybe we'd pass one or two before we'd done. I began at that point to enjoy myself, a background feeling mostly smothered by anxious concentration, but there all the same, and I knew from other days that it would be the enjoyment I remembered most afterwards, not the doubts.

Over the water-jump, still last, the others all in a group just ahead. Open ditch next; Tapestry met it just right and we pegged it back a length in mid-air. Landed nose to tail with the horse in front. Stayed there to the next fence, and again won ground in flight, setting off that time beside the next horse, not behind.

Great. I was no longer last. Just joint last. Whatever I might fear about Tapestry staying to the end, he was surging over the jumps meanwhile with zest and courage.

It was at the next fence, on the far side of the course, that the race came apart. The favourite fell, and the second favourite tripped over him. Tapestry swerved violently as he landed among the rolling bodies and crashed into the horse alongside. The rider of that horse fell off.

It happened so fast. One second, an orderly Gold Cup. Next second, a shambles. Three down, the high hopes of owners, trainers, lads and punters blown to the wind. Tapestry forged his way out like a bull, but when we tackled the hill ahead, we again lay last.

Never try to accelerate uphill, they say, because the horses you pass will pass you again on the way down. Save your strength, don't waste it. I saved Tapestry's strength in last place up the hill and it seemed to me that at the crest the others suddenly swooped away from me, piling on every ounce of everything they had, shooting off while I was still freewheeling.

Come on, I thought urgently, come on, it's now or never. Now, or absolutely never. Get on, Tapestry. Get going. I went down the hill faster than I'd ever ridden in my life.

A fence half-way down. A fractional change of stride. A leap to shame the chamoix.

Another jockey lay on the ground there, curled in a ball to avoid being kicked. Hard luck . . . Too bad . . .

Three horses in front. Two fences to go. I realized abruptly that the three horses in front were all there were. Not far in front, either. My God, I thought, almost laughing, just supposing I can pass one, I'll finish third. Third in the Gold Cup. A dream to last till death.

I urged Tapestry ever faster, and amazingly, he responded. This was the horse whose finishing speed was doubtful, who had to be nursed. This horse, thundering along like a sprinter.

Round the bend . . . only one fence to go . . . I was approaching it faster than the others . . . took off alongside the third horse, landed in front . . . with only the last taxing uphill stretch to the post. I'm third, I thought exultantly. I'm *bloody* third.

Some horses find the Cheltenham finish a painful struggle. Some wander sideways from tiredness, swish their tails and falter when in front, slow to a leaden all-spent pace that barely takes them to the post.

Nothing like that happened to Tapestry, but it did to both of the horses in front. One of them wavered up the straight at a widening angle. The other seemed to be stopping second by second. To my own and everyone else's disbelief, Tapestry scorched past both of them at a flat gallop and won the Gold Cup.

I didn't give a damn that everyone would say (and did say) that if the favourite and second favourite hadn't fallen, I wouldn't have had a chance. I didn't care a fig that it would go down in history as a 'bad' Gold Cup. I lived through such a peak of ecstasy on the lengthy walk round from the winning post to the unsaddling enclosure that nothing after, I thought, could ever match it.

It was impossible . . . and it had happened. Mrs Longerman's accountant had brought her a tax-free capital gain.

A misty hour later, changed into street clothes, with champagne flowing in the weighing room and all the hands I'd ever want slapping me on the shoulder, I was still so wildly happy that I wanted to run up the walls and laugh aloud and turn hand-springs. Speeches, presentations, Moira Longerman's excited tears, Binny's incredulous embarrassment, all had passed in a jumble which I would sort out later. I was high on the sort of glory wave which would put poppies out of business.

Into this ball of a day came a man in a St John's Ambulance uniform, asking for me.

'You Roland Britten?' he said.

I nodded over a glass of bubbles.

'There's a jockey wanting you. In the ambulance. Says he won't go off to hospital before he's talked to you. Proper fussed, he is. So would you come?'

'Who is it?' I asked, putting my drink down.

'Budley. Fell in the last race.'

'Is he badly hurt?'

We walked out of the weighing room and across the crowded stretch of tarmac towards the ambulance which stood waiting just outside the gates. It was five minutes before the time for the last race of the day, and thousands were scurrying about, making for the stands, hurrying to put on the last bet of the meeting. The ambulance man and I walked in the counter-current of those making for the car park before the greater rush began.

'Broken leg,' said the ambulance man.

'What rotten luck.'

I couldn't imagine what Bobby Budley wanted me for. There had been nothing wrong with his last annual accounts and we'd had them agreed by the Inspector of Taxes. He shouldn't have had any urgent problems.

We reached the back doors of the white ambulance, and the St John's man opened them.

'He's inside,' he said.

Not one of the big ambulances, I thought, stepping up. More like a white van, with not quite enough headroom to stand upright. They were short of regular ambulances, I supposed, on race days.

Inside there was a stretcher, with a figure on it under a blanket. I went a step towards it, head bent under the low roof.

'Bobby?' I said.

It wasn't Bobby. It was someone I'd never seen before. Young, agile, and in no way hurt. He sprang upwards off the stretcher shedding dark grey blanket like a cloud.

I turned to retreat. Found the ambulance man up beside me, inside the van. Behind him the doors were already shut. His expression was far from gentle and when I tried to push him out of the way he kicked my shin.

I turned again. The stretcher case was ripping open a plastic bag which seemed to contain a hand-sized wad of damp cotton wool. The ambulance man caught hold of one of my arms and the stretcher case the other, and despite fairly desperate heavings and struggles on my part they managed between them to hold the damp cotton wool over my nose and mouth.

It's difficult to fight effectively when you can't stand up straight and every breath you draw is pure ether. The last thing I saw in a greying world was the ambulance man's peaked cap falling off. His light brown hair tumbled out loose into a shaggy mop and turned him from an angel of mercy into a straightforward villain.

I had left racecourses once or twice before on a stretcher, but never fast asleep.

Awake in the noisy dark I could make no sense of it.

Why should they take me? Did it have anything to do with winning the Gold Cup? And if so, what?

It seemed to me that I had grown colder, and still sicker, and that the peripheral noises of creaks and rushing sounds had grown louder. There was also now an uncoordinated feeling of movement: yet I was not in a lorry.

Where, then? In an aeroplane?

The sickness suddenly identified itself into being not the aftermath of ether, as I'd vaguely thought, but a familiar malaise I'd suffered on and off from childhood.

I was seasick.

On a boat.

# CHAPTER THREE

I was lying, I realized, on a bunk. The tight net across the open side on my right was to prevent me from falling off. The rushing noises were from the waves washing against the hull. The creaks and rattles were the result of a solid body being pushed by an engine through the resistance of water.

To have made at least some sense of my surroundings was an enormous relief. I could relate myself to space again, and visualize my condition. On the other hand, sorting out the most disorientating part of the mystery left me feeling more acutely the physical discomforts. Cold. Hands tied to legs. Muscles stiff from immobility: and knowing I was on a boat, and knowing boats always made me sick, was definitely making me feel a lot sicker.

Ignorance was a great tranquillizer, I thought. The intensity of a pain depended on the amount of attention one gave it, and one never felt half as bad talking to people in daylight as alone in the dark. If someone would come and talk to me I might feel less cold and less miserable and less quite horribly sick.

No one came for a century or so.

The motion of the boat increased, and my queasiness with it. I could feel my weight rolling slightly from side to side, and had an all too distinct impression that I was also pitching lengthwise, first toe down, then head down, as the bows lifted and fell with the waves.

Out at sea, I thought helplessly. It wouldn't be so rough on a river.

I tried for a while with witticisms like 'Press-ganged, by God', and 'Shanghaied!' and 'Jim lad, Long John Silver's got you', to put a twist of lightness into the situation. Not a deafening success.

In time also I gave up trying to work out why I was there. I gave up feeling apprehensive. I gave up feeling cold and uncomfortable. Finally I was concentrating only on not actually vomiting, and the fact that I'd eaten nothing since breakfast was all that helped.

Breakfast . . .? I had lost all idea of time. I didn't know how long I'd been unconscious, or even how long I'd lain awake in the dark. Unconscious long enough to be shipped from Cheltenham to the coast, and to be carried on board. Awake long enough to long for sleep.

The engine stopped.

The sudden quiet was so marvellous that I only fully realized then how exhausting had been the assault of noise. I actively feared that it would start again. And was this, I wondered, the basis of brainwashing?

There was a new noise, suddenly, from overhead. Dragging sounds, and then metallic sounds, and then, devastatingly, a shaft of daylight.

I shut my dark-adjusted eyes, wincing, and opened them again slowly. Above my head, the shaft had grown to a square. Someone had opened a hatch.

Fresh air blew in like a shower, cold and damp. Without much enthusiasm I glanced around, seeing a small world through a wide-meshed white net.

I was in what one might call the sharp end. In the bows. The bunk where I lay grew narrower at my feet, the side walls of the cabin angling to meet in the centre, like an arrowhead.

The bunk was about two feet wide, and had another bunk above it. I was lying on a cloth-covered mattress; navy blue.

Most of the rest of the cabin was taken up by two large, open-topped, built-in, varnished wooden bins. For stowing sails, I thought. I was in the sail locker of a sailing boat.

Behind my right shoulder a door, now firmly shut, presumably led back to warmth, life, the galley and the saloon.

The matter of my wrists, too, became clear. They were indeed tied to my trousers, one on each side. From what I could see, someone had punched a couple of holes through the material in the region of each side pocket, threaded something which looked like bandage through the holes, and effectively tied each of my wrists to a bunch of cloth.

A good pair of trousers ruined: but then all disasters were relative.

A head appeared above me, framed by the hatch. Indistinctly, seeing him through the net and silhouetted against the grey sky, I got the impression he was fairly young and uncompromisingly tough.

'Are you awake?' he said, peering down.

'Yes,' I said.

'Right.'

He went away, but presently returned, leaning head and shoulders into the hatch.

'If you act sensible, I'll untie you,' he said.

His voice had the bossy strength of one accustomed to dictate, not cajole. A voice which had come up the hard way, gathering aggression on the journey.

'Have you got any dramamine?' I asked.

'No,' he said. 'There's a toilet in the cabin. You can throw up into that. You're going to have to agree you'll act quiet if I come down and untie you. Otherwise I won't. Right?'

'I agree,' I said.

'Right.'

Without more ado he lowered himself easily through the hatch and stood six feet three in his canvas shoes, practically filling all available space. His body moved in effortless balance in the boat's tossing.

'Here,' he said, lifting the lid of what had looked like a

built-in varnished box. 'Here's the head. You open the stop-cock and pump sea water through with that lever. Turn the water off when you've done, or you'll have a flood.' He shut the lid and opened a locker door on the wall above. 'In here there's a bottle of drinking water and some paper cups. You'll get your meals when we get ours.' He fished deep into one of the sail bins, which otherwise seemed empty. 'Here's a blanket. And a pillow.' He lifted them out, showed them to me, both dark blue, dropped them back.

He looked upwards to the generous square of open sky above him.

'I'll fix you the hatch so you'll have air and light. You won't be able to get out. And there's nothing to get out for. We're out of sight of land.'

He stood for a moment, considering, then began to unfasten the net, which was held simply by chrome hooks slotted into eyelets on the bunk above.

'You can hook the net up if it gets rough,' he said.

Seen without intervening white meshes, he was not reassuring. A strong face with vigorous bones. Smallish eyes, narrow-lipped mouth, open air skin and straight brown floppy hair. My own sort of age: no natural kinship, though. He looked down at me without any hint of sadistic enjoyment, for which I was grateful, but also without apology or compassion.

'Where am I?' I said. 'Why am I here? Where are we going? And who are you?'

He said, 'If I untie your hands and you try anything, I'll bash you.'

You must be joking, I thought. Six foot three of healthy muscle against a cold, stiff, seasick five foot ten. No thank you very much.

'What *is* this all about?' I said. Even to my ears, it sounded pretty weak. But then, pretty weak was exactly how I felt.

He didn't answer. He merely bent down, leaned in and over me, and unknotted the bandage from my left wrist. Extracting himself from the small space between the bunks, he repeated the process on the right.

'Stay lying down until I'm out of here,' he said.

'Tell me what's going on.'

He put a foot on the edge of the sail bins, and his hands on the sides of the hatch, and pulled himself halfway up into the outside world.

'I'll tell you,' he said unemotionally, looking down, 'that you're a bloody nuisance to me. I'm having to stow all the sails on deck.'

He gave a heave, a wriggle, and a kick, and hauled himself out.

'Tell me,' I shouted urgently. 'Why am I here?'

He didn't answer. He was fiddling with the hatch. I swung my feet over the side of the bunk and rolled in an exceedingly wobbly fashion to my feet. The pitching of the boat promptly threw me off balance and I ended in a heap on the floor.

'Tell me,' I shouted, pulling myself up again and holding on to things. 'Tell me, God dammit.'

The hatch cover slid over and shut out most of the sky. This time, though, it was not clamped down tight, but rested on metal stays, which left a three-inch gap all round: like a lid held three inches above a box.

I put a hand up through the gap and yelled again 'Tell me.'

The only reply I got was the sound of the hatch being made secure against any attempt of mine to dislodge it. Then even those sounds ceased, and I knew he'd gone away; and a minute or two later the engine started again.

The boat rolled and tossed wildly, and the sickness won with a rush. I knelt on the floor with my head over the lavatory bowl and heaved and retched as if trying to rid myself of my stomach itself. I hadn't eaten for so long that all that actually came up was bright yellow bile, but that made nothing any better. The misery of seasickness was that one's body never seemed to realize that there was nothing left to vomit.

I dragged myself onto the bunk and lay there both sweating and shivering, wanting to die.

Blanket and pillow, I thought. In the sail bin.

A terrible effort to get up and get them. I leaned down to pick them up, and my head whirled alarmingly.

Another frightful session over the bowl. Curse the blanket and pillow. But I was so cold.

I got them at the second attempt. Wrapped myself closely in the thick navy wool and put my head thankfully on the navy pillow. There was mercy somewhere, it seemed. I had a bed and a blanket and light and air and a water closet, and a lot of shipboard prisoners before me would have given their souls for all that. It seemed unreasonable to want an explanation as well.

The day passed with increasing awfulness. Anyone who has been comprehensively seasick won't need telling. Head ached and swam, skin sweated, stomach heaved, entire system felt unbelievably ill. If I opened my eyes it was worse.

How long, I thought, will this be going on? Were we crossing the Channel? Surely this relentless churning would soon end. Wherever we were going, it couldn't be far.

At some point he came back and undid the hatch.

'Food,' he said, shouting to be heard against the engine's din.

I didn't answer; couldn't be bothered.

'Food,' he shouted again.

I flapped a weak hand in the air, making go away signals.

I could swear he laughed. Extraordinary how funny seasickness is to those who don't have it. He pushed the hatch into place again and left me to it.

The light faded to dark. I slid in and out of dreams which were a good deal more comforting than reality; and during one of those brief sleeps someone came and fastened the hatch. I didn't care very much. If the boat had sunk, I would have looked upon drowning as a blessed release.

The next time the engine stopped it was only a minor relief compared with the general level of misery. I had supposed it was only in my imagination that the boat was tossing in a storm, but when the engine stopped I rolled clean off the bunk.

Climbing clumsily to my feet, holding on with one hand to the upper bunk, I felt for the door and the light switch beside it. Found the switch, and pressed it. No light. No damned light. Bloody stinking sods, giving me no light.

I fumbled my way back to the lower bunk in the blackness. Tripped over the blanket. Rolled it around me and lay down, feeling most insecure. Felt around for the net: fastened a couple of the hooks, groaning and grunting; not tidily, but enough to do the job.

From the next lot of noises from the outside world, I gathered that someone was putting up sails. On a sailing boat that merely made sense. There were rattlings and flappings and indistinct shouts, about none of which I cared a drip. It seemed vaguely strange someone should be sluicing the decks with buckets of water at such a time, until it dawned on me that the heavy intermittent splashes were made by waves breaking over the bows. The tight-closed hatch made sense. I had never wished for anything more passionately than to get my feet on warm, steady, dry land.

I entirely lost touch of time. Life became merely a matter of total wretchedness, seemingly without end. I would quite have liked a drink of water, but partly couldn't raise the energy to search for it, and partly feared to spill it in the dark, but mostly I didn't bother because every time I lifted my head the whirling bouts of sickness sent me retching to my knees. Water would be no sooner down than up.

He came and undid the hatch: not wide, but enough to let in grey daylight and a flood of fresh air. He did not, it seemed, intend me to die of suffocation.

It was raining hard outside: or maybe it was spray. I saw the bright shine of his yellow oilskins as a shower of heavy drops spattered in through the narrow gap.

His voice came to me, shouting. 'Do you want food?'

I lay apathetically, not answering.

He shouted again. 'Wave your hand if you are all right.'

I reckoned all right was a relative term, but raised a faint flap.

He said something which sounded like 'Gale', and shut the hatch again.

Bloody hell, I thought bitterly. Where were we going that we should run into gales? Out into the Atlantic? And *what for*?

The old jingle about seasickness ran through my head: 'One minute you're afraid you're dying, next minute you're afraid you're not.' For hours through the storm I groaned miserably into the pillow, incredibly ill from nothing but motion.

*

I woke from a sunny dream, the umpteenth awakening into total darkness.

Something different, I thought hazily. Same wild weather outside, the bows crashing against the seas and shipping heavy waves over the deck. Same creaking and slapping of wind-strained rigging. But inside, in me, something quite different.

I breathed deeply from relief. The sickness was going, subsiding slowly like an ebb tide, leaving me acclimatized to an alien environment. I lay for a while in simple contentment, while normality crept back like a forgotten luxury: but then, insistently, other troubles began to surface instead. Thirst, hunger, exhaustion, and an oppressive headache which I eventually put down to dehydration and a dearth of fresh air. A sour taste. An itching stubble of beard. A sweaty feeling of having worn the same clothes for a month. But worse than physical pinpricks, the mental rocks.

Confusion had had its points. Clarity brought no comfort at all. The more I was able to think straight, the less I liked the prospects.

There had to be a reason for any abduction, but the most usual reason made least sense. Ransom . . . it couldn't be. There was no one to pay a million for my release: no parents, rich or poor. Hostage . . . but hostages were mostly taken at random, not elaborately, from a public place. I had no political significance and no special knowledge: I couldn't be bartered, didn't know any secrets, had no access to Government papers or defence plans or scientific discoveries. No one would care more than a passing pang whether I lived or died, except perhaps Trevor, who would count it a nuisance to have to find a replacement.

I considered as dispassionately as possible the thought of death, but eventually discarded it. If I was there to be murdered, it would already have been done. The cabin had been made ready for a living prisoner, not a prospective corpse. Once out at sea, a weighted heave-ho would have done the trick. So, with luck, I was going to live.

However unrealistic it seemed to me, the only reason I could raise which made any sense at all was that I was there for revenge.

Although the majority of mankind think of auditing accountants as dry-as-dust creatures burrowing dimly into columns of boring figures, the dishonest regard them as deadly enemies.

I had had my share of uncovering frauds. I'd lost a dozen people their jobs and set the Revenue onto others, and seen five embezzlers go to prison, and the spite in some of those eyes had been like acid.

If Connaught Powys, for instance, had arranged this trip, my troubles had hardly started. Four years ago, when I'd last seen him, in court and newly convicted, he'd sworn to get even. He would be out of Leyhill about now. If by getting even he meant the full four years in a sail locker . . . well, it couldn't be that. It couldn't. I swallowed, convincing myself that from the solely practical viewpoint, it was impossible.

My throat was dry. From thirst, I told myself firmly: not from fear. Fear would get me nowhere.

I eased myself out of the bunk and onto the small patch of floor, holding on tight to the upper bunk. The black world went on corkscrewing around, but the vertigo had really gone. The fluid in my ears' semi-circular canals had finally got used to sloshing about chaotically: a pity it hadn't done it with less fuss.

I found the catch of the wall locker, opened it, and felt around inside. Paper cups, as promised. Bottle of water, ditto. Big plastic bottle with a screw cap. It was hopeless in the dark to use one of the cups: I wedged myself on the only available seat, which was the lowered lid of the loo, and drank straight from the bottle. Even then, with the violent rolling and pitching, a good deal of it ran down my neck.

I screwed the cap on again carefully and groped my way back to the bunk, taking the bottle with me. Hooked up the net again. Lay on my back with my head propped up on the pillow, holding the water on my chest and whistling 'Oh Susanna' to prove I was alive.

A long time passed during which I drank a good deal and whistled every tune I could think of.

After that I stood up and banged on the cabin door with my fists and the bottle, and shouted at the top of my voice that I was awake and hungry and furious at the whole bloody charade. I used a good deal of energy and the results were an absolute zero.

Back in the bunk I took to swearing instead of whistling. It made a change.

The elements went on giving the boat a bad time. I speculated fruitlessly about where we were, and how big the boat was, and how many people were sailing it, and whether they were any good. I thought about hot sausages and crusty bread and red wine, and for a fairly cheerful hour I thought about winning the Gold Cup.

At about the time that I began to wonder seriously if everyone except me had been washed overboard, the hatch-opening noises returned. He was there, still in his oilskins. I gulped in the refreshing blast of cold air and wondered just how much of a stinking fug was rushing out to meet him.

I unhooked the net and stood up, holding on and swaying. The wind outside shrieked like starlings.

He shouted, 'Do you want food?'

'Yes,' I yelled. 'And more water.' I held the nearly empty bottle up to him, and he reached down for it.

'Right.'

He shut the hatch and went away, but not before I had a terrifying glimpse of the outside world. The boat rolled heavily as usual to one side, to the left, and before it rolled back to the right I saw the sea. A huge uneven wave, towering to obliterate the sky, charcoal grey, shining, swept with gusts of spray. The next heavy crash of water over the hatch made me think happier thoughts of my dry cabin.

He came back, opened the hatch a few inches, and

lowered in a plastic carrier bag on a loop of rope. He shouted down at me.

'Next time I bring you food, you give me back this carrier. Understand?'

'Yes,' I shouted back, untying the rope. 'What time is it?'

'Five o'clock. Afternoon.'

'What day?'

'Sunday.' He pulled the rope up and began to shut the hatch.

'Give me some light,' I yelled.

He shouted something which sounded like 'Batteries' and put me back among the blind. Yes, well . . . one could live perfectly well without sight. I slid back onto the bunk, fastened the net, and investigated the carrier bag.

The water bottle, full; an apple; and a packet of two thick sandwiches, faintly warm. They turned out to be hamburgers in bread, not buns; and very good too. I ate the lot.

Five o'clock on Sunday. Three whole damned days since I'd stepped into the white van.

I wondered if anyone had missed me seriously enough to go to the police. I had disappeared abruptly from the weighing room, but no one would think it sinister. The changing room valet might be surprised that I hadn't collected from him my wallet and keys and watch, which he'd been holding as usual in safe keeping while I raced, and that I hadn't in fact paid him, either; but he would have put my absent-mindedness down to excitement. My car would still, I supposed, be standing in the jockeys' car park, but no one yet would have begun to worry about it.

I lived alone in a cottage three miles outside Newbury: my next-door neighbour would merely think I was away celebrating for the weekend. Our two office assistants, one boy, one girl, would have made indulgent allowances, or caustic allowances perhaps, when I hadn't turned up for work on Friday. The clients I had been supposed to see would have been irritated, but no more.

Trevor was away on his holidays. So no one, I concluded, would be looking for me.

On Monday morning, the bankrupt Mr Wells might make a fuss. But even if people began to realize I had vanished, how would they ever find me? The fact had to be faced that they wouldn't. Rescue was unlikely. Unless I escaped, I would be staying in the sail locker until someone chose to let me out.

Sunday to Monday was a long, cold, wild, depressing night.

# CHAPTER FOUR

On Monday, March 21st the hatch opened twice to let in air, food, sprays of water, and brief views of constantly grey skies. On each occasion I demanded information, and got none. The oilskins gave merely an impression that the crew had more than enough to do with sailing the boat in those conditions, and had no time to answer damn fool questions.

I was used to being alone. I lived alone and to a great extent worked alone; solitary by nature, and seldom lonely. An only child, long accustomed to my own company, I tended often to feel oppressed by the constant companionship of a large number of people, and to seek escape as soon as possible. All the same, as the hours dragged on, I found life alone in the sail locker increasingly wearing.

Limbo existence, I thought. Lying in a black capsule, endlessly tossing. How long did it take for the human mind to disintegrate, left alone in uncertainty in the rattling, corkscrewing dark?

A bloody long time, I answered myself rebelliously. If

the purpose of all this incarceration was to reduce me to a crying wreck, then it wasn't going to succeed. Tough thoughts, tough words . . . I reckoned more realistically that it depended on the true facts. I could survive another week of it passably, and two weeks with difficulty. After that . . . unknown territory.

Where could we be going? Across the Atlantic? Or, if the idea really was to break me up, maybe just up and down the Irish Sea? They might reckon that any suitable stretch of rough water would do the trick.

And who were 'they'?

Not him in the oilskins. He looked upon me as a nuisance, not a target for malice. He probably had instructions regarding me, and was carrying them out. How unfunny if his instructions were to take me home once I'd gone mad.

Dammit, I thought. Dammit to bloody hell. He'd have a bloody long job. Bugger him. Bugger and sod him.

There was a great sane comfort to be found in swearing.

At some long time after my second Monday glimpse of the outside, it seemed that the demented motion of the boat was slowly steadying. Standing up out of the bunk was no longer quite such a throw-around affair. Holding on was still necessary, but not holding on for dear life. The bows crashed more gently against the waves. The thuds of water over the hatch diminished in number and weight. There were shouts on deck and a good deal of pulley noise, and I guessed they were resetting the sails.

I found also that for the first time since my first awakening, I was no longer cold.

I was still wearing the clothes I had put on in the far off world of sanity: charcoal business suit, sleeveless waistcoat-shaped pullover underneath, pale blue shirt, underpants, and socks. Somewhere on the floor in the dark was my favourite Italian silk tie, worn to celebrate the Gold Cup. Shoes had vanished altogether. From being inadequate even when reinforced by a blanket, the long-suffering ensemble was suddenly too much.

I took off my jacket and rolled it into a tidy ball. As gent's natty suiting it was already a past number: as an extra pillow it added considerably to life's luxuries. Amazing how deprivation made the smallest extras marvellous.

Time had become a lost faculty. Drifting in and out of sleep with no external references was a queer business. I mostly couldn't tell whether I'd been asleep for minutes or hours. Dreams occurred in a semi-waking state, sometimes in such short snatches that I could have counted them in seconds. Other dreams were deeper and longer, and I knew that they were the product of sounder sleep. None of them seemed to have anything to do with my present predicament, and not one came up with any useful subconscious information as to why I should be there. In my innermost soul, it seemed, I didn't know.

Tuesday morning – it must have been Tuesday

morning – he came without the oilskins. The air which flowed in through the open hatch was as always fresh and clean, but now dry and faintly warm. The sky was pale blue. I could see a patch of white sail and hear the hissing of the hull as it cut through the water.

'Food,' he said, lowering one of the by now familiar plastic carriers.

'Tell me why I'm here,' I said, untying the knot.

He didn't answer. I took the carrier off, and tied on the empty one, and held on to the rope.

'Who are you? What is this boat? Why am I here?' I said.

His face showed no response except faint irritation.

'I'm not here to answer your questions.'

'Then what *are* you here for?' I said.

'None of your business. Let go of the rope.'

I held on to it. 'Please tell me why I'm here,' I said.

He stared down, unmoved. 'If you ask any more questions, and you don't leave go of the rope, you'll get no supper.'

The simplicity of the threat, and the simplicity of the mind that made it, was a bit of a stunner. I let go of the rope, but I made one more try.

'Then please just tell me how long you're going to keep me here.'

He gave me a stubborn scowl as he pulled up the carrier.

'You'll get no supper,' he said, withdrawing his head out of sight, and beginning to shut the hatch.

'Leave the hatch open,' I shouted.

I got no joy from that either. He firmly fastened me back in the dark. I stood swaying with the boat, holding onto the upper bunk, and trying to fight down a sudden overwhelming tide of furious anger. How *dared* they abduct me and imprison me in this tiny place and treat me like a naughty child. How dared they give me no reasons and no horizons. How dared they thrust me into the squalor of my own unwashed, unbrushed, unshaven state. There was a great deal of insulted pride and soaring temper in the fiery outrage with which I literally shook.

I could go berserk and smash up the place, I thought, or calm down again and eat whatever he'd brought in the carrier: and the fact that I'd recognized the choice made it certain I'd choose the latter. The bitter, frustrated fury didn't exactly go away, but at least with a sigh I had it back under control.

The intensity of what I'd felt, and its violent, unexpected onset, both alarmed me. I would have to be careful, I thought. There were so many roads to destruction, and rage, it seemed, was one of them.

If a psychiatrist had been shut up like this, I wondered, would he have had any safety nets that I hadn't? Would his knowledge of what might happen to the mind of someone in this position help him to withstand the symptoms when they occurred? Probably I should have studied psychology, not accountancy. More useful if one were kidnapped. Stood to reason.

The carrier contained two shelled hard-boiled eggs, an apple, and three small foil-wrapped triangles of processed cheese. I saved one of the eggs and two pieces of cheese for later, in case he meant it about no supper.

He did mean it. Uncountable hours passed. I ate the second egg and the rest of the cheese. Drank some water. As the day's total entertainment, hardly a riot.

When the hatch was next opened, it was dark outside, though dark with a luminous greyness quite unlike the black inside the cabin. No carrier of food materialized, and I gathered that the respite was only so that I shouldn't asphyxiate. He had opened the hatch and gone before I got round to risking any more questions.

Gone.

The hatch was wide open. Out on the deck there were voices and a good deal of activity with ropes and sails.

'Let go.'

'You're letting the effing thing fall into the sea . . .'

'Catch that effing sheet . . . Move, can't you . . .'

'You'll have to stow the gennie along the rail . . .'

Mostly his voice, from close by, directing things.

I put one foot on the thigh-high rim of the sail bin, as he had done, and hooked my hands over the side of the hatch, and heaved. My head popped out into the free world and it was about two whole seconds before he noticed.

'Get back,' he said brusquely, punctuating his remark by stamping on my fingers. 'Get down and stay down.' He kicked at my other hand. 'Do you want a bash on the head?' He was holding a heavy chromium winch handle, and he swung it in an unmistakable gesture.

'There's no land in sight,' he said, kicking again. 'So get down.'

I dropped back to the floor, and he shut the hatch. I hugged my stinging fingers and counted it fortunate that no one went sailing in hob-nailed boots.

Two seconds' uninterrupted view of the boat had been worth it, though. I sat on the lid of the loo with my feet on the side of the lower bunk opposite, and thought about the pictures still alive on my retinas. Even in night light, with eyes adjusted to a deeper darkness, I'd been able to see a good deal.

For a start, I'd seen three men.

The one I knew, who seemed to be not only in charge of me but of the whole boat. Two others, both young, hauling in a voluminous sail which hung half over the side, pulling it in with outstretched arms and trying to stop it billowing again once they'd got it on deck.

There might be a fourth one steering: I hadn't been able to see. About ten feet directly aft of the hatch the single mast rose majestically skywards, and with all the cleats and pulleys and ropes clustered around its base it had formed a block to any straight view towards the stern. There might have been a helmsman and three or four crewmen resting below. Or there might have been automatic steering and all hands visible on deck. It seemed a huge boat, though, to be managed by three.

From the roughest of guesses and distant gleams from

chromium winches I would have put it at about a cricket pitch long. Say sixty-five feet. Or say, if you preferred it, nineteen point eight one metres. Give or take an octave.

Not exactly a nippy little dinghy for Sunday afternoons on the Thames. An ocean racer, more like.

I had had a client once who had bought himself a second-hand ocean racer. He'd paid twenty-five thousand for thirty feet of adventure, and beamed every time he thought of it. His voice came back over the years: 'The people who race seriously have to buy new boats every year. There's always something new. If they don't get a better boat they can't possibly win, and the possibility of winning is what it's all about. Now me, all I want is to be able to sail round Britain comfortably at weekends in the summer. So I buy one of the big boys' cast-offs, because they're well-built boats, and just the job.' He had once invited me to Sunday lunch on board. I had enjoyed looking over his pride and joy, but privately had been most relieved when a sudden gale had prevented us leaving the moorings at his yacht club for the promised afternoon's sail.

Highly probable, I thought, that I was now being entertained on some other big boy's cast-off. The great question was, at whose expense?

The improvement in the weather was a mixed blessing, because the engine started again. The din seemed an even worse assault on my nerves than it had at the beginning. I lay on the bunk and tried to shut my ears with the pillow and my fingers, but the roaring vibration easily by-passed such frivolous barriers. I'd either got to get used to it and ignore it, I thought, or go raving, screaming bonkers.

I got used to it.

Wednesday. Was it Wednesday? I got food and air twice. I said nothing to him, and he said nothing to me. The constant noise of the engine made talking difficult. Wednesday was a black desert.

Thursday. I'd been there a week.

When he opened the hatch, I shouted, 'Is it Thursday?'

He looked surprised. Hesitated, then shouted back, 'Yes.' He looked at his watch. 'Quarter to eleven.'

He was wearing a blue cotton tee shirt, and the day outside seemed fine. The light tended to hurt my eyes.

I untied the carrier and fastened on the previous one, which as usual contained an empty water bottle. I looked up at him as he pulled it out, and he stared down at my face. He looked his normal unsmiling self: a hard young man, unfeeling rather than positively brutal.

I didn't consciously ask him, but after a pause, during which he seemed to be inspecting the horizon, he began to fix the hatch as he had done on the first day, so that it was a uniform three inches above the deck, letting in continuous air and light.

The relief at not being locked back in the dark was absolutely shattering. I found I was trembling from head to foot. I swallowed, trying to guard against the possibility that he would change his mind. Trying to tell myself that even if it proved to be only for five minutes, I should be grateful for that.

He finished securing the hatch and went away. I took some shaky deep breaths and gave myself an ineffective lecture about stoical responses, come dark, come shine.

After a while I sat on the lid of the loo and ate the first shipboard meal that I could actually see. Two hard-boiled eggs, some crispbread, three triangles of cheese and an apple. Never much variety in the diet, but at least no one intended me to starve.

He came back about half an hour after he'd gone away.

Hell, I thought. Half an hour. Be grateful for that. I had at least talked myself into facing another dose of darkness without collapsing into rubble.

He didn't, however, shut the hatch. Without altering the way it was fixed, he slid another plastic carrier through the gap. It was not this time tied to a rope, because when he let go of it, it fell to the floor; and before I could raise any remark, he had gone again.

I picked up the carrier, which seemed light and almost empty, and looked inside.

For God's sake, I thought. Laugh. Laugh, but don't bloody snivel. An ounce of kindness was more devastating than a week of misery.

He'd given me a pair of clean socks and a paperback novel.

I spent a good deal of the day trying to look out of the gap. With one foot on the rim of the sail bins, and my hands grasping the hatch opening, I could get my head up to the top well enough, but the view would have been more comprehensive if either the gap had been a couple of inches deeper or my eyes had been located halfway up my forehead. What I did see, mostly by tilting my head and applying one eye at a time, was a lot of ropes, pulleys, and rolled up sails, a lot of green sea, and a dark line of land on the horizon ahead.

None of these things changed all day except that the smudge of land grew slowly thicker, but I never tired of looking.

At closer quarters I also looked at the fittings of the hatch itself, which, I realized after a time, had been modified slightly for my visit. The metal props which held it open were hinged, and folded down inside the cabin when the hatch was closed. Out on deck the hatch cover was mounted on two heavier extending hinges, which allowed it to open outwards completely and lie flat on its back.

Inside the cabin there were two sturdy clips for securing the hatch shut from below, and outside there were two others, for securing the hatch from above.

So far, all as planned by the ship builders. What had been added, though, was extra provision to prevent someone inside the cabin from pushing the hatch wide open after releasing it from the hinged props. Normally, one could have done this. Sail locker hatches were supposed to open easily and wide, so that the sails could be pulled in and out. There was no point in ordinary circumstances in making things difficult. But now, outside, crossing from fore to aft and from port to starboard over the top of the hatch cover, were two lengths of chain, each secured at both ends to cleats which to my eyes looked newly screwed to the deck. The chains held the hatch cover down on the props like guy ropes, taut and forceful. If I could dislodge those chains, I thought, I could get out. If I had anything to dislodge them with. A couple of Everest-sized ifs. I could get my hands out through the three inch gap, but not much arm. Not enough to reach the cleats, let alone undo the chains. As for levers, screwdrivers, hammers and files, all I had were paper cups, a flimsy carrier and a plastic water bottle. Tantalizing, all those hours looking out at unreachable freedom.

In between the long bouts of balancing up by the ceiling I sat on the loo lid and read the book, which was an American private-eye thriller with a karate-trained hero who would have chopped his way out of a sail locker in five minutes.

Inspired by him, I had another go at the cabin door. It withstood my efforts like a stolid wall. Obviously I should have studied karate as well as psychiatry. Better luck next time.

The day whizzed past. The light began to fade. Outside the smudge of land had grown into an approaching certainty, and I had no idea what land it was.

He came back, lowered the carrier, and waited while I tied on the empty ones.

'Thank you,' I shouted, as he pulled them up, 'for the book and socks.'

He nodded, and began to close the hatch.

'Please don't,' I shouted.

He paused and looked down. It seemed to be still be-kind-to-prisoners day, because he provided his first explanation.

'We are going into port. Don't waste your breath making a noise when we stop. We'll be anchored. No one will hear you.'

He shut the hatch. I ate sliced tinned ham and a hot baked potato in the noisy stupefying dark, and to cheer myself up thought that now that the journey was ending they surely wouldn't keep me there much longer. Tomorrow, perhaps, I would be out. And after that I might get some answers.

I stifled the gloomy doubts.

*

The engine slowed, the first time it had changed its note. There were footsteps on deck, and shouts, and the anchor went over with a splash. The anchor chain rattled out, sounding as if it were passing practically through the sail locker; behind the panelling, no doubt.

The engine was switched off. There was no sound from anywhere. The creakings and rushing noises had stopped. No perceptible motion any more. I had expected the peace to be a relief, but as time passed it was the opposite. Even aggravating stimuli, it seemed, were better than none at all. I slept in disjointed snatches and lay emptily awake for hours and hours wondering if one really could go mad from too much nothing.

When he next opened the hatch it was full daylight outside. Friday; mid-morning. He lowered the carrier, waited for the exchange, raised the rope, and began to close the hatch.

I made involuntarily a vague imploring gesture with my hands. He paused, looking down.

'I can't let you see where we are,' he said.

It was the nearest he had come to an apology, the nearest to admitting that he might have treated me better, if he didn't have his orders.

'Wait,' I yelled, as he pulled the hatch over.

He paused again: prepared at least to listen.

'Can't you put screens round if you don't want me to see the land?' I said. 'Leave the hatch open . . .'

He considered it. 'I'll see,' he said, 'later.'

It seemed an awfully long time later, but he did come

back, and he did open the hatch. While he was fastening it, I said, 'When are you going to let me out?'

'Don't ask questions.'

'I *must*,' I said explosively. 'I have to know.'

'Do you want me to shut the hatch?'

'No.'

'Then don't ask questions.'

It may have been spineless of me, but I didn't ask any more. He hadn't given me one useful answer in eight days, and if I persevered, all I would get would be no light and no supper and an end to the new era of partial humanity.

When he'd gone I climbed up for a look, and found he had surrounded the hatch area with bulging bolsters of rolled sails. My field of vision had come down to about eighteen inches.

I lay on the top bunk for a change, and tried to imagine what it was about the port, so hopelessly near, that I might recognize. The sky was pale blue, with sun shining through high, hazy cloud. It was warm, like a fine spring day. There were even seagulls.

It evoked in me such a strong picture that I became convinced that if I could only see over the sail bolsters, I would be looking at the harbour and beaches where I'd played as a child. Maybe all that frantic sailing had been nowhere but up and down the English Channel, and we were now safe back home in Ryde, Isle of Wight.

I shook the comforting dream away. All one could

actually tell for sure was that it was not in the Arctic Circle.

There were occasional sounds from outside, but all distant, and nothing of any use. I read the American thriller again, and thought a good deal about escape.

When the day was fading he came back with supper, but this time, after I'd swopped the carriers, he didn't shut the hatch. That evening I watched the light die to dusk and night, and breathed sweet air. Small mercies could be huge mercies, I thought.

Saturday, March 26th. The morning carrier contained fresh bread, fresh cheese, fresh tomatoes: someone had been shopping ashore. It also contained an extra bottle of water and a well-worn piece of soap. I looked at the soap and wondered if it was there from kindness or because I stank; and then with wildly leaping hope wondered if it was there so that I should at least be clean when they turned me loose.

I took off all my clothes and washed from head to foot, using a sock as a sponge. After the week's desultory efforts with salt water from the loo, the lather was a fantastic physical delight. I washed my face and ears and neck and wondered what I looked like with a beard.

After that, dressed in shirt and underpants which were both long overdue for the same treatment, I ate the morning meal.

After that, I tidied the cabin, folding the blanket and my extra clothes and stacking everything neatly.

After that, I still couldn't face for a long time that my soaring hope was unfounded. No one came to let me out.

It was odd how soon the most longed-for luxury became commonplace and not enough. In the dark, I had ached for light. Now that I had light, I took it for granted and ached for room to move.

The cabin was triangular, its three sides each about six feet long. The bunks on the port side, and the loo and sail bins on the starboard side, took up most of the space. The floor area in the centre was roughly two feet wide by the cabin door, but narrowed to a point about four feet in, where the bunks and the forward sail bin met. There was room to take two small paces, or one large. Any attempt at knees-bend-arms-stretch involved unplanned contact with the surrounding woodwork. There was more or less enough space to stand on one's head by the cabin door. I did that a couple of times. It just shows how potty one can get. The second time I bashed my ankle on the edge of the sail bin coming down, and decided to give Yoga a miss. If I'd tried the Lotus position, I'd have been wedged for life.

I felt a continuous urge to scream and shout. I knew that no one would hear me, but the impulse had nothing to do with reason. It stemmed from frustration, fury and induced claustrophobia. I knew that if I gave way to it, and yelled and yelled, I would probably end up sobbing.

The thought that maybe that was precisely what someone wanted to happen to me was an enormous support. I couldn't stop the screaming and shouting from going on inside my head, but at least it didn't get out.

After I'd finally come to terms with the thought that it wasn't Exodus day, I spent a good deal of time contemplating the loo. Not metaphysically: mechanically.

Everything in the cabin was either built-in, or soft. From the beginning I'd been given no possible weapons, no possible implements. All the food had been for eating with my fingers, and came wrapped only in paper or plastic, if at all. No plates. Nothing made of metal, china or glass. The light bulb had not only been unscrewed from its socket, but the glass cover for it, which I guessed should be there, was not.

The pockets of my suit had been emptied. The nail file I usually carried in my breast pocket was no longer there: nor were my pens clipped inside: and my penknife had gone from my trousers.

I sat on the floor, lifted the lid, and at close quarters glared at the loo's mechanics.

Bowl, flushing lever, pump. A good deal of tubing. The stopcock for turning the sea water on and off. Everything made with the strength and durability demanded by the wild motions of the sea, which shook flimsy contraptions to pieces.

The lever was fastened at the back, hinged to the built-in casing of the fitment. At the front, it ended in a wooden handle. Attached at about a third of the way back was the rod which led directly down into the pump, to pull the piston there up and down. The whole lever, from handle to hinge, measured about eighteen inches.

I lusted for that lever like a rapist, but I could see no way, without tools, of getting it off. The hinge and the piston linkage were each fastened with a nut and bolt, and appeared to have been tightened by Atlas. Nut versus thumb and finger was no contest. I had tried on and off for two days.

A spanner. My kingdom for a spanner, I thought.

Failing a spanner, what else?

I tried with my shirt. The cloth saved the pressure on skin and bones, but gave no extra purchase. The nuts sat there like rocks. It was like trying to change a wheel with only fingers and a handkerchief.

Trousers? The cloth itself tended to slip more easily than my shirt. I tried the waistband, and found it a great deal better. Around the inside of the waist was a strip with two narrow rows of rough-surfaced rubber let into it. The real purpose of the strip was to help belt-less trousers stay up by providing a friction grip against a tucked-in shirt. Applying trouser-band to nut gave a good grip and slightly more hope, but despite a lot of heavy effort, no results.

The day ground on. I went on sitting on the floor futilely trying to unscrew nuts which wouldn't unscrew, simply because there was nothing else to do.

*

Tinned ham again for supper. I carefully peeled off all the fat, and ate the lean.

The hatch stayed open.

I said thanks for the soap, and asked no questions.

Sunday. Another Sunday. How *could* anyone keep me locked up so long without explanation? The whole modern world was churning along outside, and there I was cooped up like the man in the iron mask, or as near as dammit.

I applied the strips of ham fat to the nuts, to see if grease would have any effect. I spent most of the day warming the piston-rod nut in my fingers, rubbing fat round its edges, and hauling at it with my trousers.

Nothing happened.

Now and again I stood up and stretched, and climbed up to see if the sail bolsters were still obstructing the view, which they always were. I read bits of the thriller again. I closed the loo lid and sat on it, and looked at the walls. I listened to the seagulls.

My ordinary life seemed far removed. Reality was inside the sail locker. Reality was a mystery. Reality was mind-cracking acres of empty time.

Sunday night drifted in and darkened and slowly became Monday. He came much earlier than usual with my breakfast, and when he had lifted out the exchange carrier, he began to close the hatch.

'Don't,' I yelled.

He paused only briefly, staring down unmoved.

'Necessary,' he said.

I went on yelling for him to open it for a long time after he'd gone away and left me in the dark. Once I'd started making a noise, I found it difficult to stop: all the stifled screams and shouts were trying to burst out through the hole in the dam. If the dam broke up, so would I. I stuffed the pillow into my mouth to make myself shut up, and resisted a desire to bang my head against the door instead.

The engine started. Din and vibration and darkness, all as before. It's too much, I thought. Too much. But there were only two basic alternatives. Stay sane or go crazy. Sanity was definitely getting harder.

Think rational thoughts, I told myself. Repeat verses, do mental arithmetic, remember all the tricks that other solitary prisoners have used to see them through weeks and months and years.

I tore my mind away from such impossible periods and directed it to the present.

The engine ran on fuel. It had used a good deal of fuel on the journey. Therefore if the boat was going far, it would need more.

Engines were always switched off during refuelling. If I made the most colossal racket when we refuelled, just possibly someone might hear. I didn't honestly see how any noise I could make would attract enough attention, but I could try.

The chain rattled back through its hidden chute as the anchor came up, and I presumed the boat was moving, although there was no feeling of motion.

Then someone came and put a radio on top of the hatch, and turned the volume up loud. The music fought a losing battle against the engine for a while, but shortly I felt the boat bump, and almost at once the engine switched off.

I knew we were refuelling. I could hear only loud pop music. And no one on the quayside, whatever I did, could possibly have heard *me*.

After a fairly short while the engine started again. There were a few small thuds outside, felt through the hull, and then nothing. Someone came and collected the radio: I yelled for the hatch to be opened, but might as well not have bothered.

Motion slowly returned to the boat, bringing hopeless recognition with it.

Going out to sea again.

Out to sea, in the noise and the dark. Still not knowing why I was there, or for how long. Growing less fit from lack of exercise and less able to deal with mental pressure. Starting last week's torments all over again.

I sat on the floor with my back against the cabin door, and folded my arms over my knees, and put my head on my arms, and wondered how I could possibly endure it.

Monday I spent in full-blown despair.

On Tuesday, I got out.

# CHAPTER FIVE

Monday night the boat was anchored somewhere, but it stopped after I got my supper and started again before Tuesday mid-morning. It rained most of the time, drumming on the hatch. I was glad of the respite from the engine but in general the misery level was a pain.

When he brought the morning food he fixed the hatch open. The extent of my relief was pathetic.

Shortly after, they stopped the engine and put up the sails, and the grey sky outside slowly cleared to blue.

I ate the hard boiled eggs and the apple and thought about the thick slice of bread, upon which, for the first time, he had given me butter. Then I pulled a button off my shirt to use as a scraper, and transferred as much of the butter as I could to the stubborn nuts and bolts on the flushing lever. Then I ate the bread. Then I sat on the floor and one after the other warmed the nuts with my hand in the hope that the butter and ham fat would melt into the screw threads.

After that I ripped a length of the rubberized waistband from my trousers, and fished out of the bottom of one of the sail bins the white net which I had stored there after the storms.

It was activity for activity's sake, more than any real hope. I wound the waistband twice round the piston-rod nut, because it was the nearest, and fitted over that the chromium hook which had attached the net to the upper berth. Then I tugged the net.

After a second of gripping, the hook slid round on the cloth and fell off. I tried again, folding the waistband so that it had an elasticated side against the hook as well as against the nut. That time the hook stayed in place; but so did the nut.

I tugged several times. If I tugged very hard, hook, waistband and all came off. Nothing else happened. I slung the net back into the sail bin in depression.

After that I sat for ages with my hand on the piston-rod nut, until it was as warm as a handful of pennies clutched by a child. Then I wound the strip of waistband round quickly three times, to make the nut larger to grip, and then I tried it with all my remaining muscle power.

The waistband turned in my hand.

Damn it to hell, I thought hopelessly. I pulled it off and wound it on again, trying to grip it more tightly.

It turned again.

It may seem ridiculous, but it was not until it turned more easily the third time that I realized I was turning the nut on the bolt, not the waistband on the nut.

Unbelievable. I sat there looking idiotic, with my

mouth open. Excitement fluttered in my throat like a stifled laugh. If I could get one off, what about the other?

Time hadn't mattered for the first one. I'd had nothing else to do. For the second one, the hinge, I was feverishly impatient.

I warmed the nut, and wound on the waistband, and heaved; and nothing happened.

Heaved again.

A blob.

It had to move, I thought furiously. It simply had to. After several more useless attempts, I went back to basics.

Perhaps after all the tugging session with the hook had had some effect. I scooped out the net and applied it to the hinge nut, and tugged away with enthusiasm, replacing the hook every time it fell off. Then I made myself warm the nut as thoroughly as I had the other one, so that the heat from my hand was conducted right to the inside, where the melted grease and the minute heat-expansion of the metal could do their work. Then I wound on the waistband again and practically tore all the ligaments in my arm and back with a long and mighty heave.

And that time, the waistband turned. That time again I couldn't be sure until the third turn, when the nut started moving more freely, that I'd really done it.

I climbed up on the sail bin and squinted out at the free world. To the left all I could see was sky and a sparkle of sun on the water. I turned my head to the right and nearly fell off my perch. To the right there was a sail, and shining below it, green and rocky and moderately close, there was land.

I thought that if he came along at that moment to shut the hatch I would perversely be grateful.

Only desperation made me do what I did next, because I was sure that if he caught me in mid-escape he'd tie my hands and leave me in the dark on starvation rations.

The risk that I wouldn't get out unseen was appalling. My present conditions were just about bearable; my future afterwards wouldn't be.

Yet if I hadn't meant to risk it, why had I laboured so long on the nuts?

I went back to the loo and unscrewed the nuts completely. I knocked the bolts out, and pulled the whole lever free.

Without it, no one could flush the loo. I thought grimly that it would be an added complication if I found myself back in the cabin with it gone.

There was no sign of anyone on deck, and as usual I couldn't see if the boat was on automatic steering or whether there was anyone at the helm.

Hesitation was only in my mind. Looking back, it seemed as if I did everything very fast.

I pulled the hinged props of the hatch down inside the cabin, which one would do in the normal way if one wanted to shut the hatch oneself from the inside. This had the effect of slackening the guy-rope action of the chains crossed over the top.

Through the much reduced gap, little more than a slit, I poked the lever, aiming at where a link of chain was hooked over the top.

Long hours of inspection had given me the impression that those chains had no other fastening. Putting a link over the hook of the cleat must have seemed safe enough, because they were certain I had no means of dislodging them. I stuck the lever into the chain on the right, wedged it securely, and pushed. With almost miraculous elegance the whole chain slid loosely outwards, and the link fell off the cleat.

Without pausing for anything but mental hip-hoorays I applied the lever again, this time to where the fore and aft chain was fastened on the bow side. Again, with no more fuss, the link slid off.

I was committed. I couldn't get the chains back on again. I had to open the hatch now, and climb out. There was no retreat.

I took the lever with me as a last resort against recapture, putting it out first onto the deck. Then with both hands I released the hatch from the hinged props and pushed it wide. Eased it down gently until it lay flat, fearing to let it crash open and bring them running.

I snaked out onto the deck on my stomach. Rolled to the right, under the jib sail. Reached the railing, grabbed it with both hands, and bunny-hopped fast over the side, going down into the sea straight and feet first, like a pillar.

It wasn't the safest way of disembarking, but I survived it, staying down under the surface until my lungs protested. Surfacing was one of the most anxious moments of my life, but when I cautiously lifted mouth, nose and eyes above the water, there was the boat a hundred yards away, steadily sailing on.

With a great intake of air I sank down again and began to swim underwater towards the shore; gently, so as to make no notice-attracting splash.

The water was chilly, but not as cold as I'd expected. The shore, when I came up again, looked about a mile away, though distances at sea were deceptive.

The boat sailed on peacefully. It must have had a name on it, I supposed, though in the flurry I hadn't seen one. I wondered how long it would be before they found I had gone. Supper time, with luck.

The land ahead looked a most promising haven. To the left it was rocky, with grassy cliffs, but straight ahead lay a much greener part, with houses and hotels, and a strip of sand. Civilization, hot baths, freedom and a razor. I swam towards them steadily, taking rests. A mile was a long way for a moderate swimmer, and I was nothing like as strong as I had been twelve days earlier.

I looked back at the boat. It had gone a good way along the coast: growing smaller.

The big mainsail was sagging down the mast.

God, I thought, my heart lurching, if they're taking down the sails they'll see the open hatch.

Time had run out. They knew I had gone.

I ploughed for the shore until I felt dizzy with the effort. Swam until I had grey dots before the eyes and even greyer dots in the mind.

I wasn't going back into that dark hole. I absolutely couldn't.

When I next looked back all the sails were down and the boat was turning.

The hotels ahead were in a sandy bay. Two big hotels, white, with rows of balconies, and a lot of smaller buildings all around. There were some people on the beach, and four or five standing in the water.

Five hundred yards, perhaps.

It would take me years to swim five hundred yards.

I pushed my absolutely useless muscles into frantic efforts. If I could only reach the other bathers, I would be just one more head.

The boat had not been travelling very fast under sail. They would motor back faster. I feared to look around; to see them close. My imagination heard him shouting and pointing, and steering the boat to intercept me, felt them grabbing me with boathooks and pulling me in. When in the end I did nerve myself for a look, it was bad enough, but still too far to distinguish anyone clearly.

Next time I looked, it was alarming. They were catching up like hares. The nearest point of land was still about three hundred yards away, and it was uneven rock, not easy shelving beach. The sand lay in the centre of the bay: the curving arms were shallow cliffs. I would never reach the sand, I thought.

And yet . . . sailing boats had deep keels. They wouldn't be able to motor right up to the beach. Perhaps, after all, I could get there.

I had never felt so tired, so leaden. The hardest steeplechase had never demolished me so completely, even those I'd lost from being unfit. My progress through the water grew slower and slower, when speed was all that mattered. In the end it took me all my time to stay afloat.

There was a current, which I hadn't noticed at first, carrying me to the left, drifting me off my line to the beach. Nothing fierce; but simply sapping. I hadn't enough kick left to overcome it.

Another look back.

Literally terrifying. I could see him on deck, standing in the bows, shading his eyes with his hand. He had come back on a course closer to the shore than when I'd jumped, and it was the shoreline he seemed to be scouring most closely.

I swam on with feeble, futile strokes. I could see that I was not going to reach the sand. The current was taking me inexorably towards the higher, left hand side of the bay, where there were trees to within ten feet of the waterline, and rocks below the trees.

When I'd got to the numb stage of thinking drowning would be preferable to recapture, and doubting if one *could* drown oneself in cold blood, I found suddenly that I could no longer see for miles along the coast. I had at last got within the embracing arms of the bay. When I looked back, I couldn't see the boat.

It didn't stay out of sight long. It crept along in a straight line until it reached the centre of the bay, and there dropped anchor. I watched it in sick glimpses over my shoulder. Saw them unbuckle a black rubber dinghy and lower it over the side. Caught an impression of them lowering an outboard engine, and oars, and of two of them climbing down into the boat.

I heard the outboard splutter into life. Only about thirty feet to go to touch the land. It seemed like thirty miles.

There was a man-made strip of concrete set into the rocks ahead of me at the water's edge. I glanced along the shore towards the beach, and saw that there were others. Aids to bathers. The most heartening aid in the world to the bather approaching at snail's pace with the hounds of hell at his back.

The dinghy pulled away from the anchored boat and pointed its bulky black shape towards the shore.

I reached the strip of concrete. It was a flat step, set only inches above the water.

No grips for hauling oneself out. Just a step. I put one hand flat on it and raised a foot to it, and used jelly muscles to flounder up onto my stomach.

Not enough. Not enough. The dinghy would come while I was lying there.

My heart was pounding. Effort and fear in equal measures. Utter desperation took me to hands and knees and set me crawling up the rocks to find shelter.

Ordinarily it would have been easy. It was a gentle shore, undemanding. A child could have jumped where I laboured. I climbed up about six feet of tumbled rocks and found a shallow gully, half full of water. I rolled into the hollow and lay there panting, hopelessly exhausted, listening to the outboard engine grow steadily louder.

They must have seen me, I thought despairingly. Seen me climbing up out of the sea. Yet if I'd stayed at the water's edge they would have found me just as surely. I lay in defeated misery and wondered how on earth I could live through whatever was coming.

The dinghy approached. I kept my head down. They were going to have to come and find me and carry me, and if I could raise enough breath I'd yell until some of the people on the beach took notice, except that they were far enough away to think it was all a game.

The engine died and I heard his voice, raised but not exactly shouting.

He said, 'Excuse me, but have you seen a friend of ours swim in from the sea? We think he fell overboard.'

A woman's voice answered him, from so close to me that I almost fainted.

'No, I haven't seen anybody.'

He said, 'He takes drugs. He might have been acting funny.'

'Serves him right, then,' she said, sanctimoniously.

'I've been reading. I haven't seen him. Have you come from that boat?'

'That's right. We think he fell overboard about here. We heard a splash, but we thought it was just a fish. Till after.'

'Sorry,' she said. 'Why don't you ask along the beach?'

'Just starting this side,' he said. 'We'll work round.'

There was a noise of oars being fitted into rowlocks, and the splash and squeak as they pulled away. I stayed where I was without moving, hoping she wouldn't have hysterics when she saw me, dreading that she would call them back.

I could hear him, away along the shore, loudly asking the same question of someone else.

Her voice said, 'Don't be frightened. I know you're there.'

I didn't answer her. She'd taken away what was left of my breath.

After a pause she said, 'Do you take drugs?'

'No,' I said. It was little more than a whisper.

'What did you say?'

'No.'

'Hm. Well, you'd better not move. They're methodical. I think I'll go on reading.'

Incredulously, I took her advice, lying half in and half out of the water, feeling heart and lungs subside slowly to a more manageable rhythm.

'They've landed on the beach,' she said.

My heart stirred up again. 'Are they searching?' I said anxiously.

'No. Asking questions, I should think.' She paused. 'Are they criminals?'

'I don't know.'

'But . . . would they take you from here by force? With people watching?'

'Yes. You heard them. If I shouted for help, they'd say I was crazy with drugs. No one would stop them.'

'They're walking round the far side of the bay,' she said. 'Asking people.'

'My name is Roland Britten,' I said. 'I live in Newbury, and I'm an accountant. I was kidnapped twelve days ago, and they've kept me on that boat ever since, and I don't know why. So please, whoever you are, if they do manage to get me back there, will you tell the police? I really do most desperately need help.'

There was a short silence. I thought that I must have overdone it; that she didn't believe me. Yet I'd had to tell her, as a precaution.

She apparently made up her mind. 'Well then,' she said briskly, 'time for you to vanish.'

'Where to?'

'My bedroom,' she said.

She was a great one for punches in the mental solar plexus. In spite of the grimness of things in general, I almost laughed.

'Can you see me?' I said.

'I can see your feet. I saw all of you when you climbed out of the sea and scrambled up here.'

'And how do I get to your bedroom dressed in a wet shirt and underpants and nothing else?'

'Do you want to avoid those men, or don't you?'

There was no answer to that.

'Stay still,' she said sharply, though I had not in fact moved. 'They're looking this way. Someone over there seems to be pointing in this direction.'

'Oh God.'

'Stay still.' There was a longish pause, then she said, 'They are walking back along the beach, towards their boat. If they don't stop there, but come on this way, we will go.'

I waited dumbly, and more or less prayed.

'There's a path above us,' she said. 'I will hand you a towel. Wrap it round you, and climb up to the path.'

'Are they coming?'

'Yes.'

A triangle of brightly striped bathing towel appeared over the rock by my head. There was little I'd ever wanted to do less than stand up out of my secure hiding place. My nerves were all against it.

'Hurry up,' she said. 'Don't look back.'

I stood up, dripping, with my back to the sea. Pulled the towel towards me, wrapped it round like a sarong, and tackled the rocky upgrade to the path. The respite in the gully had given me back a surprising amount of energy: or perhaps it was plain fear. In any case I climbed the second stage a great deal more nimbly than the first.

'I'm behind you,' her voice said. 'Don't look back. Turn right when you reach the path. And don't run.'

'Yes ma'am,' I said under my breath. Never argue with a guardian angel.

The path was fringed on both sides with trees, with a mixture of sand and bare rock underfoot. The sunshine dappled through the branches and at any other time would have looked pretty.

When the path widened she fell into step beside me, between me and the sea.

'Take the branch path to the left,' she said, drawing level. 'And don't walk too fast.'

I glanced at her, curious to see what she looked like. She matched her voice: a no-nonsense middle-aged lady with spectacles and a practical air. Self-confident. Tall: almost six feet. Thin, and far from a beauty.

She was wearing a pale-pink blouse, fawn cotton trousers, and sandshoes, and she carried a capacious canvas beach bag.

Beach. Swimming. In March.

'Where is this place?' I said.

'Cala St Galdana.'

'Where's that?'

'Minorca, of course.'

'*Where*?'

'Don't stop walking. Minorca.'

'Island next to Majorca?'

'Of course.' She paused. 'Didn't you know?'

I shook my head. The branch path reached the top of a shallow gradient and began to descend through more trees on the far side.

She peered to the right as we went over the brow.

'Those men are just coming along the lower path, heading towards where I was sitting. I think it would be a good idea to hurry a little now, don't you?'

'Understatement,' I said.

Hurrying meant stubbing my bare toes on various half-buried stones and feeling the dismal weakness again make rubber of my legs.

'While they are looking for you on the rocks, we will reach my hotel,' she said.

I shuffled along and saved my breath. Glanced over my shoulder. Only empty path. No pursuing furies. So why did I feel that they could see through earth and trees and know exactly where to find me?

'Over that little bridge, and across the road. Over there.' She pointed. 'That's the hotel.'

It was one of the two big white ones. We reached the wide glass doors and went inside. Made it unchallenged across the hall and into the lift. Rose to the fifth floor. She scooped some keys out of her beach bag, and let us into 507.

We had seen almost nobody on the way. Still enough warm sun for holidaymakers to be out on the beach and for the staff to be sleeping.

507 had a sea-view balcony, twin beds, two armchairs,

a yellow carpet, and orange and brown curtains. Regulation hotel room, with almost none of my saviour's belongings in sight.

She walked over to the glass door, which was wide open, and half stepped onto the balcony.

'Do you want to watch?' she said.

I looked cautiously over her shoulder. From that height one could see the whole panorama of the bay. There was the boat, anchored in the centre. There was the dinghy on the sand. The headland where I'd crawled out of the sea was to the right, the path leading to it from the beach showing clearly through the trees like a dappled yellow snake.

Along the path came the two men, my familiar warder in front, making for the sand. They trudged slowly across to the dinghy, still looking continually around, and pushed it into the sea.

They both climbed in. They started the outboard. They steered away from the beach.

I felt utterly drained.

'Do you mind if I sit down?' I said.

# CHAPTER SIX

Thanks to telephones, consul, bank, and friends, I flew back to England the following evening, but not before I had collected further unforgettable memories of Miss Hilary Margaret Pinlock.

She asked me my measurements, descended to the local boutiques, and returned with new clothes.

She lent me her bathroom, inspected me cleaned and dressed, and decided to go shopping for a razor. I protested. She went. It was as easy to stop Miss Pinlock as an avalanche.

With some relief I scratched the twelve days' scruffy dark stubble off my face, one glance in the looking glass having persuaded me that I was not going to look better in a beard. The twelve days of indoor life had left me thin and pale, with grey hollows in cheeks and eye sockets which I didn't remember having before. Nothing that a little freedom wouldn't fix.

On her second expedition she had also bought bread, cheese and fruit, explaining that she was there on a package holiday, and that the hotel didn't cater for random visitors.

'I'll go down to dinner at seven as usual,' she said. 'You can eat here.'

Throughout all her remarks and actions ran the positive decision-making of one accustomed to command.

'Are you a children's nurse?' I asked curiously.

'No,' she said, unsmiling. 'A headmistress.'

'Oh.'

The smile came, briefly. 'Of a girls-only comprehensive, in Surrey.'

With a touch of sardonic humour she watched me reassess her in the light of that revelation. Not a do-gooding bossy spinster, but a fulfilled career woman of undoubted power.

'Yes. Well . . .' she shrugged. 'If you give me the numbers, I'll ask the switchboard for your calls.'

'And I need a bedroom,' I said.

'Your friends might return and ask about strangers needing bedrooms,' she said.

It had occurred to me too. 'Yes, but . . .' I said.

She pointed to one of the twin beds. 'You can sleep there. I am here alone. The friend who was coming with me had to cry off at the last minute.'

'But . . .' I stopped.

She waited calmly.

'All right,' I said. 'Thank you.'

When she returned from dinner she brought with her a piece of news and a bottle of wine.

'Your friend from the boat was downstairs in the lobby, asking everyone who speaks English if they saw a crazy young man come ashore today. Everyone said no. He looks extremely worried.'

'Probably thinks I drowned.'

The boat had gone from the bay. He must have reached another mooring and returned to Cala St Galdana by road. I wondered how long and how thoroughly he would persevere in his search: the more he feared whoever he was working for, the less he would give up.

The evening air was chilly. Miss Pinlock shut the glass door against the night sky and expertly opened her bottle of Marqués de Riscal.

'Tell me about your journey,' she said, handing me a glass.

I told her the beginning and the end, and not much of the middle.

'Extraordinary,' she said.

'When I get home I'll have a go at finding out what it was all about . . .'

She looked at me gravely. 'It may not be over.'

She had an uncomfortable habit of putting my worst fears into speech.

We drank the excellent wine and she told me a little of her busy life.

'I enjoy it,' she said positively.

'Yes, I see that.'

There was a pause. She looked carefully at the wine in her glass.

She said, 'Will you go to bed with me?'

I suppose I sat in an ungentlemanly heap with my mouth open. I closed it, conscious of the insult it conveyed.

When I'd got over the first shock, she looked up. Her face was calm and businesslike as before, but also suddenly there was vulnerability and self-consciousness. A blush started on her neck, and spread painfully upwards.

She was between forty-two and forty-six, I guessed. She had dark brown wavy hair, going grey, cut with shape but not much style. A broad, lined forehead, large nose, mouth turning down naturally at the corners, and small chin. Behind her glasses her eyes were brown and looked small, probably the effect of the lenses. Wrinkles grew where wrinkles grow; and there was no glow to her skin. A face of character, but not sexually attractive, at least not to me.

'Why?' I said, which was a pretty stupid question.

She blushed a little deeper and shook her head.

'Look,' I said, 'it isn't as simple as that. I can't . . . I mean, one can't just sort of switch that sort of thing on and off, like a tap.'

We sat in awkward silence. She put down her glass, and said, 'I'm sorry. It was a ridiculous thing to say. Please try and forget it.'

'You said it because it was in your mind. So . . . well . . . you must have meant it.'

She half smiled, ruefully. 'It's been in my mind, now and again, for a long time. You will find it extraordinary, but I have never . . . so to speak, slept with a man.'

'In this permissive age?' I said.

'There you are, you see. You find it hard to believe. But I've never been pretty, even as a child. And also I've always been, well . . . able to do things. Learn. Teach. Organize. Administrate. All the unfeminine things. All my life people have relied on me, because I was capable. I've always had health and energy, and I've enjoyed getting on, being given senior posts, and five years ago, being offered a headship. In most ways my life has been absorbing and gratifyingly successful.'

'But?' I suggested.

She nodded. 'But. I was never interested in boys when I was in my teens, and then I thought them callow, and at university I worked all hours to get a First, and after that I've always taught in girls' schools because frankly it is usually a man who's given the headship in a mixed school, and I've never fancied the role of male-ego-massager in second place. Nothing I've ever been or done has been geared to romance.'

'So why *now*?'

'I hope you won't be angry, but it is mostly curiosity, and the pursuit of knowledge.'

I wasn't angry. Just astounded.

Her blush had subsided as fast as it had risen. She was back on surer ground.

'For some time I've thought I ought to have had the

experience. Of sexual intercourse, that is. It didn't come my way when I was young, but I didn't expect it, you see. I think now that I should have tried to find a man, but then, when I was at college, I was half scared of it, and I didn't have any great urge, and I was engrossed in my work. Afterwards for years it didn't bother me, until I was thirty or so, and of course by that time all the men one meets are married, and in any case, teaching among women, one rarely meets any men, except officials, and so on. I go to many official functions, of course, but people tend not to ask unmarried women to private social occasions.'

'What changed your mind?' I asked, fascinated.

'Oh, having to cope with highly-sexed young girls. The modern lot are so clued up. So brash and outspoken. I like them. But I have to arrange their sex-education lessons, and in my time I've even taught them, from text books. I feel it would be a great deal better if I knew . . . what the sex act felt like. I feel at a disadvantage with many of the older girls, particularly as this last term I had to advise a pregnant fourteen-year-old. Fourteen! She knows more than I do. How can I advise her?'

'Catholic priests don't have this problem,' I commented.

'Catholic priests may be respected for virginity, but school-mistresses are not.' She paused, hesitating, and went on. 'To be honest, I also find myself at a disadvantage with the married members of my staff. Some of them have a tendency to patronize me, even unconsciously. I don't like it. I would be able to cope with it perfectly, though, if I actually knew what they know.'

'Am I,' I said slowly, 'the first man you have asked?'

'Oh yes.' She smiled slightly and drank some wine. 'There are practically no men one *can* ask. Especially if one is a headmistress, and widely known. I certainly wouldn't jeopardize my job.'

'I can see that it would be difficult,' I said, thinking about it.

'So of course holidays are the only possibility,' she said. 'I've been on archaeological cruises to Greece, and all that sort of thing, and I've seen other couples join up, but it never happened to me. And then I've heard that some lonely women throw themselves at ski-instructors and waiters and men who perform for money, but somehow that isn't what I want. I mean, I don't want to despise myself. I want knowledge without guilt or shame.'

'The dream of Eden,' I said.

'What? Oh, yes.'

'What about your friend?' I said, pointing to the second bed.

She smiled twistedly. 'No friend, just an excuse for having come alone.'

'Friends being death to the pursuit of knowledge?'

'Exactly.'

We drank some more wine.

'I've been here since last Saturday,' she said. 'I always

take a complete break straight after the end of term, and then go back refreshed for the new work.'

'A perfect system,' I said absently. 'Why didn't you . . . er . . . throw me back, when the men in the dinghy came after me?'

'If you mean, did I immediately see you as a . . . *possible* . . . then no, of course not. I was fascinated, in a way. I'd never seen anyone in such terror before. I watched you from quite a long way out. Swimming, and looking back. It wasn't until you reached the concrete step, though, and I saw your face clearly, that I realized that you were being *hunted*. It would take a certain mentality to point the hounds at an exhausted quarry gone to ground, and I don't have it.'

'And thank God for that,' I said.

I stood up, and opened the glass door, and went out onto the balcony. The cool night was clear, with bright stars over the ageless Mediterranean. Waves rippled softly round the edges of the bay, and the gentle moonlight shone on the wide, empty expanse where the boat had been anchored.

It was the weirdest of debts. She had saved me from recapture. I certainly owed her my wholeness of mind, if not life itself. If the only payment she wanted was something I didn't much want to give, then that was simply too bad. One extreme favour, I thought sardonically, deserved another.

I went in, and sat down. Drank some wine with a dry mouth.

'We'll try, if you like,' I said.

She sat very still. I had a swift impression that now I'd agreed she was hastily retreating: that the half-fear of her student days was definitely still there.

'You don't have to,' she said.

'No. I want to.' Heaven forgive all liars.

She said, as if speaking to herself, and not to me: 'I'll never have another chance.'

The voice of longing teetering on the brink of the leap in the dark. Her strength of mind, I saw, would carry her through. I admired her. I determined to make Hilary Pinlock's leap something that at least she wouldn't regret: if I could.

'First of all,' I said, 'we'll switch off the lights and sit by the window for a while, and talk about it.'

We sat facing each other in dim reflected moonlight, and I asked her some fairly medical questions, to which she gave straightforward replies.

'What if you get pregnant?' I said.

'I'd solve that later.'

'You want to go ahead?'

She took a deep breath. 'If you do.'

If I *can*, I thought.

'Then I think the best thing to do first would be to get undressed,' I said. 'Do you have a nightdress? And could you lend me a dressing gown?'

I reflected, as I put on her blue candlewick in the privacy of the bathroom, that deep physical tiredness was a rotten basis for the matter in hand. I yawned. I wanted above all to go to sleep.

When I went out she was sitting by the window in a long cotton nightgown which had a frill round the neck-line, but was not, of course, transparent.

'Come on,' I said. 'We'll sit on the bed.'

She stood up. The nightgown accentuated her height and thinness, and revealed long narrow feet. I pulled back the bed-clothes, sat on the white sheet, and held my hand out towards her. She came, gripped my hand, and sat beside me.

'Right,' I said. 'Now, if at any point you want to stop, you've only got to say so.'

She nodded.

'Lie down, then,' I said, 'and imagine you are twenty.'

'Why?'

'Because this is not a brain matter. It's about the stimulation of nerve endings. About feeling, not thinking. If you think all the time of who you are, you may find it inhibiting. Age doesn't exist in the dark. If you imagine you are twenty, you will be twenty, and you'll find it liberating.'

'You're a most unusual man.'

'Oh sure,' I said. 'And you're a most unusual woman. So lie down.'

She gave a small unexpected chuckle, and did as I said.

'Take off your glasses,' I said, and she put them without comment on the bedside table. In the dim light her eyes looked larger, as I'd guessed, and her big nose smaller, and her determined mouth softer. I leaned over and kissed her lips, and if it was basically a nephew-to-aunt gesture it brought a smile to her face and a grin to my own.

It was the strangest lovemaking, but it did work. I looked back afterwards to the moment when she first took pleasure in the sensation of my stroking her skin; the ripple of surprise when she felt with her hands the size of an erect man; the passion with which she finally responded; and the stunning release into gasping incredulity.

'Is that,' she said, out of breath, 'is that what every woman feels?'

I knew she had reached a most satisfactory climax. 'I guess so,' I said. 'On good days.'

'Oh my goodness,' she said in a sort of exultation. 'So now I *know*.'

# CHAPTER SEVEN

Thursday morning I went back to the office and tried to take up my life where it had left off.

The same smell of typewriters, filing cabinets, reams of paper. Same bustle, adding machines, telephones. Same heaps of too much work. All familiar, all unreal.

Our two assistants, Debbie and Peter, had had a rough time, they said aggrievedly, trying to account to everyone for my unaccountable absence. They had reported my disappearance to the police, who had said I was over twenty-one and had the right to duck out if I wanted to, and that they would look for me only if I'd committed a crime, or was clearly a missing victim. They had thought I had merely gone off on a celebratory binge after winning the Gold Cup.

'We told them you wouldn't have gone away for so long,' Peter said. 'But they didn't show much interest.'

'We wanted them to get in touch with Mr King, through Interpol,' Debbie complained. 'And they laughed at the idea.'

'I expect they would,' I said. 'So Trevor is still on his holiday?'

'He's not due back until Monday,' Peter said, surprised that I should have forgotten something I knew so well.

'Oh yes . . .'

I spent the morning re-organizing the timetable and getting Peter to make new appointments to replace those I'd missed, and the afternoon discovering that as far as the police were concerned, my troubles were still of little interest. I was back home, wasn't I? Unharmed. Without having to pay a ransom? Was there any form of extortion? No. Was I starved? No. Beaten? No. Tied with ropes, straps, shackles? No. Was I sure it wasn't a practical joke? They would look into it, they said: but one of them remarked that *he* wouldn't mind a free fortnight's trip to the Mediterranean, and his colleague laughed. I gathered that if I seriously wanted to get to know, I would have to do the investigating myself.

I did want to know. Not knowing felt dangerously unsafe, like standing behind a bad-tempered horse. If I didn't know why I'd been taken the first time, how was I to stop it happening again?

Thursday evening I collected my Dolomite, which had been moved to the Cheltenham racecourse manager's front drive. ('Where on earth have you been? We traced that it was your car through the police.') Next I drove to the house of the racecourse valet to pick up my wallet and keys and racing saddle. ('Where on earth have you been? I gave the racecourse manager your car keys, I hope that's all right.') Then I drove back to my cottage (having spent the previous night in an airport hotel), and with faint-hearted caution let myself in.

No one was waiting there in the dark, with coshes or ether or one-way tickets to sail lockers. I switched on all the lights and poured myself a stiff Scotch and told myself to calm down and take a better grip.

I telephoned the trainer I regularly rode early morning exercise for ('Where on earth have you been?') and arranged to start again on Monday: and I rang a man who had asked me to ride in a hunter 'chase, to apologize for not turning up. I saw no reason not to answer the questions about where I'd been, so I told them all: abducted and taken on a boat to Minorca, and I didn't know why. I thought at least that someone might come up with a possible explanation, but everyone I told sounded as flummoxed as I felt.

There wasn't much food in the cottage, and the steak in the fridge had grown whiskers. I decided on spaghetti, with chopped up cheese melting on it, but before starting to cook I went upstairs to change new jacket for old sweater, and to make a detour to the bathroom.

I glanced casually out of the bathroom window and spent a frozen instant in pure panic.

There was a man in the garden, looking towards the downstairs rooms of the cottage. The light from the sitting-room window fell brightly on his face.

I hadn't consciously remembered him, but I knew him

at once, in one heart-stopping flash of the inner eye. He was the fake St John's Ambulance man from Cheltenham races.

Behind him, in the road, stood a car, with gleams of light edging its roof and windows. A second man was levering himself out of the passenger's seat, carrying what looked like a plastic bag containing cotton wool. A third figure, dimly seen, was heading through the garden to the back of the house.

They couldn't, I thought: surely they couldn't think they would trick me again. But with three of them, they hardly needed tricks.

The St John's man waved his arm to the man by the car, and pointed, and the two of them took up positions, one on each side of my front door, out of sight of anyone opening it from the inside. The St John's man stretched out an arm and rang my bell.

I unfroze.

Wonderful how terror sharpened the wits. There was only one place I could hide, and that was in my bedroom. The speed with which I'd gone over the side of the boat was nothing compared with my disappearance inside the cottage.

Downstairs in the sitting-room the huge old fireplace had at one side incorporated a bread oven, which the people living there before me had removed, constructing instead a head-high alcove with display shelves. Wanting a safe place in which to keep valuables, they had opened the upper part of the bread oven space into the bedroom above, where it formed a sort of box below the floor of the built-in wardrobe. Not having much in the way of valuables, I stored my two suitcases in there instead.

I opened the wardrobe door, and pulled up the hinged flap of flooring, and hauled out the cases.

The door bell rang again, insistently.

Lowering myself into the space took seconds, and I had the wardrobe door shut and the flap of floor almost in place when they burst in through the front door.

They rampaged through the place, opening and slamming doors, and shouting, and finally gathering all together downstairs.

'He must be bloody here.'

'Britten! Britten, come out, we know you're here.'

'The effing bastard's scarpered.'

I could hear every loud word through the chipboard partition between my hiding place and the sitting-room. I felt horribly vulnerable sitting there, level with the picture over the mantelshelf, practically in the room with them, hidden only by a thin piece of wall.

'He couldn't have seen us coming.'

'He never got out of the back, I'll tell you that for sure.'

'Then where the bleeding hell is he?'

'How about those suitcases of his upstairs?'

'No. He ain't in them. They're too small. And I looked.'

'He must be meaning to bleeding scarper.'

'Yeah.'

'Take another butcher's upstairs. He must be here somewhere.'

They searched the whole house again, crashing about with heavy boots.

One of them opened the wardrobe above me for the second time, and saw nothing but clothes, as before. I sat under their feet and sweated, and felt my pulse shoot up to the hundreds.

'Look under the bed,' he said.

'Can't. The bed's right on the floor.'

'How about the other bedroom, then?'

'I looked. He ain't there.'

'Well, bleeding well look again.'

The wardrobe door closed above me. I wiped the sweat out of my eyes and tried to ease my legs without scraping my shoes on the wall and making a noise. I was half sitting, half lying, in a recess about three feet long by two feet deep, and just wide enough for my shoulders. My knees were bent acutely, with my heels against the backs of my thighs. It was a bad position for every muscle I could think of.

Two of them came into the sitting-room, one after the other.

'What you got there? Here, let me see.'

'None of your bleeding business.'

'It's his wallet. You've got his wallet.'

'Yeah. Well, it was in his bedroom.'

'Well, bleeding well put it back.'

'Not likely, he's got thirty quid in it.'

'You'll effing well do as I say. You know the orders, same as I do. Don't steal nothink, don't break nothink. I told you.'

'You can have half, then.'

'Give it to me. I'll put it back. I don't trust you.' It was the St John's man talking, I thought.

'It's bloody stupid, not nicking what we can get.'

'You want the fuzz on our necks? They didn't bloody look for him last time, and they won't bloody look for him this time, either, but they will if they find his place has been turned over. Use your bloody loaf.'

'We ain't got him yet.'

'Matter of time. He's round here some place. Bound to be.'

'He won't come back if he sees us in here.'

'No, you got a point there. Tell you what, we'll turn the lights off and wait for him, and jump him, like.'

'He left all the lights on, himself. He won't come in if they're off.'

'Best if one of us waits in the kitchen, like, and the other two in the garden. Then when he gets here we can jump him from both sides, right, just as he's coming back through the door.'

'Yeah.'

Into these plans there suddenly came a fresh voice, female and enquiring.

'Mr Britten? Mr Britten, are you there?'

I heard her push the front door open and take the step into the sitting-room.

The voice of my next-door neighbour.

Yes, Mrs Morris, I'm here, I thought. And it would take more than me and a small plump senior citizen to fight off my unwanted guests.

'Who are you?' she said.

'Friends of his. Calling on him, like.'

'He's away,' she said sharply.

'No he's not. He's back. His car's round the side. And he's having a drink, see? Whisky.'

'Then where is he? Mr Britten?' she called.

'Ain't no use, lady. He's out. We're waiting for him, like.'

'I don't think you should be in here.' A brave lady, old Mrs Morris.

'We're friends of his, see.'

'You don't look like his friends,' she said.

'Know his friends, then, do yer?'

A certain nervousness crept into her voice, but the resolution was still there.

'I think you'd better wait outside.'

There was a pause, then the St John's man said, 'Where do you think he could be? We've searched all over for him.'

Let her not know about this hiding place, I prayed. Let her not think of it.

'He might've gone to the pub,' she said. 'Why don't you go down there? To the Fox.'

'Yeah, maybe.'

'Anyway, I think I'll just see you out.'

Intrepid little Mrs Morris. I heard them all go out, and shut the front door behind them. The lock clicked decisively. The cottage was suddenly still.

I lay quiet, listening for their car to start.

Nothing happened.

They were still there, I thought. Outside. Round my house. Waiting.

On the mantelshelf, the clock ticked.

I cautiously pushed up the flap over my head, and sat up, straightening knees, back and neck, with relief.

The light in my bedroom was still on, shining in a crack under the wardrobe door. I left the door shut. If they saw so much as a shadow move they would know for sure I was inside the house.

I reflected that I had had a good deal too much practice at passing uncertain hours in small dark places.

The lock clicked on my front door.

One gets to know the noises of one's own house so well that sight is unnecessary for interpretation. I heard the unmistakable sound of the hinges, and the gritty sound of a shoe on the bare flagstones of the entrance hall. Then there were quiet noises in the sitting-room itself, and low voices, and the squeak of the door to the kitchen. They had come back in a way that would not bring Mrs Morris.

I sat rigidly, wondering whether to slide down into the smaller space and risk them hearing my movements, or stay with head and shoulders above floor level and risk them searching my clothes cupboard yet again. If I coughed or sneezed, or as much as knocked the chipboard with my elbow as I slid down into the safer hiding place, they would hear me. I sat immobile, stretching my own ears and wondering despairingly how long they would stay.

Breathing evenly was difficult, controlling my heartbeat was impossible. Acute anxiety over a period of hours was highly shattering to the nerves.

From time to time I could hear them moving and murmuring, but could no longer distinctly hear their words. I supposed that they too were hiding, waiting out of sight for me to come home. It was almost funny when one thought of it: them hiding behind the furniture and me within the walls.

Unfunny if they found me. More like unfaceable.

I took a deep, shaky breath, one of many.

Someone began to come quietly upstairs. The familiar creaks of the old treads fizzed through my body like electric shocks. The risk of moving had to be taken. I tucked my elbows in and bent my knees, and eased myself back under the floor. The flap came down hard on my hair and I thought wildly that they must have heard it: but no one arrived with triumphant shouts, and the awful suspense just went on and on.

I got pains from being bent up, and I got cramps, but there was nothing I could do about that except surrender.

One of them spent a good time in my bedroom. I could hear his footfall through the floorboards, and the small thuds of drawers shutting. Guessed he was no longer looking for me, but at what I owned. It didn't make his nearness to me any safer.

The fear seemed endless; but everything ends. I heard them murmuring again in the sitting-room, and shutting the kitchen door. The man upstairs went down again. More murmurings: a chorus. Then silence for a while. Then a step or two in the hall, and the click of the front door closing.

I waited, thinking that only one of them had gone out.

Their car started. Shifted quietly into gear. Drove off.

I still lay without moving, not trusting that it was over, that it wasn't a trick: but the absolute quietness persisted, and in the end I pushed up the flap of the floor and levered myself with much wincing and pins and needles onto my bedroom carpet.

The lights were still on, but the black square of window was grey. The whole night had passed. It was dawn.

I threw a few things into one of the suitcases and left the cottage ten minutes later.

The Yale lock on the front door showed no signs of forcing, and I guessed they must have opened it with a credit card, as I myself had done once when I'd locked myself out. My car stood untouched where I'd left it, and even my half-drunk glass of Scotch was still on the sitting-room table.

Feeling distinctly unsettled I had a wash, shave and breakfast at the Chequers Hotel, and then went to the police.

'Back again?' they said.

They listened, made notes, asked questions.

'Do you know who they were?'

'No.'

'Any evidence of a forced entry?'

'No.'

'Anything stolen?'

'No.'

'Nothing we can do, sir.'

'Look,' I said, 'these people are trying to abduct me. They've succeeded once, and they're trying again. Can't you do a damn thing to help?'

They seemed fairly sympathetic, but the answer was no. They hadn't enough men or money to mount a round-the-clock guard on anyone for an indefinite period without a very good reason.

'Isn't the threat of abduction a very good reason?'

'No. If you believe the threat, you could hire yourself a private bodyguard.'

'Thanks very much,' I said. 'But if anyone reports me missing again, I won't have gone by choice, and you might do me a favour and start looking.'

'If they do, sir, we will.'

*

I went to the office and sat at my desk and watched my hands shake. Whatever I normally had in the way of mental and physical stamina was at a very low ebb.

Peter came in with a cable and his usual expression of not quite grasping the point, and handed me the bad news. CAR BROKEN DOWN RETURNING WEDNESDAY APOLOGIES TREVOR.

'You read this?' I asked Peter.

'Yes.'

'Well, you'd better fetch Mr King's list, for next week, and his appointment book.'

He went on the errand and I sat and looked blankly at the cable. Trevor had sent it from some town I'd never heard of in France, and had given no return address. He wouldn't be worried, wherever he was. He would be sure I could take his extra few days in my stride.

Peter came back with the list and I laced my fingers together to keep them still. What did people take for tranquillizers?

'Get me some coffee,' I said to Peter. His eyebrows rose. 'I know it's only a quarter past nine,' I said, 'but get me some coffee . . . please.'

When he brought the coffee I sent him to fetch Debbie, so that I could share between them the most urgent jobs. Neither of them had a good brain, but they were both persistent, meticulous plodders, invaluable qualities in accountants' assistants. In many offices the assistants were bright and actively studying to become accountants themselves, but Trevor for some reason seemed always to prefer working with the unambitious sort. Peter was twenty-two, Debbie twenty-four. Peter, I thought, was a latent homosexual who hadn't quite realized it. Debbie, mousy-haired, big-busted, and pious, had a boyfriend working in a hardware shop. Peter occasionally made jokes about screws, which shocked her.

They sat opposite my desk with notebooks poised, both of them looking at me with misgiving.

'You really look awfully ill,' Debbie said. 'Worse even than yesterday. Grey, sort of.' There seemed to be more ghoulish relish in her voice than concern.

'Yes, well, never mind that,' I said. 'I've looked at Mr King's list, and there are a few accounts that won't wait until he gets back.' There were two he should have seen to before he went, but no one was perfect. 'Certificate for the solicitors, Mr Crest, and Mr Grant. I'm afraid they are already overdue. Could you bring all the papers for those two in here, Debbie? Later, I mean. Not this instant. Then there are the two summonses to appear before the Commissioners next Thursday. I'll apply for postponements for those, but you'd better bring all the books in here, Debbie, anyway, and I'll try and make a start on them.'

'That's the Axwood stables, is it? And Millrace Stud?'

'Not the stud; that's the week after. Mr King can deal with that. The Axwood stables, yes, and those corn merchants, Coley Young.'

'The Coley Young books aren't here yet,' Peter said.

'Well, for crying out loud, didn't you do what I said two weeks ago, and tell them to send them?' I could hear the scratch in my voice and did my best to stop it. 'OK,' I said slowly. 'Did you ask them to send them?'

'Yes, I did.' Peter tended to look sulky. 'But they haven't come.'

'Ring them again, would you? And what about the Axwood stables?'

'You checked those yourself, if you remember.'

'Did I?' I looked back as if to a previous existence. The two summonses to appear before the Commissioners were not particularly serious. We seldom actually went. The summonses were issued when the Inland Revenue thought a particular set of accounts were long overdue: a sort of goad to action. It meant that Trevor or I asked for a postponement, did the accounts, and sent them in before the revised date. End of drama. The two summonses in question had arrived after Trevor had left for his holidays, which was why he hadn't dealt with them himself.

'You said the petty cash book hadn't arrived,' Peter said.

'Did I? Did you ask them to send it?'

'Yes, I did, but it hasn't come.'

I sighed. 'Ring them again.'

A great many clients saw no urgency at all in getting their accounts done, and requests from us for further information or relevant papers were apt to be ignored for weeks.

'Tell them both they really will have to go before the Commissioners if they don't send those books.'

'But they won't really, will they?' Peter said. Not the brightest of boys, I thought.

'I'll get adjournments anyway,' I said patiently, 'but Trevor will need those books to hand the second he gets back.'

Debbie said, 'Mr Wells rang three times yesterday afternoon.'

'Who is Mr Wells? Oh yes. Mr Wells.'

'He says one of his creditors is applying to have him made bankrupt and he wants to know what you're going to do about it.'

I'd forgotten all the details of Mr Wells' troubles. 'Where are his books?' I asked.

'In one of those boxes,' Debbie said, pointing. A three-high row of large cardboard boxes ran along the wall under the window. Each box had the name of the client on it, in large black letters, and each contained the cash books, invoices, receipts, ledgers, paying-in books, bank statements, petty cash records, stocktakings and general paraphernalia needed for the assessment of taxes. Each of the boxes represented a task I had yet to do.

It took me an average of two working days to draw up the annual accounts for each client. Some audits took longer. I had roughly two hundred clients. The thing was impossible.

Trevor had collared the bigger firms and liked to

spend nearly a week on each. He dealt with seven clients. No wonder Commissioners' summonses fell on us like snow.

Peter and Debbie did most of the routine work, checking bank statements against cheque numbers, and against invoices paid. Someone extra to share that work would only help Trevor and me to a certain extent. Taking a third, fully equal partner would certainly reduce the pressure, but it would also entail dividing the firm's profits into three instead of two, which would mean a noticeable drop in income. Trevor was totally opposed. Amalgamation with the London firm meant Trevor not being boss and me not going racing . . . a fair sized impasse, all in all.

'Debbie and I didn't get our pay cheques last week,' Peter said. 'Nor did Bess.' Bess was the typist.

'And the water heater in the washroom is running cold,' Debbie added. 'And you did say I could go to the dentist this afternoon at three-thirty.'

'Sorry about all the extra work,' Peter said, not sounding it, 'but I'm afraid it's my Friday for the Institute of Accounting Staff class.'

'Mm,' I said. 'Peter, telephone to Leyhill Prison and ask if Connaught Powys is still there.'

'What?'

'Leyhill Prison. Somewhere in Gloucestershire. Get the number from directory enquiries.'

'But . . .'

'Just go and do it,' I said. 'Connaught Powys. Is he still there.'

He went out looking mystified, but then he, like Debbie, dated from after the searchingly difficult court case. Debbie went to fetch the first batch of the papers I needed, and I began on the solicitors' certificates.

Since embezzlement of clients' trust monies had become a flourishing industry, laws had been passed to ensure that auditors checked every six months to see that the cash and securities which were supposed to be in a solicitor's care actually were there. If they weren't, Nemesis swiftly struck the solicitor off the Roll. If they were, the auditor signed the certificate and pocketed his fee.

Peter returned as if he'd come from a dangerous mission, looking noble.

'The prison said he was released six weeks ago, on February 16th.'

'Thanks.'

'I had a good deal of trouble in getting through.'

'Er . . . well done,' I said. He still looked as if he thought more praise was due, but he didn't get it.

If Connaught Powys had been out for six weeks, he would have had a whole month to fix me up with a voyage. I tried hard to concentrate on the checking for the certificates but the sail locker kept getting in the way.

Solicitor Grant's affair tallied at about the third shot, but I kept making errors with Denby Crest's. I realized I'd always taken clarity of mind for granted, like walking:

one of those things you don't consciously value until you've lost it. Numbers, from my infancy, had been like a second language, understood without effort. I checked Denby Crest's figures five times and kept getting a fifty thousand pounds' discrepancy, and knowing him, as he occasionally did work for us, it was ridiculous. Denby Crest was no crook, I thought in exasperation. It's my useless muddle-headed thought processes. Somewhere I was transposing a decimal point, making a mountain out of a molehill discrepancy of probably five pounds or fifty pence.

In the end I telephoned his office and asked to speak to him.

'Look, Denby,' I said, 'I'm most awfully sorry, but are you sure we've got all the relevant papers?'

'I expect so,' he said, sounding impatient. 'Why don't you leave it for Trevor? He gets back to England tomorrow, doesn't he?'

I explained about the broken-down car. 'He won't be back in the office until Wednesday or Thursday.'

'Oh.' He sounded disconcerted and there was a perceptible pause. 'All the same,' he said, 'Trevor is used to our ways. Please leave our certificate until he gets back.'

'But it's overdue,' I said.

'Tell Trevor to call me,' he said. 'And now, I'm sorry, but I have a client with me. So if you'll excuse me . . .'

He disconnected. I shuffled his papers together thankfully and thought that if he wanted to risk waiting for Trevor it was certainly all right by me.

At twelve-thirty Peter and Debbie went out to lunch, but I didn't feel hungry. I sat in shirtsleeves before the newly tackled sea of Mr Wells' depressing papers: put my elbows on the desk, and propped my forehead on the knuckles of my right hand, and shut my eyes. Thought a lot of rotten thoughts and wondered about buying myself a one-way ticket to Antarctica.

A voice said, 'Are you ill, asleep or posing for Rodin?'

I looked up, startled.

She was standing in the doorway. Young, fair, slender pretty.

'I'm looking for Trevor,' she said.

One couldn't have everything, I supposed.

# CHAPTER EIGHT

'Don't I know you?' I said, puzzled, standing up.

'Sure.' She looked resigned, as if this sort of thing happened often. 'Cast your mind back to long hair, no lipstick, dirty jeans and ponies.'

I looked at the short bouncy bob, the fashionable make-up, the swirling brown skirt topped by a neat waist-length fur-fabric jacket. Someone's daughter, I thought; recently and satisfactorily grown up.

'Whose daughter?' I said.

'My own woman.'

'Reasonable.'

She was enjoying herself, pleased with her impact on men.

'Jossie Finch, actually.'

'Wow,' I said.

'Every grub spreads its wings.'

'To where will you fly?'

'Yes,' she said, 'I've heard you were smooth.'

'Trevor isn't here, I'm afraid.'

'Mm. Still on his hols?'

I nodded.

'Then I was to deliver the same message to you, if you were here instead.'

'Sit down?' I suggested, gesturing to a chair.

'Can't stop. Sorry. Message from Dad. What are you doing about the Commissioners? He said he was absolutely not going before any so-and-so Commissioners next Thursday, or lurid words to that effect.'

'No, he won't have to.'

'He also says he would have sent the petty cash book, or whatever, in with me this morning, but his secretary is sick, and if you ask me she's the sickest thing that ever broke fingernails on a typewriter, and she has not done something or other with petty cash receipts or vouchers, or whatever it is you need. However . . .' she paused, drawing an exaggerated breath. 'Dad says, if you would like to drop in this evening you could go round the yard with him at evening stables, and have a noggin afterwards, and he will personally press into your hot little palms the book your assistant has been driving him mad about.'

'I'd like that,' I said.

'Good. I'll tell him.'

'And will you be there?'

'Ah,' she said, her eyes laughing, 'a little uncertainty is the HP sauce on the chips.'

'And the spice of life to you, too.'

She gave me an excellent smile, spun on her heel so

that the skirt swirled and the hair bounced, and walked out of the office.

Jossie Finch, daughter of William Finch, master of Axwood Stables. I knew her father in the way all long-time amateur riders knew all top trainers; enough to greet and chat to at the races. Since his was one of the racing accounts which pre-dated my arrival in the firm, and which Trevor liked to do himself, I had never before actually visited his yard.

I was interested enough to want to go, in spite of all my troubles. He had approximately ninety horses in his care, both jumpers and flat racers, and winners were taken for granted. Apart from Tapestry, most of the horses I usually rode were of moderate class, owned with more hope than expectation. To see a big stableful of top performers was always a feast. I would be safe from abduction there. And Jossie looked a cherry on the top.

When Peter and Debbie came back I laid into them for going out and leaving the outer door unlocked, and they adopted put-upon expressions and said they thought it was all right, as I was there, which would stop people sneaking in to steal things.

My fault, I thought more reasonably. I should have locked it after them myself. I would have to reshape a lot of habits. It could easily have been the enemy who walked in, not Jossie Finch.

I spent part of the afternoon on Mr Wells, but more of it trying to trace Connaught Powys.

We had his original address on file, left over from the

days when he had rigged the computer and milked his firm of a quarter of a million pounds in five years. The firm's audit was normally Trevor's affair, but one year, when Trevor was away a great deal with an ulcer, I had done it instead, and by some fluke had discovered the fraud. It had been one of those things you don't believe even when it is in front of your eyes. Connaught Powys had been an active director, and had paid his taxes on a comfortable income. The solid, untaxed lolly had disappeared without trace, but Connaught himself hadn't been quick enough.

I tried his old address. A sharp voice on the telephone told me the new occupants knew nothing of the Powys' whereabouts, and wished people would stop bothering them, and regretted the day they'd ever moved into a crook's house.

I tried his solicitors, who froze when they heard who was trying to find him. They could not, they said, divulge his present address without his express permission: which, their tone added, he was as likely to give as Shylock to a church bazaar.

I tried Leyhill Prison. No good.

I tried finally a racing acquaintance called Vivian Iverson who ran a gambling club in London and always seemed to know of corruption scandals before the stories publicly broke.

'My dear Ro,' he said, 'you're fairly non gratis in that quarter, don't you know.'

'I could guess.'

'You put the shivers up embezzlers, my friend. They're leaving the Newbury area in droves.'

'Oh sure. And I pick the Derby winner every year.'

'You may well jest, my dear chap, but the whisper has gone round.' He hesitated. 'Those two little dazzlers, Glitberg and Ownslow, have been seen talking to Powys, who has got rid of his indoor pallor under a sun lamp. The gist, so I'm fairly reliably told, was a hate-Britten chorus.'

'With vengeance intended?'

'No information, my dear chap.'

'Could you find out?'

'I only *listen*, my dear Ro,' he said. 'If I hear the knives are out, I'll tell you.'

'You're a pet,' I said dryly.

He laughed. 'Connaught Powys comes here to play, most Fridays.'

'What time?'

'You do ask a lot, my dear chap. After dinner to dawn.'

'How about making me an instant member?'

He sighed heavily. 'If you are bent on suicide, I'll tell the desk to let you in.'

'See you,' I said. 'And thanks.'

I put down the receiver and stared gloomily into space. Glitberg and Ownslow. Six years apiece, reduced for good behaviour . . . They could have met Connaught Powys in Leyhill, and it would have been no joy to any of them that I had put them all there.

Glitberg and Ownslow had served on a local council and robbed the ratepayers blind, and I'd turned them up through some dealings they'd done with one of my clients. My client had escaped with a fine, and had removed his custom from me with violent curses.

I wondered how much time all the embezzlers and bent solicitors and corrupted politicians in Leyhill Prison spent in thinking up new schemes for when they got out. Glitberg and Ownslow must already have been out for about six months.

Debbie had gone to the dentist and Peter to his Institute of Accounting Staff class, and this time I did lock the door behind them.

I felt too wretchedly tired to bother any further with Mr Wells. The shakes of the morning had gone, but even the swift tonic of Jossie Finch couldn't lift the persistent feeling of threat. I spent an hour dozing in the armchair we kept for favoured clients and when it was time, locked the filing cabinets and my desk and every door in the office, and went down to my car.

There was no one hiding behind the front seats. No one lurking round the edges of the car park. Nothing in the boot except the suitcase I'd stowed there that morning. I started up and drove out into the road, assaulted by nothing but my own nerves.

William Finch's yard lay south-west of Newbury: a huge spread of buildings sheltering in a hollow, with a creeper-covered Victorian mansion rising on the hillside above. I arrived at the house just as Finch was coming out of it, and we walked down together to the first cluster of boxes.

'Glad you could come,' he said.

'It's a treat.'

He smiled with easy charm. A tall man, going grey at about fifty, very much in command of himself and everything else. He had a broad face, fine well-shaped mouth, and the eyes of experience. Horses and owners thrived in his care, and years of success had given him a stature he plainly enjoyed.

We went from box to box, spending a couple of minutes in each. Finch told me which horse we were looking at, with some of its breeding and form. He held brief reassurance conversations in each case with the lad holding the horse's head, and with his head lad, who walked round with us. If all was well, he patted the horse's neck and fed him a carrot from a bag which his head lad carried. A practised important routine evening inspection, as carried out by every trainer in the country.

We came to an empty box in a full row. Finch gestured to it with a smile.

'Ivansky. My National runner. He's gone up to Liverpool.'

I almost gaped like an idiot. I'd been out of touch with the normal world so much that I had completely forgotten that the Grand National was due that Saturday.

I cleared my throat. 'He should . . . er . . . have a fair chance at the weights.' It seemed a fairly safe comment, but he disagreed.

'Ten twelve is far too much on his Haydock form. He's badly in with Wasserman, don't you think?'

I raked back for all the opinions I'd held in the safe and distant life of three weeks ago. Nothing much surfaced.

'I'm sure he'll do well,' I said.

He nodded as if he hadn't noticed the feebleness of the remark, and we went on. The horses were truly an impressive bunch, glowing with good feeding, thorough grooming and well-judged exercise. I ran out of compliments long before he ran out of horses.

'Drink?' he said, as the head lad shut the last door.

'Great.'

We walked up to the house, and he led the way into a sitting-room-cum-office. Chintz-covered sofa and chairs, big desk, table with drinks and glasses, walls covered with framed racing photographs. Normal affluent trainer ambience.

'Gin?' he said.

'Scotch, if you have it.'

He gave me a stiff one and poured gin like water for himself.

'Your health,' he said.

'And yours.'

We drank the ritual first sip, and he gestured to me to sit down.

'I've found that damned cash book for you,' he said, opening a drawer in the desk. 'There you are. Book, and file of petty cash receipts.'

'That's fine.'

'And what about these Commissioners?'

'Don't worry, I've applied for a postponement.'

'But will they grant it?'

'Never refused us yet,' I said. 'They'll set a new date about a month ahead, and we'll do your accounts and audit before then.'

He relaxed contentedly over his draught of gin. 'We can expect Trevor here next week, then? Counting hay bales and saddles?' There was humour in his voice at the thoroughness ahead.

'Well,' I said, 'maybe at the end of the week, or the one after. He won't be back until Wednesday or Thursday.' Did 'Returning Wednesday', I wondered, mean *travelling* Wednesday, or turning up for work? 'I'll do a lot of the preliminary paperwork for him, to save time.'

Finch turned to the drinks table and unscrewed the gin. 'I thought he was due back on Monday.'

'His car's broken down somewhere in France.'

'That'll please him.' He drank deeply. 'Still, if you make a start on things, the audit should get done in time.'

'Don't worry about the Commissioners,' I said; but everyone did worry when the peremptory summons dropped through their door. If one neither asked for a postponement nor attended at the due hour, the Commissioners would fix one's year's tax at whatever figure they cared to, and to that assessment there was no appeal. As such assessments were customarily far higher than the amount of tax actually due, one avoided them like black ice.

To my pleasure, the swirly brown skirt and bouncy fair hair made a swooping entrance. She was holding a marmalade cat which was trying to jump out of her arms.

'Damn thing,' she said, 'why won't he be *stroked*.'

'It's a mouser,' said her father, unemotionally.

'You'd think it would be glad of a cuddle.'

The cat freed itself and bolted. Jossie shrugged. 'Hello,' she said to me. 'So you got here.'

'Mm.'

'Well,' she said to her father, 'what did he say?'

'Eh? Oh . . . I haven't asked him yet.'

She gave him a fond exasperated smile and said to me, 'He wants to ask you to ride a horse for him.'

Finch shook his head at her, and I said, 'When?'

'Tomorrow,' Jossie said. 'At Towcester.'

'Er,' I said, 'I'm not really ultra fit.'

'Nonsense. You won the Gold Cup a fortnight ago. You must be.'

'Josephine,' her father said. 'Clam up.' He turned to me. 'I'm flying up to Liverpool in the morning, but I have this horse in at Towcester, and to be blunt he's still entered there only because someone forgot to scratch him by the eleven o'clock deadline this morning . . .'

'The chronically sick secretary,' muttered Jossie.

'So we've either got to run him after all or pay a fine, and I was toying with the idea of sending him up there, if I could get a suitable jockey.'

'Most of them having gone to the National,' Jossie added.

'Which horse?' I said.

'Notebook. Novice hurdler. Four-year-old chestnut gelding, in the top yard.'

'The one with the flaxen mane and tail?'

'That's right. He's run a couple of times so far. Shows promise, but still green.'

'Last of twenty-six at Newbury,' Jossie said cheerfully. 'It won't matter a curse if you're not fit.' She paused. 'I've been delegated to saddle it up, so you might do us a favour and come and ride it.'

'Up to you,' Finch said.

The delegated saddler was a powerful attraction, even if Notebook himself was nothing much.

'Yes,' I said weakly. 'OK.'

'Good.' Jossie gave me a flashing smile. 'I'll drive you up there, if you like.'

'I would like,' I said regretfully, 'but I'll be in London tonight. I'll go straight to Towcester from there.'

'I'll meet you outside the weighing room, then. He's in the last race, by the way. He would be.'

Novice hurdles were customarily first or last (or both), on a day's programme: the races a lot of racegoers chose to miss through lunch or leaving early to avoid the crush. The poor-relation races for the mediocre majority, where every so often a new blazing star scorched out of the ruck on its way to fame.

Running horses in novice hurdles meant starting from

home early or getting back late; but there were far more runners in novice hurdles than in any other type of race.

When I left it was Jossie who came back with me through the entrance hall to see me off. As we crossed a vast decrepit Persian rug I glanced at the large dark portraits occupying acres of wall space.

'Those are Nantuckets, of course,' she said, following my gaze. 'They came with the house.'

'Po-faced lot,' I said.

'You did know that Dad doesn't actually own all this?'

'Yes, I actually did know.' I smiled to myself, but she saw it.

She said defensively, 'All right, but you'd be surprised how many people make up to me, thinking that they'll marry the trainer's daughter and step into all this when he retires.'

'So you like to establish the ground rules first?'

'OK, greyhound-brain, I'd forgotten you'd know from Trevor.'

I knew in general that Axwood Stables Ltd belonged to an American family, the Nantuckets, who rarely took much personal interest in the place except as a business asset. It had been bought and brought to greatness in the fifties by a rumbustious tycoon thrown up atypically from prudent banking stock. Old Naylor Nantucket had brought his energies and enterprise to England, had fallen in love with English racing, had built a splendid modern stable yard and filled it with splendid horses. He had engaged the young William Finch to train them for him, and the middle-aged William Finch was still doing it for his heirs, except that nowadays nine tenths of the horses belonged to other owners, and the young Nantuckets, faintly ashamed of Uncle Naylor, never crossed the Atlantic to see their own horses perform.

'Doesn't your father ever get tired of training for absent owners?' I said.

'No. They don't argue. They don't ring him up in the middle of the night. And when they lose, they don't complain. He says training would be a lot easier if *all* owners lived in New York.'

She stood on the doorstep to wave me goodbye, assured and half-mocking, a girl with bright brown eyes, graceful neck, and neat nose and mouth in between.

I booked into the Gloucester Hotel, where I'd never stayed before, and ate a leisurely and much needed dinner in a nearby restaurant. I shouldn't have accepted the ride on Notebook, I thought ruefully; I'd hardly enough strength to cut up a steak.

A strong feeling of walking blindfold towards a precipice dragged at my feet all the way to Vivian Iverson's gambling club. I didn't know which way the precipice lay: ahead, behind, or all round. I only suspected that it was still there, and if I did nothing about finding it, I could walk straight over.

The Vivat Club proved as suave and well-manicured as its owner, and was a matter of interconnecting small rooms, not open expanses like casinos. There were no croupiers in eye-shades with bright dramatic spotlights over the tables, and no ladies tinkling with diamonds in half shadow. There were however two or three discreet chandeliers, a good deal of cigar smoke, and a sort of reverent hush.

Vivian, good as his word, had left a note for me to be let in, and as an extra, treated as a guest. I walked slowly from room to room, balloon glass of brandy in hand, looking for his elegant shape, and not finding it.

There were a good many businessmen in lounge suits earnestly playing chemin-de-fer, and women among them with eyes that flicked concentratedly from side to side with every delivered card. I'd never had an urge towards betting for hours on the turn of a card, but everyone to his own poison.

'Ro, my dear fellow,' Vivian said behind me. 'Come to play?'

'On an accountant's earnings?' I said, turning to him and smiling. 'What are the stakes?'

'Whatever you can afford to lose, my dear fellow.'

'Life, liberty, and a ticket to the Cup Final.'

His eyes didn't smile as thoroughly as his mouth. 'Some people lose honour, fortunes, reputation, and their heads.'

'Does it disturb you?' I asked.

He made a small waving gesture towards the chemin-de-fer. 'I provide a pastime to cater for an impulse. Like bingo.'

He put his hand on my shoulder as if we were long-lost friends and steered me towards a further room. There were heavy gold links in his cuffs, and a silk cord edging to his blue velvet jacket. Dark glossy hair on a well-shaped head, flat stomach, faint smell of fresh talc. About thirty-five, and shrewdly succeeding where others had fallen to bailiffs.

There was a green baize raised-edge gaming table in the further room, but no one was playing cards.

Behind the table, in the club's ubiquitous wooden-armed, studded-leather armchairs, sat three men.

They were all large, smoothly dressed, and unfriendly. I knew them, from way back.

Connaught Powys. Glitberg. Ownslow.

'We hear you're looking for us,' Connaught Powys said.

# CHAPTER NINE

I stood still. Vivian closed the door behind me and sat in another armchair on the edge of my left-hand vision. He crossed one leg elegantly over the other and eased the cloth over the knee with a languid hand.

Ownslow watched with disfavour.

'Piss off,' he said.

Vivian's answer was an extra-sophisticated drawl. 'My dear fellow, I may have set him up, but you've no licence to knock him down.'

There were several other empty chairs, pulled back haphazardly from the centre table. I sat unhurriedly in one of them and did my best with Vivian's leg-crossing ritual, hoping that casualness would reduce the atmosphere from bash-up to boardroom. Ownslow's malevolent stare hardly persuaded me that I'd succeeded.

Ownslow and Glitberg had run a flourishing construction racket for years, robbing the ratepayers of literally millions. Like all huge frauds, theirs had been done on paper, with Glitberg in the council's Planning Office, and

Ownslow in the Works and Maintenance. They had simply invented a large number of buildings: offices, flats and housing estates. The whole council having approved the buildings in principle, Glitberg, in his official capacity, advertised for tenders from developers. The lowest good-looking tender often came from a firm called National Construction (Wessex) Ltd and the council confidently entrusted the building to them.

National Construction (Wessex) Ltd did not exist except as expensively produced lettterheads. The sanctioned buildings were never built. Huge sums of money were authorized and paid to National Construction (Wessex) Ltd, and regular reports of the buildings' progress came back as Glitberg, from Planning, made regular inspections. After the point when the buildings were passed as ready for occupation the Maintenance department took over. Ownslow's men maintained bona-fide buildings, and Ownslow also requisitioned huge sums for the maintenance of the well-documented imaginary lot.

All the paperwork had been punctiliously, even brilliantly, completed. There were full records of rents received from the imaginary buildings, and rates paid by the imaginary tenants; but as all councils took it for granted that council buildings had to be heavily subsidized, the permanent gap between revenue and expenditure was accepted as normal.

Like many big frauds it had been uncovered by accident, and the accident had been my digging a little too deeply into the affairs of one of the smaller operators sharing in the crumbs of the greater rip-off.

The council, when I'd informed them, had refused to believe me. Not, that was, until they toured their area in detail, and found weedy grass where they had paid for, among other things, six storeys of flats for low-income families, a cul-de-sac of maisonettes for single pensioners, and two roadfuls of semi-detached bungalows for the retired and handicapped.

Blind-eye money had obviously been passed to various council members, but bribery in cash was hard to prove. The council had been publicly embarrassed and had not forgiven me. Glitberg and Ownslow, who had seen that the caper could not continue for ever, had been already preparing a quiet departure when the police descended on them in force on a Sunday afternoon. They had not exactly forgiven me either.

In line with all their other attention to detail, neither of them had made the mistake of living above his legal income. The huge sums they had creamed off had been withdrawn from the National Construction (Wessex) Ltd bank account over the years as a stream of cheques and cash which had aroused no suspicion at the bank, and had then apparently vanished into thin air. Of the million-plus which they had each stolen, not a pound had been recovered.

'Whatever you want from us,' Glitberg said, 'you're not going to get.'

'You're a danger to us,' Connaught Powys said.

'And like a wasp, you'll get swatted,' said Ownslow.

I looked at their faces. All three showed the pudgy roundness of self-indulgence, and all three had the sharp, wary eyes of guilt. Separately, Connaught Powys, with his sun-lamp tan and smoothly brushed hair, looked a high-up City gent. Heavy of body, in navy blue pin-stripes. Pale grey silk tie. Overall air of power and opulence, and not a whisper of cell-fug and slopping-out in the mornings.

Ownslow in jail was an easier picture. Fairish hair straggled to his collar from a fringe round a bald dome. Thick neck, bull shoulders, hands like baseball gloves. A hard, tough man whose accent came from worlds away from Connaught Powys.

Glitberg, in glasses, had short bushy grey hair and a fanned-out spread of white side-whiskers, which made him look like a species of ape. If Connaught Powys was power, and Ownslow was muscle, Glitberg was venom.

'Have you already tried?' I said.

'Tried what?' Ownslow said.

'Swatting.'

They stared, all three of them, without expression, at some point in the air between myself and Vivian.

'Someone has,' I said.

Connaught Powys smiled very slightly. 'Whatever we have done, or intend to do, about you,' he said, 'we are not going to be so insane as to admit it in front of a witness.'

'You'll be looking over your shoulder for the rest of your life,' Glitberg said, with satisfaction.

'Don't go near building sites on a dark night,' Ownslow said. 'There's a bit of advice, free, gratis and for nothing.'

'How about a sailing boat on a dark night?' I said. 'An ocean-going sailing boat.'

I wished at once that I hadn't said it. The unfriendliness on all three faces hardened to menace, and the whole room became very still.

Into the silence came Vivian's voice, relaxed and drawling. 'Ro . . . time you and I had a drink together, don't you think?'

He unfolded himself from his chair, and I, feeling fairly weak at the knees, stood up from mine.

Connaught Powys, Glitberg, and Ownslow delivered a collective look of such hatred that even Vivian began to look nervous. His hand fumbled with the door knob, and as he left the room, behind me, he almost tripped over his own feet.

'Whew,' he said in my ear. 'You do play with big rough boys, my dear fellow.' He steered me this time into a luxurious little office; three armchairs, all safely unoccupied. He waved me to one of them and poured brandy into two balloons.

'It's not what they say,' he said, 'as how they say it.'

'And what they don't say.'

He looked at me speculatively over his glass.

'Did you get what you wanted? I mean, was it worth your while, running under their guns?'

I smiled twistedly. 'I think I got an answer.'

'Well then.'

'Yes. But it was to a question I didn't ask.'

'I don't follow you.'

'I'm afraid,' I said slowly, 'that I've made everything a great deal worse.'

I slept soundly at the Gloucester, but more from exhaustion than an easy mind.

From the racing page of the newspaper delivered under my door in the morning I saw that my name was down in the list of runners as the rider of Notebook in the last race at Towcester. I sucked my teeth. I hadn't thought of asking William Finch not to include me in his list for the press, and now the whole world would learn where I would be that afternoon at four-thirty. If, that was, they bothered to turn to an insignificant race at a minor meeting on Grand National day.

'You'll be looking over your shoulder for the rest of your life,' Glitberg had said.

I didn't intend to. Life would be impossible if I feared for demons in every shadow. I wouldn't climb trustingly into any ambulances at Towcester, but I would go and ride there. There was an awfully thin line, it seemed to me, between cowardice and caution.

Jossie, waiting outside the weighing room, sent the heeby-jeebies flying.

'Hello,' she said. 'Notebook is here, looking his usual noble self and about to turn in his standard useless performance.'

'Charming.'

'The trainer's orders to the jockey,' she said, 'are succinct. Stay on, and stay out of trouble. He doesn't want you getting hurt.'

'Nor do I,' I said with feeling.

'He doesn't want anything to spoil the day if Ivansky wins the National.'

'Ah,' I said. 'Does he think he will?'

'He flew off in the air-taxi this morning in the usual agonized euphoria,' she said, with affection. 'Hope zig-zagging from conviction to doubt.'

Finch had sent two horses to Towcester, the second of them, Stoolery, being the real reason for Jossie's journey. I helped her saddle it for the two mile handicap 'chase, and cheered with her on the stands when it won. The Grand National itself was transmitted on television all over the racecourse straight afterwards, so that Jossie was already consoled when Ivansky finished fifth.

'Oh well.' She shrugged. 'That's that. Dad will feel flat, the owners will feel flat, the lads will get gloomily drunk, and then they'll all start talking about next year.'

We strolled along without much purpose and arrived at the door to the bar.

'Like a drink?' I asked.

'Might pass the time.'

The bar was crowded with people dissecting the National result, and the elbowing customers jockeying for service were four deep.

'Don't let's bother,' Jossie said.

I agreed. We turned to leave, and a thin hand stretched out from the tight pressed ranks and gripped my wrist hard.

'What do you want?' a voice shouted over the din. 'I've just got served. What do you want? Quick!'

The hand, I saw, belonged to Moira Longerman, and beyond her, scowling as usual, stood Binny Tomkins.

'Jossie?' I said.

'Fruit juice. Grapefruit if poss.'

'Two grapefruit juice,' I said.

The hand let go and disappeared, shortly to reappear with a glass in it. I took it, and also the next issue, and finally Moira Longerman herself, followed by Binny, fought her way out of the throng, holding two glasses high to avoid having the expensive thimblefuls knocked flying.

'How super!' she said. 'I saw you in the distance just now. I've been trying to telephone you for weeks and now I hear some extraordinary story about you being kidnapped.'

I introduced Jossie who was looking disbelievingly at what Moira had said.

'Kidnapped?' Her eyebrows rose comically. 'You?'

'You may well laugh,' I said ruefully.

Moira handed a glass to Binny, who nodded a scant thanks. Graceless man, I thought. Extraordinary to leave any woman to fight her way to get him a drink, let alone the owner of the most important horse in his yard. She was paying, of course.

'My *dear*,' Moira Longerman said to Jossie. 'Right after Ro won the Gold Cup on my darling Tapestry, someone kidnapped him from the racecourse. Isn't that right?' She beamed quizzically up at my face, her blue eyes alight with friendly interest.

'Sure is,' I agreed.

Binny scowled some more.

'How's the horse?' I said.

Binny gave me a hard stare and didn't answer, but Moira Longerman was overflowing with news and enthusiasm.

'I do so want you to ride Tapestry in all his races from now on, Ro, so I hope you will. He's ready for Ascot next Wednesday, Binny says, and I've been trying and trying to get hold of you to see if you'll ride him.'

Binny said sourly, 'I've already engaged another jockey.'

'Then disengage him, Binny dear.' Underneath the friendly birdlike brightness there was the same touch of steel which had got me the Gold Cup ride in the first place. Moira might be half Binny's physical weight but she had twice the mental muscle.

'It might be better to let this other chap ride . . .' I began.

'No, no,' she interrupted. 'It's you I want, Ro. I won't have anyone else. I told Binny that, quite definitely, the very moment after you'd won the Cup. Now you're back and safe again it will either be you on my horse or I won't run him.' She glanced defiantly at Binny, impishly at Jossie, and with a determined nod of her blonde curly head, expectantly turned to me. 'Well? What do you say?'

'Er,' I said, which was hardly helpful.

'Oh go on,' Jossie said. 'You'll have to.'

Binny's scowl switched targets. Jossie caught the full blast and showed no discomfiture at all.

'He did win the Gold Cup,' she said. 'You can't say he isn't capable.'

'He does say that, my dear,' beamed Moira Longerman happily. 'Isn't it odd?'

Binny muttered something blackly of which the only audible word was 'amateurs'.

'I think that what Binny really means,' said Moira sweetly and distinctly. 'is that Ro, like most amateurs, always tries very hard to win, and won't listen to propositions to the contrary.'

Binny's face turned a dark red. Jossie practically giggled. Moira looked at me with limpid blue eyes as if not quite aware of what she'd said, and I chewed around helplessly for a sensible answer.

'Like most *jockeys*,' I said finally.

'You're so nice, Ro,' she said. 'You think everyone's honest.'

I tended, like most accountants, to think exactly the opposite, but as it happened I had never much wondered about Binny. To train a horse like Tapestry should have been enough, without trying to rig his results.

Binny himself had decided to misunderstand what Moira had said, and was pretending that he hadn't seen the chasm that was opening at his feet. Moira gave him a mischievous glance and allowed him no illusions about her power to push him in.

'Binny dear,' she said, 'I'll never desert the man who trained a Gold Cup winner for me. Not as long as he keeps turning out my horses beautifully fit, and I choose who rides them.'

Jossie cleared her throat in the following silence and said encouragingly to Binny, 'I expect you had a good bet in the Gold Cup? My father always puts a bit on in the Cup and the National. Too awful if you win, and you haven't. Makes you look such an ass, he says.'

If she had tried to rub salt into his raw wounds, it appeared she couldn't have done a better job. Moira Longerman gave a delighted laugh.

'You naughty girl,' she said, patting Jossie's arm. 'Poor Binny had so little faith, you see, that not only did he not back Tapestry to win, but I've heard he unfortunately laid it to lose. Such a pity. Poor Binny, winning the Gold Cup and ending up out of pocket.'

Binny looked so appalled that I gathered the extent of her information was a nasty shock to him.

'Never mind,' Moira said kindly. 'What's past is past.

And if Ro rides Tapestry next Wednesday, all will be well.'

Binny looked as if everything would be very far from well. I wondered idly if he could possibly have already arranged that Tapestry should lose on Wednesday. On his first outing after a Gold Cup win, any horse would start at short odds. Many a bookmaker would be grateful to know for certain that he wouldn't have to pay out. Binny could already have sold that welcome information, thinking that I wasn't around to upset things. Binny was having a thoroughly bad time.

I reflected that I simply couldn't afford to take Wednesday off. The mountains of undone work made me feel faintly sick.

'Ro?' Moira said persuasively.

'Yes,' I said. 'Nothing I'd like better in the world.'

'Oh goody!' Her eyes sparkled with pleasure. 'I'll see you at Ascot, then. Binny will ring you, of course, if there's a change of plan.'

Binny scowled.

'Tell me all,' Jossie demanded as we walked across to the trainers' stand to watch the next race. 'All this drama about you being kidnapped.'

I told her briefly, without much detail.

'Do you mean they just popped you on a boat and sailed off with you to the Med?'

'That's right.'

'What a lark.'

'It was inconvenient,' I said mildly.

'I'll bet.' She paused. 'You said you escaped. How did you do that?'

'Jumped overboard.'

Her mouth twisted with sympathy. I reflected that it was only four days since that frantic swim. It seemed another world.

Jossie was of the real, sensible world, where things were understandable, if not always pleasant. Being with her made me feel a great deal more settled, more normal, and safer.

'How about dinner,' I said, 'on the way home?'

'We've got two cars,' she said.

'Nothing to prevent them both stopping at the same place.'

'How true.'

She was again wearing swirly clothes: a soft rusty red, this time. There was nothing tailored about her, and nothing untidy. An organized girl, amusing and amused.

'There's a fair pub near Oxford,' I said.

'I'll follow you, then.'

I changed in due course for Notebook's race, and weighed out, and gave my lightest saddle to the Axwood travelling head lad, who was waiting for it by the door.

'Carrying overweight, are you?' he said sardonically.

'Four pounds.'

He made an eyes-to-heaven gesture, saying louder than words that trainers should put up professionals in novice hurdle races, not amateurs who couldn't do ten stone six. I didn't mention that on Gold Cup day I'd weighed eight pounds more.

When I went out to the parade ring, he and Jossie were waiting, while a lad led the noble Notebook round and round, now wearing my saddle over a number cloth. Number thirteen. So who was superstitious?

'He bucks a bit,' said the travelling head lad, with satisfaction.

'When you get home,' Jossie said to him, 'please tell my father I'm stopping on the way back for dinner with Roland. So that he doesn't worry about car crashes.'

'Right.'

'Dad fusses,' Jossie said.

The travelling head lad gave me another look which needed no words, and which speculated on whether I would get her into bed. I wasn't so sure that I cared all that much for the travelling head lad.

A good many people had already gone home, and from the parade ring one could see a steady drift to the gate. There were few things as disheartening, I thought, as playing to a vanishing audience. On the other hand, if one made a frightful mess, the fewer who saw it, the better.

'They said "jockeys get mounted" half an hour ago,' Jossie said.

'Two seconds,' I said. 'I was listening.'

The travelling head lad gave me a leg up. Notebook gave a trial buck.

'Stay out of trouble,' Jossie said.

'It's underneath me,' I said, feeling the noble animal again try to shoot me off.

She grinned unfeelingly. Notebook bounced away, hiccupped sideways down to the start, and then kept everyone waiting while he did a circus act on his hind legs. 'Bucks a bit', I thought bitterly. I'd fall off before the tapes went up, if I wasn't careful.

The race started, and Notebook magnanimously decided to take part, setting off at an uncoordinated gallop which involved a good deal of head-shaking and yawing from side to side. His approach to the first hurdle induced severe loss of confidence in his rider, as he seemed to be trying to jump it sideways, like a crab.

As I hadn't taken the precaution of dropping him out firmly at the back, always supposing I could actually have managed it, as he was as strong as he was wilful, his diagonal crossing of the flight of hurdles harvested a barrage of curses from the other jockeys. 'Sorry' was a useless word in a hurdle race, particularly from an unfit amateur who should have known better than to be led astray by a pretty girl. I yanked Notebook's head straight at the next hurdle with a force which would have had the Cruelty to Animals people swooning. He retaliated by screwing his hindquarters sideways in mid-air and landing on all four feet at once, pointing east-north-east to the rails.

This manoeuvre at least dropped him out into last place, which he tried to put right by running away with me up the stretch in front of the stands. As we fought each other on the way outwards round the mile-and-a-half circuit I understood the full meaning of the trainer's orders to his jockey. 'Stay on, and stay out of trouble.' My God.

I was not in the least surprised that Notebook had finished last of twenty-six at Newbury. He would have been last of a hundred and twenty-six, if his jockey had had any sense. Last place on Notebook was not exactly safe, but if one had to be anywhere on him, last place was wisest. No one, however, had got the message through to the horse.

The circuit at Towcester went out downhill from the stands, flattened into a straight stretch on the far side, and ended with a stamina-sapping uphill pull to the finishing straight and the winning post. Some of the world's slowest finishes had been slogged out there on muddy days at the end of three-mile 'chases. Notebook however set off downhill on firm going at a graceless rush, roller-coastered over the most distant hurdles, and only began to lose interest when he hit the sharply rising ground on the way back.

By that time the nineteen other runners were ahead as of right, as Notebook's stop-go and sideways type of jumping lost at every flight the lengths he made up on the flat.

I suppose I relaxed a little. He met the next hurdle all wrong, ignored my bid to help him, screwed wildly in mid-air, and landed with his nose on the turf and all four feet close together behind it. Not radically different from six other landings, just more extreme.

Being catapulted off at approximately thirty miles an hour is a kaleidoscopic business. Sky, trees, rails and grass somersaulted around my vision in a disjointed jumble, and if I tucked my head in it was from instinct, not thought. The turf smacked me sharply in several places, and Notebook delivered a parting kick on the thigh. The world stopped rolling, and half a ton of horse had not come crashing down on top of me. Life would go on.

I sat up slowly, all breath knocked out, and watched the noble hindquarters charge heedlessly away.

An ambulance man ran towards me, in the familiar black St John's uniform. I felt a flood of panic. A conditioned reflex. He had a kind face: a total stranger.

'All right, mate?' he said.

I nodded weakly.

'You came a proper purler.'

'Mm.' I unclipped my helmet, and pulled it off. Speech was impossible. My chest heaved from lack of air. He put a hand under one of my armpits and helped me as far as my knees, and from there, once I could breathe properly, to my feet.

'Bones OK?'

I nodded.

'Just winded,' he said cheerfully.

'Mm.'

A Land Rover arrived beside us with a jerk, and the vet inside it said that as there were no injured horses needing his attention, he could offer me a lift back to the stands.

'You fell off,' Jossie observed, as I emerged with normal breath and clean bill of health from the doctor in the First Aid room.

I smiled, 'Granted.'

She gave me a sideways glance from the huge eyes.

'I thought all jockeys were frightfully touchy about being told they fell off,' she said. 'All that guff about it's the horse that falls, and the jockey just goes down with the ship.'

'Quite right,' I said.

'But Notebook didn't actually fall, so you fell off.' Her voice was lofty, teasing.

'I don't dispute it.'

'No, aren't you boring.' She smiled. 'They caught Notebook in the next parish, so while you change I'll go along to the stables and see he's OK, and I'll meet you in the car park.'

'Fine.'

I changed into street clothes, fixed with the valet to take my saddles, helmet, and other gear to Ascot for the following Wednesday, and walked the short distance to the car park.

The crowds had gone, and only the stragglers like me were leaving now in twos and threes. The cars still remaining stood singly, haphazardly scattered instead of in orderly rows.

I looked into the back of mine, behind the front seats.

No one there.

I wondered with a shiver what I would have done if there had been. Run a mile, no doubt. I stood leaning on my car waiting for Jossie, and no one looked in the least like trying to carry me off. A quiet spring-like Saturday evening in the Northamptonshire countryside, as friendly as beer.

# CHAPTER TEN

She followed me in her pale blue Midget to the pub on the south side of Oxford, and chose a long cold drink with fruit on the top and a kick in the tail.

'Dad has schooled Notebook until he's blue in the face,' she said, pursing her lips to the straw which stuck up like a mast from the log-jam of fruit.

'Some of them never learn,' I said.

She nodded. Polite transaction achieved, I thought: she had obliquely apologized for the horse's frightful behaviour, and I had accepted that her father had done his best to teach him to jump. Some trainers, but not those of William Finch's standing, seemed to think that the best place for a green novice to learn to jump was actually in a race: rather like urging a child up the Eiger without showing him how to climb.

'What made you become an accountant?' she said. 'It's such a dull sort of job.'

'Do you think so?'

She gave me the full benefit of the big eyes. 'You obviously don't,' she said. She tilted her head a little, considering. 'You don't *look* boring and stuffy, and you don't *act* boring and stuffy, so give.'

'Judges are sober, nurses are dedicated, miners are heroes, writers drink.'

'Or in other words, don't expect people to fit the image?'

'As you say,' I said.

She smiled. 'I've known Trevor since I was six.'

A nasty one. Trevor, without any stretch of imagination, could fairly be classed as stuffy and boring.

'Carry on,' she said. 'Why?'

'Security. Steady employment. Good pay. The usual inducements.'

She looked at me levelly. 'You're lying.'

'What makes you think so?'

'People who risk their necks for nothing in jump races are not hell-bent on security, steady employment, and money.'

'Because of me Mum, then,' I said flippantly.

'She bossed you into it?'

'No.' I hesitated, because in fact I never had told anyone why I'd grown up with a fiery zeal as powerful as a vocation. Jossie waited with quizzical expectation.

'She had a rotten accountant,' I said. 'I promised her that when I grew up I would take over. As corny as that.'

'And did you?'

'No. She died.'

'Sob story.'

'Yes, I told you. Pure corn.'

She stirred the fruit with her straw, looking less mocking. 'You're afraid I'll laugh at you.'

'Sure of it,' I said.

'Try me, then.'

'Well . . . she was a rotten businesswoman, my Mum. My father got killed in a pointless sort of accident, and she was left having to bring me up alone. She was about thirty. I was nine.' I paused. Jossie was not actually laughing, so I struggled on. 'She rented a house just off the sea-front at Ryde and ran it as a holiday hotel, half a step up from a boarding house. Comfortable, but no drinks licence; that sort of thing. So she could be there when I got home from school, and in the holidays.'

'Brave of her,' Jossie said. 'Go on.'

'You can guess.'

She sucked down to the dregs of her glass and made a bubbling noise through the straw. 'Sure,' she said. 'She was good at cooking and welcoming people and lousy at working out how much to charge.'

'She was also paying tax on money she should have claimed as expenses.'

'And that's bad?'

'Crazy.'

'Well, go on,' she said encouragingly. 'Digging a story out of you is worse than looking for mushrooms.'

'I found her crying sometimes, mostly in the winter when there weren't any guests. It's pretty upsetting for a kid of ten or so to find his mother crying, so you can say I was upset. Protective also, probably. Anyway, at first

I thought it was still because of losing Dad. Then I realized she always cried when she'd been seeing Mr Jones, who was her accountant. I tried to get her to open up on her troubles, but she said I was too young.'

I stopped again. Jossie sighed with exasperation and said, 'Do get *on* with it.'

'I told her to ditch Mr Jones and get someone else. She said I didn't understand, I was too young. I promised her that when I got older I would be an accountant, and I'd put her affairs to rights.' I smiled lopsidedly. 'When I was thirteen she went down to Boots one morning and bought two hundred aspirins. She stirred them into a glass of water, and drank them. I found her lying on her bed when I came home from school. She left me a note.'

'What did it say?'

'It said "Dear Ro, Sorry, Love, Mum." '

'Poor girl.' Jossie blinked. Not laughing.

'She'd made a will,' I said. 'One of those simple things on a form from the stationers. She left me everything, which was actually nothing much except her own personal things. I kept all the account books and bank statements. I got shuttled around uncles and aunts for a few years, but I kept those account books safe, and then I got another accountant to look at them. He told me Mr Jones seemed to have thought he was working for the Inland Revenue, not his client. I told him I wanted to be an accountant, and I got him to show me exactly what Mr Jones had done wrong. So there you are. That's all.'

'Are you still killing Mr Jones to dry your mother's tears?' The teasing note was back, but gentler.

I smiled, 'I enjoy accountancy. I might never have thought of it if it hadn't been for Mr Jones.'

'So God bless villains.'

'He was ultra-righteous. A smug pompous ass. There are still a lot of Mr Joneses around, not pointing out to their clients all the legitimate ways of avoiding tax.'

'Huh?'

'It's silly to pay tax when you don't have to.'

'That's obvious.'

'A lot of people do, though, from ignorance or bad advice.'

I ordered refill drinks and told Jossie it was her turn to unbutton with the family skeletons.

'My Ma?' she said in surprise. 'I thought the whole world knew about my Ma. She canoes up and down the Amazon like a yo-yo, digging up ancient tribes. Sends back dispatches in the shape of earnest papers to obscure magazines. Dad and I haven't seen her for years. We get telegrams in January saying Happy Christmas.'

Revelation dawned. 'Christabel Saffray Finch! Intrepid female explorer, storming about in rain forests?'

'Ma,' Jossie nodded.

'Good heavens.'

'Good grief, more like.'

'Trevor never told me,' I said. 'But then he wouldn't, I suppose.'

Jossie grinned. 'Trevor disapproves. Trevor also

always disapproves of Dad's little consolations. Aunts, I used to call them. Now I call them Lida and Sandy.'

'He's very discreet.' Even on the racecourse, where gossip was a second occupation, I hadn't heard of Lida and Sandy. Or that Christabel Saffray Finch, darling of anthropological documentaries, was William's wife.

'Sandy is his ever-sick secretary,' Jossie said, 'perpetually shuttling between bronchitis, backache and abortion.'

I laughed. 'And Lida?'

Jossie made a face, suddenly vulnerable under all the bright froth.

'Lida's got her hooks into him like a tapeworm. I can't stand her. Let's talk about food; I'm starving.'

We read the menu and ordered, and finished our drinks, and went in to dinner in the centuries-old dining-room: stone walls, uncovered oak beams, red velvet and soft lights.

Jossie ate as if waistlines never expanded, which was refreshing after the finicky picker I'd taken out last.

'Luck of the draw,' she said complacently, smothering a baked-in-the-skin potato with a butter mountain. I reflected that she'd drawn lucky in more ways than metabolism. A quick mind, fascinating face, tall, slender body: there was nothing egalitarian about nature.

Most of the tables around us were filled with softly chattering groups of twos and fours, but over by a far wall a larger party were making the lion's share of the noise.

'They keep looking over here,' Jossie said. 'Do you know them?'

'It looks like Sticks Elroy with his back to us.'

'Is it? Celebrating his winner?'

Sticks Elroy, named for the extreme thinness of his legs, had studiously avoided me in the Towcester changing room, and must have been thoroughly disconcerted to find me having dinner in his local pub. He was one of my jockey clients, but for how much longer was problematical. I was not currently his favourite person.

The noise, however, was coming not from him but from the host of the party, a stubborn-looking man with a naturally loud voice.

'Avert your gaze,' I said to Jossie.

The large eyes regarded me over salad and steak.

'An ostrich act?' she said.

I nodded. 'If we bury our heads, maybe the storm won't notice us.'

The storm, however, seemed to be gathering force. Words like 'bastard' rose easily above the prevailing clatter and the uninvolved majority began to look interested.

'Trouble,' Josie said without visible regret, 'is on its feet and heading this way.'

'Damn.'

She grinned. 'Faint heart.'

Trouble arrived with the deliberate movements of the slightly drunk. Late forties, I judged. About five feet eight, short dark hair, flushed cheeks and aggressive eyes. He stood four-square and ignored Jossie altogether.

'My son tells me you're that bastard Roland Britten.' His voice, apart from fortissimo, was faintly slurred.

To ignore him was to invite a punch-up. I laid down my knife and fork. Leaned back in my chair. Behaved as if the enquiry was polite.

'Is Sticks Elroy your son?'

'Too right, he bloody is,' he said.

'He had a nice winner today,' I said. 'Well done.'

It stopped him for barely two seconds.

'He doesn't need your bloody "well done".'

I waited mildly, without answering. Elroy senior bent down, breathed alcohol heavily, and pointed an accusing finger under my nose.

'You leave my son alone, see? He isn't doing anyone any harm. He doesn't want any bastard like you snitching on him to the bloody tax man. Judas, that's what you are. Going behind his back. Bloody informer, that's what you are.'

'I haven't informed on him.'

'What's that?' He wagged the finger to and fro, belligerently. 'Costing him hundreds, aren't you, with the bloody tax man. Bastard like you ought to be locked up. Serve you bloody well right.'

The head waiter arrived smoothly at Elroy's shoulder.

'Excuse me, sir,' he began.

Elroy turned on him like a bull. 'You trot off. You majordomo, or whatever you are. You trot off. I'll have my say, and when I've had my say I'll sit down, see? Not before.'

The head waiter cravenly retired, and Elroy returned to his prime target. Jossie's eyes stared at him with disfavour, which deflected him not at all.

'I hear someone locked you up for ten days or so just now, and you got out. Bloody shame. You deserve to be locked up, you do. Bastard like you. Whoever it was locked you up had the right idea.'

I said nothing. Elroy half turned away, but he had by no means finished. Merely addressing a wider audience.

'You know what this bastard did to my son?' The audience removed its eyes in thoroughly British embarrassment, but they got told the answer whether they liked it or not.

'This boot-licking, creeping bastard went crawling to the tax man and told him my son had some cash he hadn't paid taxes on.'

'I didn't,' I said to Jossie.

He swung round to me again and poked the finger rigidly under my nose. 'Bloody liar. Locking up's too bloody good for bastards like you.'

The manager arrived, with the head waiter hovering behind.

'Mr Elroy,' the manager said courteously. 'A bottle of wine for your party, compliments of the management.' He beckoned a finger to the head waiter, who deftly proffered a bottle of claret.

The manager was young and well-dressed, and

reminded me of Vivian Iverson. His unexpected oil worked marvels on the storm, which abated amid a few extra 'bastards' and went back to its table muttering under its breath.

The people at the other tables watched from the cover of animated conversation, while the head waiter drew the cork for Elroy and poured the free wine. The manager drifted casually back to Jossie and me.

'There will be no charge for your dinner, sir.' He paused delicately. 'Mr Elroy is a valued customer.' He bowed very slightly and drifted on without waiting for an answer.

'How cool of him,' Josie said, near explosion.

'How professional.'

She stared at me. 'Do you often sit still and let people call you a bastard?'

'Once a week and twice on Sundays.'

'Spineless.'

'If I'd stood up and slogged him, our steaks would have gone cold.'

'Mine has, anyway.'

'Have another,' I said. I started to eat again where I had left off, and so, after a moment or two, did Jossie.

'Go on,' she said. 'I'm all agog. Just what was that all about?' She looked round the restaurant. 'You are now the target of whispers, and the consensus looks unfavourable.'

'In general,' I said, spearing lettuce, 'people shouldn't expect their accountants to help them break the law.'

'Sticks?'

'And accountants unfortunately cannot discuss their clients.'

'Are you being serious?'

I sighed. 'A client who wants his accountant to connive at a massive piece of tax-dodging is not going to be madly pleased when the accountant refuses to do it.'

'Mm.' She chewed cheerfully. 'I do see that.'

'And,' I went on, 'an accountant who advises such a client to declare the loot and pay the tax, because otherwise the nasty Revenue men will undoubtedly find out, and the client will have to pay fines on top of tax and will end up very poorly all round, because not only will he get it in the neck for that one offence, but every tax return he makes in the future will be inspected with magnifying glasses and he'll be hounded for evermore over every penny and have inspectors ransacking every cranny of his house at two in the morning . . .' I took a breath ' . . . such an accountant may be unpopular.'

'Unreasonable.'

'And an accountant who refuses to break the law, and says that if his client insists on doing so he will have to take his custom somewhere else, such an accountant may possibly be called a bastard.'

She finished her steak and laid down her knife and fork. 'Does this hypothetical accountant snitch to the tax man?'

I smiled. 'If the client is no longer his client, he doesn't know whether his ex-client is tax-dodging or not. So no, he doesn't snitch.'

'Elroy had it all wrong, then.'

'Er,' I said, 'it was he who set up the scheme from which Sticks drew the cash. That's why he is so furious. And I shouldn't be telling you that.'

'You'll be struck off, or strung up, or whatever.'

'Sky high.' I drank some wine. 'It's quite extraordinary how many people try to get their accountants to help them with tax fiddles. I reckon if someone wants to fiddle, the last person he should tell should be his accountant.'

'Just get on with it, and keep quiet?'

'If they want to take the risk.'

She half laughed. 'What risk? Tax-dodging is a national sport.'

People never understood about taxation, I thought. The ruthlessness with which tax could be collected put Victorian landlords in the shade, and the Revenue people now had frightening extra powers of entry and search.

'It's much safer to steal from your employer than the tax man,' I said.

'You must be joking.'

'Have some profiteroles,' I said.

Jossie eyed the approaching trolley of super-puds and agreed on four small cream-filled buns smothered in chocolate sauce.

'Aren't you having any?' she demanded.

'Think of Tapestry on Wednesday.'

'No wonder jockeys get fat when they finally let themselves eat.' She spooned up the dark brown goo with satisfaction. 'Why is it safer to steal from your employer?'

'He can't sell your belongings to get his money back.'

The big eyes widened.

'Golly!' she said.

'If you run up debts, the courts can send bailiffs to take your furniture. If you steal instead, they can't.'

She paused blankly in mid-mouthful, then went on chewing, and swallowed. 'Carry right on,' she said. 'I'm riveted.'

'Well . . . it's theft which is the national sport, not tax-dodging. Petty theft. Knocking off. Nicking. Most shop-lifting is done by the staff, not the customers. No one really blames a girl who sells tights all day if she tucks a pair into her handbag when she goes home. Pinching from employers is almost regarded as a rightful perk, and if ever a manufacturing firm puts an efficient checker on the staff exits there's practically a riot until he's removed.'

'Because he stops the outward march of spanners and fork-lift trucks?'

I grinned. 'You could feed an army on what disappears from the fridges of hotels.'

'Accountants,' she said, 'shouldn't find it amusing.'

'Especially as they spend their lives looking for fraud.'

'Do you?' she said, surprised. 'Do you really? I thought accountants just did sums.'

'The main purpose of an audit is to turn up fiddles.'

'I thought it was . . . well . . . to add up the profit or loss.'

'Not really.'

She thought. 'But when Trevor comes to count the hay and saddles and stuff, that's stocktaking.'

I shook my head. 'More like checking on behalf of your father that he hasn't got a stable lad selling the odd bale or bridle on the quiet.'

'Good heavens.' She was truly astounded. 'I'll have to stop thinking of auditors as fuddy-duddies. Change their image to fraud squad policemen.'

'Not that, either.'

'Why not?'

'If an auditor finds that a firm is being swindled by its cashier, for instance, he simply tells the firm. He doesn't arrest the cashier. He leaves it to the firm to decide whether to call in the handcuffs.'

'But surely they always do.'

'Absolutely not. Firms get red faces and tend to lose business if everyone knows their cashier took them for a ride. They sack the cashier and keep quiet, mostly.'

'Are you bored with telling me all this?'

'No,' I said truthfully.

'Then tell me a good fraud.'

I laughed. 'Heard any good frauds lately?'

'Get on with it.'

'Um . . .' I thought. 'A lot of the best frauds are complicated juggling with figures. It's the paperwork which deceives the eye, like a three card trick. I paused, then smiled. 'I know a good one, though they weren't my clients, thank God. There was a manager of a broiler-chicken factory farm which sold thousands of chickens every week to a freezing firm. The manager was also quietly selling a hundred a week to a butcher who didn't know the chickens had fallen off the back of a lorry, so to speak. No one could ever tell how many chickens there actually were on the farm, because the turnover was so huge and fast, and baby chicks tend to die. The manager pocketed a neat little untaxed regular income, and like most good frauds it was discovered by accident.'

'What accident?'

'The butcher used to pay the manager by cheque, made out in the manager's name. One day he happened to meet one of the directors of the firm which owned the chicken farm, and to save postage he got out his chequebook, wrote a cheque in the manager's name, and asked the director to give it to him, to pay for that month's delivery of chickens.'

'And the lid blew off.'

'With a bang. They sacked the manager.'

'No prosecution?'

'No. The last I heard, he was selling rose bushes by mail order.'

'And you wondered for whose nursery he was working?'

I grinned and nodded. She was quick and funny, and it seemed incredible that I'd met her only the day before.

We drank coffee and talked about horses. She said she had been trying her hand at three-day-eventing, but would be giving it up soon.

'Why?' I asked.

'Lack of talent.'

'What will you do instead?'

'Marry.'

'Oh.' I felt obscurely disappointed. 'Who?'

'I've no idea. Someone will turn up.'

'Just like that?'

'Of course just like that. One finds husbands in the oddest places.'

'What are you doing tomorrow?' I said.

Her eyes gleamed with light and life. 'Visiting a girl friend. What will you do instead?'

'Sums, I expect.'

'But tomorrow's Sunday.'

'And I can have the office to myself all day, without any interruption. I often work on Sundays. Nearly always.'

'Good grief.'

We went out to where the Midget and the Dolomite stood side by side in the car park.

'Thanks for the grub,' Jossie said.

'And for your company.'

'Do you feel all right?'

'Yes,' I said, surprised. 'Why?'

'Just checking,' she said. 'Dad'll ask. It looked such a crunching fall.'

I shook my head. 'A bruise or two.'

'Good. Well, goodnight.'

'Goodnight.' I kissed her cheek.

Her eyes glinted in the dim light from the pub's windows. I kissed her mouth, rather briefly, with closed lips. She gave me the same sort of kiss in return.

'Hm,' she said, standing back. 'That wasn't bad. I do hate wet slobbers.'

She slid expertly into the Midget and started the engine.

'See you in the hay,' she said. 'Counting it.'

She was smiling as she drove away, probably with a mirror expression of my own. I unlocked my car door, and, feeling slightly silly, I looked into the dark area behind the front seats.

No one there.

I sat in the car and started it, debating whether or not to risk going home to the cottage. Friday and Saturday had passed safely enough; but maybe the cats were still watching the mousehole. I decided that another night away would be prudent, and from the pub drove north-wards around Oxford again, to the anonymity of the large motel and service station built beside a busy route-connecting roundabout.

The place as usual was bright with lights and bustle: flags flying on tall poles and petrol pumps rattling. I booked in at the reception office, took the key, and drove round to the slightly quieter wing of bedrooms at the rear.

Sleep would be no problem, I thought. The constant rumble of traffic would be soporific. A lullaby.

I yawned, took out my suitcase, locked the car, and fitted the key into the bedroom door.

Something hit me very hard between the shoulders. I fell against the still closed door, and something immediately hit me very hard on the head.

This time, it was brutal. This time, no ether.

I slid in a daze down the door and saw only dark unrecognizable figures bending over to punch and kick. The thuds shuddered through my bones, and another bang on the head slid me deep into peaceful release.

# CHAPTER ELEVEN

I awoke in the dark. Black, total darkness.

I couldn't make out why I should be lying on a hard surface in total darkness, aching all over.

A fall, I thought. I had a fall at Towcester. Why couldn't I remember?

I felt cold. Chilled through and through. When I moved, the aches were worse.

I suddenly remembered having dinner with Jossie. Remembered it all clearly, down to kissing her goodnight in the car park.

So then what?

I tried to sit up, but raising my head was as far as I got. The result was whirling nausea and a pile-driving headache. I inched my fingers tentatively through my hair and found a wince-making area of swelling. I let my head down again, gingerly.

There was no sound except the rustle of my clothes. No engine. No creakings or rushings or water noises. I was not lying on a bunk, but on a larger surface, hard and flat.

I might not be in a sail locker, but I was certainly still in the dark. In the dark in every sense. Weak frustrated anger mocked me that in four days of freedom I hadn't found out enough to save me from the gloomy present.

Every movement told me what I still couldn't remember. I knew only that the fall off Notebook could not be the source of the soreness all over my body. There would have been a few bruises which would have stiffened up overnight, but nothing like the overall feeling of having been kneaded like dough. I rolled with a grunt on to my stomach and put my head on my folded arms. The only good thing that I could think of was that they hadn't tied my hands.

They. Who were *they?*

When my head stopped hammering, I thought, I would have enough energy to find out where I was and try to get out. Meanwhile it was enough just to lie still and wait for things to get better.

Another thing to be grateful for, I thought. The hard flat surface I was lying on was not swaying about. With luck, I was not on a boat. I wasn't going to be sick. A bruised body was absolutely nothing compared with the agonies of seasickness.

I had no shoes on, just socks. When I squinted at my wrist there was no luminous dial there: no watch. I couldn't be bothered to check all my pockets. I was certain they'd be empty.

After a while I remembered deciding to go to the

motel, and after that, bit by bit, I remembered booking in, and the affray on the doorstep.

They must have followed me all the way from Towcester, I thought. Waited through dinner with Jossie. Followed me to the motel. I hadn't spotted them once. I hadn't even heard their footsteps behind me, against the constant noise of traffic.

My instinctive feeling of being safe with Jossie had been dead right.

Ages passed.

The racket inside my skull gradually subsided. Nothing else happened.

I had a feeling that it was nearly dawn, and time to wake up. It had been ten-thirty when I'd been knocked out. There was no telling how long I'd been unconscious, or lain feebly in my present state, but the body had its own clock, and mine was saying six in the morning.

The dawn feeling stirred me to some sort of action, though if there was dawn outside it was not making its way through to me. Perhaps, I thought uneasily, I was wrong about the time. It was still night outside. I prayed for it to be still night outside.

I had another go at sitting up. One couldn't say that I felt superbly healthy. Concussion took a while to go away, and cold was notoriously bad for bruised muscles. The combination made every movement a nuisance. A familiar sort of pain, because of racing falls in the past. Just worse.

The surface beneath me was dirty: I could feel the gritty dust. It smelled faintly of oil. It was flat and smooth and not wood.

I felt around me in all directions, and on my left connected with a wall. Slithering on one hip, I inched that way and cautiously explored with my fingers.

Another smooth flat surface, at right angles to the floor. I banged it gently with my fist, and got back the noise and vibration of metal.

I thought that if I sat for a while with my back against the wall it would soon get light, and it would be easy then to see where I was. It had to get light, I thought forlornly. It simply had to.

It didn't, of course.

When they'd given me light on the boat, I'd escaped. A mistake to be avoided.

It had to be faced. The darkness was deliberate, and would go on. It was no good, I told myself severely, sitting in a miserable huddle feeling sorry for myself.

I made a further exploration into unmapped territory, and found that my world was a good deal smaller than Columbus's. It seemed prudent to move while still sitting down, on the flat-earth theory that one might fall over the edge; but two feet of shuffling to the right brought me to a corner.

The adjacent wall was also flat, smooth, and metal. I

shifted my spine round on to it, and set off again to the right.

The traverse was short. I came almost at once to another corner. I found that if I sat in the centre of the wall I could reach both side walls at once quite easily with my fingertips. Five feet, approximately, from side to side.

I shuffled round the second corner and pressed on. Three feet down that side, I knew where I was. The flatness of the metal wall was broken there by a big rounded bulge, whose meaning was as clear to my touch as if I'd been seeing it.

It was the semi-circular casing over a wheel; and I was inside a van.

I had a powerful, immediate picture of the fake ambulance I'd climbed into at Cheltenham. A white van, of a standard pattern, with the doors opening outwards at the rear. If I continued past the wheel, I would come to the rear doors.

And I would feel a proper fool, I thought, if all I had to do was open the doors and step out.

I wouldn't have minded feeling a proper fool. The doors were firmly shut, and likely to remain so. There was no handle on the inside.

In the fourth corner I came across what I had this time been given in the way of life support systems, and if my spirits had already been at zero, at that point they went way below.

There was a five-gallon plastic jerrycan full of liquid, and a large carrier bag.

I unscrewed the cap of the jerrycan and sniffed at the contents. No smell. Sloshed some of the liquid out on to my hand, and tasted it.

Water.

I screwed the cap on again, fumbling in the dark.

*Five gallons* of water.

Oh no, I thought numbly. Oh dear God.

The carrier was packed to the top with flat plastic packets, each about four inches square. There was again no smell. I pulled one of the packets open, and found the contents were thin four-inch squares of sliced processed cheese.

I counted the packets with a sinking heart, taking them one by one from the carrier and stacking them on the floor. There were sixty of them. All, as far as I could tell, exactly the same.

Wretchedly I counted them from the floor back into the carrier, one by one, and there were still sixty. They had given me enough food and water to last for at least four weeks. There were going to be no twice a day visits: no one to talk to at all.

Sod them, I thought violently. If this was revenge, it was worse than anything I'd ever brought on any crook.

Spurred by anger, I stood without caution to explore the top part of the van, and banged my sore head on the roof. It was very nearly altogether too much. I found myself back on my knees, cursing and holding my head, and trying not to weep. A battered feeble figure, sniffing in the dark.

It wouldn't do, I thought. It was necessary to be sternly unemotional. To ignore the aches and pains. To take a good cold grip of things, and make a plan and routine for survival.

When the fresh waves of headache passed, I got on with it.

The presence of food and drink meant, I thought, that survival was expected. That one day, if I didn't manage a second escape, I would be released. Death, again, was not apparently on the agenda. Well, then, why was I getting into such a fuss?

I had read once of a man who had spent weeks down a pothole in silence and darkness to see how a total lack of external reference would affect the human body. He had survived with his mind intact and his body none the worse for wear, and his sense of time had gone remarkably little astray. What he could do, so could I. It was irrelevant, I thought sternly, that the scientist had volunteered for his incarceration, and had had his heartbeat and other vital signs monitored on the surface, and could have got out again any time he felt he'd had enough.

Feeling a good deal steadier for the one-man pep-talk, I got more slowly to my feet, sliding my spine up the side wall, and feeling for the roof with my hands. It was too low for me to stand upright, by four or six inches. With head and knees bent, I felt my way again right round the van.

Both sides were completely blank. The front wall was broken by the shape of a small panel which must have opened through to the driving cab. It seemed to be intended to slide, but was fastened shut as firmly as if it had been welded. There was no handle or bolt on the inside; only smoothed metal.

The rear doors at first seemed to be promising, as I discovered they were not entirely solid, but had windows. One each side, about twelve inches across, the distance from my wrist to my elbow, and half as high.

There was no glass in the windows. I stretched my hand cautiously through the one on the right, and immediately came to a halt. Something hard was jammed against the doors on the outside, holding them shut.

I was concentrating so much on the message from my fingers that I realized that I was crouching there with my eyes shut. Funny, really. I opened them. No light. What good were eyes without light?

Outside each window there was an area of coarse cloth, which felt like heavy canvas. At the outer sides of the window it was possible to push the canvas, to move it three or four inches away from the van. On the inner halves it was held tight against the van by whatever was jamming the doors shut.

I put an arm out of each outer section of window in turn, and felt as much of the outside of the van as I could reach. It was very little, and of no use. The whole of the back of the van was sheeted in canvas.

I slid down again to the floor and tried to visualize

what I'd felt. A van covered in canvas with its rear doors jammed shut. Where could one park such a thing so that it wouldn't be immediately discovered? In a garage? A barn? If I banged on the sides, would anyone hear me?

I banged on the sides of the van, but my fists made little noise, and there was nothing else to bang with. I shouted 'Help' a good many times through the windows, but no one came.

There was air perceptibly leaking in through the missing windows: I could feel it when I pushed the canvas outwards. No fear of asphyxiation.

It irritated me that I could do nothing useful with those windows. They were too small to crawl through, even without the canvas and whatever was holding it against the van. I couldn't get my head through the spaces, let alone my shoulders.

I decided to eat some cheese and think things over. The cheese wasn't bad. The thoughts produced the unwelcome reflection that this time I had no mattress, no blanket, no pillow, and no loo. Also no paperback novel, spare socks, or soap. The sail locker had been a Hilton compared with the van.

On the other hand, in an odd sort of way the time in the sail locker had prepared me better for this dourer cell. Instead of feeling more frightened, more hysterical, more despairing, I felt less. I had already been through all the horrors. Also, during the four days of freedom, I had not gone to the South Pole to avoid capture. I'd feared it and done my best to dodge it, but in returning to my usual life, I'd known it might come.

The reason for the first abduction presumably still existed. I had escaped before the intended time, and in someone's eyes this had been a very bad thing. Bad enough to send the squad to retake me, from the cottage, within a day of my return to England. Bad enough to risk carting me off again when this time there would, I hoped, be a police search.

I was pretty sure I must still be in England. I certainly had no memory of being transported from the motel to wherever I was now, but the impression that I'd been unconscious for only an hour or two was convincingly strong.

Sunday morning. No one would miss me. It would be Monday before Debbie and Peter began to wonder. Tuesday, perhaps, before the police took it seriously, if indeed they did, in spite of their assurance. A day or two more before anyone really started looking: and I had no wife or parents to keep the search alive, if I wasn't to be found soon after that.

Jossie might have done, I thought regretfully, if I'd known her for longer. Jossie with her bright eyes and forthright tongue.

At the very least, at the most hopeful assessment, the future still looked a long, hard, weary grind.

Shortening the perspective dramatically, it was becoming imperative to solve immediately the question of liquid waste disposal. I might be having to live in a tin box, but not, if I could help it, in a filthy stinking tin box.

Necessity concentrated the mind wonderfully, as others before me had observed. I took the cheese slices out of one of the thick plastic packets, and used that, and emptied it in relays out of the rear window, pushing the canvas away from the van as far as I could. Not the most sanitary of arrangements, but better than nothing.

After that little excitement, I sat down again. I was still cold, though not now with the through-and-through chill of injury-shock. I could perhaps have done some warming-up arm-swinging exercises, if it hadn't been for protesting bruises. As things were, with every muscle movement a reminder, I simply sat.

Exploration had kept me busy up to that point, but the next few hours revealed the true extent of my isolation.

There was absolutely no external sound. If I suppressed the faint noise of my own breathing, I could hear literally nothing. No traffic, no hum of aircraft, no wind, no creak, no rustle. Nothing.

There was absolutely no light. Air came steadily in from between the outside of the van and its canvas shroud, but no light came with it. Eyes wide open, or firmly shut, it was all the same.

There was no perceptible change in temperature. It remained just too low for comfort, defying my body's efforts to acclimatize. I had been left trousers, underpants, shirt, sports jacket and socks, though no tie, no belt, no loose belongings of any sort. It was Sunday, April 3rd. It might have been a sunny spring day outside, but wherever I was, it was simply too cold.

People would be reading about the Grand National in their Sunday newspapers, I thought. Lying in bed, warm and comfortable. Getting up and strolling to the pub. Eating hot meals, playing with the kids, deciding not to mow the lawn for another week. Millions of people, living their Sunday.

I served myself a Sunday lunch of cheese slices, and with great care drank some water from the can. It was heavy, being full, and I couldn't afford to tip it over. Enough water went down my neck to make me think of the uses of cheese packets as drinking cups.

After lunch, a snooze, I thought. I made a fairly reasonable pillow by rearranging the cheese packets inside the carrier, and resolutely tried to sleep, but the sum of discomfort kept me awake.

Well, then, I thought, lying on my back and staring at the invisible ceiling, I could sort out what I'd learned during my four free days.

The first of them could be discounted, as I'd spent it in Minorca, organizing my return home. That left two days in the office and one at the races. One night hiding in the cottage, one sleeping soundly in the Gloucester hotel. For all of that period I'd been looking for reasons, which made this present dose of imprisonment a great deal different from the first. Then, I'd been completely bewildered. This time I had at least one or two ideas.

Hours passed.

Nothing got any better.

I sat up for a while, and lay down again, and everything hurt, just the same. I cheered myself up with the thought that the stiff ache of bruises always finally got better, never worse. Suppose, for instance, it had been appendicitis. I'd heard that people going off to Everest or other Backs of Beyond had their perfectly healthy appendix removed, just in case. I wished on the whole that I hadn't thought of appendicitis.

Or toothache.

I had a feeling that it was evening, and then that it was night.

There was no change, except in me. I grew slowly even colder, but as if from the inside out. My eyelids stayed heavily shut. I drifted gradually in and out of sleep, a long drowsy twilight punctuated by short groaning awakenings every time I moved. When I woke with a clear mind, it felt like dawn.

If the cycle held, I thought, I could keep a calendar. One empty cheese packet for every day, stacked in the right-hand front corner of the van. If I put one there at every dawn, I would know the days. One for Sunday: a second for Monday. I extracted two wads of cheese slices and shuffled carefully a couple of feet forward to leave the empties.

I ate and drank what I thought of as breakfast: and I had become, I realized, much more at home in the dark. Physically, I was less clumsy. I found it easier to manage the water can, for instance, and no longer tended to put the cap on the floor and feel frustrated when I couldn't at once find it after I'd drunk. I now put my hand back automatically to where I'd parked the cap in the first place.

Mentally, too, it was less of a burden. On the boat I'd loathed it, and of all the rotten prospects of a second term of imprisonment, it had been being thrown back into the dark which I had shrunk from most. I still hated it, but its former heavy oppression was passing. I found that I no longer feared that the darkness on its own would set me climbing the walls.

I spent the morning thinking about reasons for abduction, and in the afternoon made an abacus out of pieces of cheese arranged in rows, and did a string of mathematical computations. I knew that other solitary captives had kept their minds occupied by repeating verses, but I'd always found it easier to think in numbers and symbols, and I'd not learned enough words by heart for them to be of any present use. Goosey goosey gander had its limitations.

*

Monday night came and went. When I woke I planted another cheese packet in the front right-hand corner, and flexed arms and legs which were no longer too sore to be worth it.

Tuesday morning I spent doing exercises and thinking about reasons for abduction, and Tuesday afternoon I felt my way delicately round the abacus, enlarging its scope as a calculator. Tuesday evening I sat and hugged my knees, and thought disconsolately that it was all very well telling myself to be staunch and resolute, but that staunch and resolute was not really how I felt.

Three days since I'd had dinner with Jossie. Well . . . at least I had her to think about, which I hadn't had on the boat.

The dozing period came round again. I lay down and let it wash over me for hours, and counted it Tuesday night.

Wednesday, for the twentieth time, I felt round the van inch by inch, looking for a possible way out. For the twentieth time, I didn't find one.

There were no bolts to undo. No levers. There was nothing. No way out. I knew it, but I couldn't stop searching.

Wednesday was the day I was supposed to be riding Tapestry at Ascot. Whether because of that, or simply because my body was back approximately to normal, the time passed more slowly than ever.

I whistled and sang, and felt restless, and wished passionately that there was room to stand up straight. The only way to straighten my spine was to lie down flat. I could feel my hard-won calm slipping away round the edges, and it was a considerable effort to give myself something to do with the pieces-of-cheese slide rule.

Wednesday I lost track of whether it was noon or evening, and the idea of days and days more of that existence was demoralizing. Dammit, I thought mordantly. Shut up, shut up with the gloomsville. One day at a time. One day, one hour, one minute at a time.

I ate some cheese and felt sleepy, and that at long last was Wednesday done.

Thursday midday, I heard a noise.

I couldn't believe it.

Some distant clicks, and a grinding noise. I was lying on my back doing bicycling exercises with my legs in the air, and I practically disconnected myself getting to my knees and scrambling over to the rear doors.

I pushed the canvas away from one of the windows, and shouted at the top of my lungs.

'Hey . . . hey . . . Come here.'

There were footsteps; more than one set. Soft footsteps, but in that huge dead silence, quite clear.

I swallowed. Whoever it was, there was no point in keeping quiet.

'Hey,' I shouted again. 'Come here.'

The footsteps stopped.
A man's voice, close to the van, spoke very loudly.
'Are you Roland Britten?'
I said weakly, 'Yes . . . who are you?'
'Police, sir,' he said.

# CHAPTER TWELVE

They took a good long while getting me out, because, as the disembodied voice explained, they would have to take photographs and notes for use in any future prosecution. Also there was the matter of fingerprints, which would mean further delay.

'And we can't get you out without moving the van, you see, sir,' said the voice. 'On account of it's backed hard up against a brick pillar, and we can't open the rear doors. On top of that the driving cab doors are both locked, and the brake's hard on, and there's no key in the ignition. So if you'll be patient, sir, we'll have you out as soon as we can.'

He sounded as if he were reassuring a small child who might scream the place down at any minute, but I found it easy to be patient, if only he knew.

There were several voices outside after a while, and from time to time they asked me if I was all right, and I said yes; and in the end they started the van's engine and drove it forward a few feet, and pulled off the canvas cover.

The return of sight was extraordinary. The two small windows appeared as oblongs of grey, and I had difficulty in focusing. A face looked in, roundly healthy, enquiring and concerned, topped by a uniform cap.

'Have you out in a jiffy now, sir,' he said. 'We're having a bit of difficulty with these doors, see, as the handle's been sabotaged.'

'Fine,' I said vaguely. The light was still pretty dim, but to me a luxury like no other on earth. A half-forgotten joy, newly discovered. Like meeting a dead friend. Familiar, lost, precious, and restored.

I sat on the floor and looked around my prison. It was smaller than I'd imagined: cramped and claustrophobic, now that I could see the grey enclosing walls.

The jerrycan of water was of white plastic, with a red cap. The carrier was brown, as I'd imagined it. The little calendar stack of five empty packets lay in its corner, and the hardening pieces of cheese from my counting machine, in another. There was nothing else, except me and dust.

They opened the doors eventually and helped me out, and then took notes and photographs of where I'd been. I stood a pace or two away and looked curiously at my surroundings.

The van was indeed the white one from Cheltenham, or one exactly like it. An old Ford. No tax disc, and no number-plates. The canvas which had covered it was a huge, dirty dark grey tarpaulin, the sort used for sheeting loads on lorries. The van had been wrapped in it like a parcel, and tied with ropes threaded through eyelets in the tarpaulin's edges.

The van, the police and I were all inside a building of about a hundred feet square. All round the walls rose huge lumpy heaps of dust-covered unidentifiable bundles, grey shapes of boxes and things that looked like sandbags. Some of the piles reached the low flat ceiling, which was supported at strategic points by four sturdy brick pillars.

It was against one of these, in the small clear area in the centre, that the van had been jammed.

'What is this place?' I said to the policeman beside me.

'Are you all right, sir?' he said. He shivered slightly. 'It's cold in here.'

'Yes,' I said. 'Where exactly are we?'

'It used to be one of those army surplus stores, selling stuff to the public. Went bust a while back, though, and no one's ever shifted all the muck.'

'Oh. Well . . . whereabouts is it?'

'Down one of those tracks that used to be the railway branch line, before they closed it.'

'Yes,' I said apologetically. 'But what town?'

'Eh?' He looked at me in surprise. 'Newbury, of course, sir.'

The town clocks pointed to five o'clock when the police drove me down to the station. My body's own time had proved remarkably constant, I thought. Much better than on the boat, where noise and tossing and sickness had upset things.

I was given a chair in the office of one of the same policemen as before, who showed no regrets at having earlier thought I was exaggerating.

'How did you find me?' I said.

He tapped his teeth with a pencil, a hard-working Detective Inspector with an air of suspecting the innocent until they were found guilty.

'Scotland Yard had a call,' he said grudgingly. 'We'll want a statement from you, sir, if you don't mind.'

'A cup of tea first,' I suggested.

His gaze wandered over my face and clothes. I must have looked a wreck. He came somewhere near a smile, and sent a young constable on the errand.

The tea tasted marvellous, though I daresay it wasn't. I drank it slowly and told him fairly briefly what had happened.

'So you didn't see their faces at all, this time?'

'No,' I said.

'Pity.'

'Do you think,' I said tentatively, 'that some one could drive me back to the motel, so I can collect my car?'

'No need, sir,' he said. 'It's parked beside your cottage.'

'What?'

He nodded. 'With a lot of your possessions in it. Suitcase. Wallet. Shoes. Keys. All in the boot. Your assistants notified us on Monday that you were missing again. We sent a man along to your cottage. He reported your car was there, but you weren't. We did what you asked, sir. We did look for you. The whole country's been looking for you, come to that. The motel rang us yesterday to say you'd booked in there last Saturday but hadn't used the room, but apart from that there was nothing to go on. No trace at all. We thought you might have been taken off on another boat, to be frank.'

I finished the tea, and thanked him for it.

'Will you run me back to the cottage, then?'

He thought it could be arranged. He came with me out to the entrance hall, to fix it.

A large man with an over-anxious expression came bustling in from the street, swinging the door wide and assessing rapidly the direction from which he would get most satisfaction. My partner at his most bombastic, his deep voice echoing round the hall as he demanded information.

'Hello, Trevor,' I said. 'Take it easy.'

He stopped in mid-commotion, and stared at me as if I were an intrusive stranger. Then he recognized me, and took in my general appearance, and his face went stiff with shock.

'Ro!' He seemed to have trouble with his voice. 'Ro, my dear fellow. My dear fellow. I've just heard . . . My God, Ro . . .'

I sighed. 'Calm down, Trevor. All I need is a razor.'

'But you're so *thin*.' His eyes were appalled. I reflected

that I was probably a good deal thinner than when he'd seen me last, some time in the dim, distant, and safe past.

'Mr King has been bombarding us all day,' said the Detective Inspector with a touch of impatience.

'My dear Ro, you must come back with me. We'll look after you. My *God*, Ro . . .'

I shook my head. 'I'm fine, Trevor. I'm grateful to you, but I'd really rather go home.'

'Alone?' he said anxiously. 'Suppose . . . I mean . . . do you think it's safe?'

'Oh yes,' I nodded. 'Whoever put me in, let me out. It's all over, I think.'

'What's all over?'

'That,' I said soberly, 'is a whole new ball game.'

The cottage embraced me like a balm.

I had a bath, and shaved, and a grey face of gaunt shadows looked at me out of the mirror. No wonder Trevor had been shocked. Just as well, I thought, that he hadn't seen the black and yellow blotches of fading bruises which covered me from head to foot.

I shrugged, and thought the same as before: nothing that a few days' freedom wouldn't fix. I put on jeans and a jersey and went downstairs in search of a large Scotch, and that was the last peaceful moment of the evening.

The telephone rang non-stop. Reporters, to my amazement, arrived at the doorstep. A television camera appeared. When they saw I was astounded, they said hadn't I read the papers.

'What papers?'

They produced them, and spread them out.

*The Sporting Life*: headline on Tuesday: 'Where is Roland Britten?' followed by an article about my sea trip, as told by me to friends. I had not been seen since Towcester. Friends were worried.

On Wednesday, paragraphs in all the dailies: 'Tapestry's rider again missing' in one of the staider, and 'Fun Jock Twice Removed?' from a tits-and-bums.

Thursday – that day – many front pages carried a broadly smiling picture of me, taken five minutes after the Gold Cup. 'Find Roland Britten' ordered one, and 'Fears for Jockey's Life' gloomed another. I glanced over them in amazement, remembering ironically that I'd been afraid no one would really look for me at all.

The telephone rang beside my hand. I picked up the receiver and said hello.

'Ro? Is that you?' The voice was fresh and unmistakable.

'Jossie!'

'Where the hell have you been?'

'Have dinner with me tomorrow, and I'll tell you.'

'Pick me up at eight,' she said. 'What's all that noise?'

'I'm pressed by Press,' I said. 'Journalists.'

'Good grief.' She laughed. 'Are you all right?'

'Yes, fine.'

'It was on the news, that you'd been found.'

'I don't believe it.'

'Big stuff, buddy boy.' The mockery was loud and clear.

'Did you start it . . . all this publicity?' I said.

'Not me, no. Moira Longerman. Mrs Tapestry. She tried to get you Sunday, and she tried your office on Monday, and they told her you were missing, and they thought you might have been kidnapped again, so she rang up the editor of *The Sporting Life*, who's a friend of hers, to ask him to help.'

'A determined lady,' I said gratefully.

'She didn't run Tapestry yesterday, you know. There's a sob-stuff bit in *The Sporting Life*. "How can I run my horse while Roland is missing" and all that guff. Fair turns your stomach.'

'Fair turned Binny Tomkins's, I'll bet.'

She laughed. 'I can hear the wolves howling for you. See you tomorrow. Don't vanish before eight.'

I put the telephone down, but the wolves had to wait a little longer, as the bell immediately rang again.

Moira Longerman, excited and twittering, coming down the wire like an electric current.

'Thank heavens you're free. Isn't it marvellous? Are you all right? Can you ride Tapestry on Saturday? Do tell me all about the horrible place where they found you . . . and Roland, dear, I don't want you listening to a word Binny Tomkins says about you not being fit to ride after all you've been through.'

'Moira,' I said, vainly trying to stop the flow. 'Thank you very much.'

'My dear,' she said, 'it was rather *fun*, getting everyone mobilized. Of course I was truly dreadfully worried that something awful had happened to you, and it was quite clear that somebody had to do *something*, otherwise you might stay kidnapped for *weeks*, and it seemed to me that a jolly good fuss was what was wanted. I thought that if the whole country was looking for you, whoever had taken you might get cold feet and turn you loose, and that's precisely what happened, so I was right and the silly police were all wrong.'

'What silly police?' I said.

'Telling me I might have put you in danger by getting *The Sporting Life* to say you'd vanished again. I ask you! They said if kidnappers get panicky they could kill their victim. Anyway, they were wrong, weren't they?'

'Fortunately,' I agreed.

'So do tell me all about it,' she said. 'Is it true you were shut up in a van? What was it like?'

'Boring,' I said.

'Roland, *really*. Is that all you've got to say?'

'I thought about you all day on Wednesday, imagining you'd be furious when I didn't turn up at Ascot.'

'That's better.' She laughed her tinkly laugh. 'You can make up for it on Saturday. Tapestry's in the Oasthouse Cup at Kempton, though of course he's got top weight there, which was why we wanted to run at Ascot instead. But now we're going to Kempton.'

'I'm afraid . . .' I said, 'that Binny's right. This time, I'm really not fit enough. I'd love to ride him, but . . . well . . . at the moment I couldn't go two rounds with a kitten.'

There was a short silence at the other end.

'Do you mean it?' she demanded doubtfully.

'I hate to say so, but I do.'

The doubt in her voice subsided. 'I'm sure you'll be a hundred per cent after a good night's sleep. After all, you'll have nearly two days to recover, and even Binny admits you're pretty tough as amateurs go . . . so *please*, Roland, *please* ride on Saturday, because the horse is jumping out of his skin, and the opposition is not so strong as it will be in the Whitbread Gold Cup in two weeks' time, and I feel in my bones that he'll win this race but not the other. And I don't want Binny putting up any other jockey, as to be frank I only trust you, which you know. So *please* say you will. I was so *thrilled* when I heard you were free, so that you could ride on Saturday.'

I rubbed my hand across my eyes. I knew I shouldn't agree, and that I was highly unlikely to be fit enough even to walk the course on my feet, let alone control half a ton of thoroughbred muscle on the rampage. Yet to her, if I refused, it would seem like gross ingratitude after her lively campaign to free me, and I too suspected that if Tapestry started favourite with a different jockey of Binny's choice, he wouldn't win. There was also the insidious old desire to race which raised its head in defiance of common sense. Reason told me I'd fall off from weakness at the first fence, and the irresistible temptation of a go at another of the season's top 'chases kidded me not to believe it.

'Well . . .' I said, hesitating.

'Oh, you *will*,' she said delightedly. 'Oh Roland, I'm so *glad*.'

'I shouldn't.'

'If you don't win,' she said gaily, 'I promise I won't blame you.'

I'd blame myself, I thought, and I'd deserve it.

I went to the office at nine the next morning, and Trevor fussed about a great deal too much.

'You need rest, Ro. You should be in bed.'

'I need people and life and things to do.'

He sat in the clients' armchair in my office and looked worried. The sun-tan of his holiday suited him, increasing his air of distinction. His silvery hair was fluffier than usual, and his comfortable stomach looked rounder.

'Did you have a good time,' I said, 'in Spain?'

'What? Oh yes, splendid. Splendid. Until the car broke down, of course. And all the time, while we were enjoying ourselves, you . . .' He stopped and shook his head.

'I'm afraid,' I said wryly, 'that I'm dreadfully behind with the work.'

'For heaven's sake . . .'

'I'll try to catch up,' I said.

'I wish you'd take it easy for a few days.' He looked as

if he meant it, his eyes full of troubled concern. 'It won't do either of us any good if you crack up.'

My lips twitched. That was more like the authentic Trevor.

'I'm made of plasticine,' I said; and despite his protests I stayed where I was and once again tried to sort out the trail of broken appointments.

Mr Wells was in a worse mess than ever, having sent a cheque which had promptly bounced. A prosecution for that was in the offing.

'But you knew the bank wouldn't pay it,' I protested when he telephoned with this latest trouble.

'Yes . . . but I thought they *might*.'

His naïvety was frightening: the same stupid hopefulness which had got him enmeshed in the first place. He blanked out reality and believed in fantasies. I'd known others like him, and I'd never known them change.

'Come on Monday afternoon,' I said resignedly.

'Supposing someone kidnaps you again.'

'They won't,' I said. 'Two-thirty, Monday.'

I went through the week's letters with Debbie and sorted out the most urgent. Their complexity made me wilt.

'We'll answer them on Monday morning,' I said.

Debbie fetched some coffee and said at her most pious that I wasn't fit to be at work.

'Did we get those postponements from the Commissioners for Axwood Stables and Coley Young?' I said.

'Yes, they came on Wednesday.'

'And what about Denby Crest's certificate?'

'Mr King said he'd see about that this morning.'

I rubbed a hand over my face. No use kidding myself. However much I disliked it, I did feel pathetically weak. Agreeing to ride Tapestry had been a selfish folly. The only sensible course was to ring Moira Longerman at once, and cry off: but when it came to race-riding, I'd never been sensible.

'Debbie,' I said, 'please would you go down to the store in the basement, and bring up all the old files on Connaught Powys, and on Glitberg and Ownslow.'

'Who?'

I wrote the names down for her. She glanced at them, nodded, and went away.

Sticks Elroy telephoned, words tumbling out in a rush, incoherent and thick with Oxfordshire accent. A lot more talkative than he'd been at dinner in the pub, when overshadowed by his bull-like dad.

'Stop,' I said. 'I didn't hear a word. Say it slowly.'

'I said I was ever so sorry you got shut up in that van.'

'Well . . . thanks.'

'My old man couldn't have done it, you know.' He sounded anxious, more seeking to convince than convinced.

'Don't you think so?'

'I know he said . . . Look, well, he went on cursing all evening, and I know he's got a van, and all, which is off somewhere getting the gearbox fixed, or something, and I know he was that furious, and he said you should be locked up, but I don't reckon he could have done it, not for real.'

'Did you ask him?' I said curiously.

'Yeah.' He hesitated. 'See . . . we had a bloody big row, him and me.' Another pause. 'He always knocked us about when we were kids. Straps, boots, anything.' A pause. 'I asked him about you . . . he punched me in the face.'

'Mm,' I said. 'What did you decide to do about that cash?'

'Yeah, well, that's what the row was about, see. I reckoned you were right and I didn't want any trouble with the law, and Dad blew his top and said I'd never been grateful for everything he'd done for me. He says if I declare that cash and pay tax on it he'll be in trouble himself, see, and I reckon he was mad enough to do anything.'

I reflected a bit. 'What colour is his van?'

'White, sort of. An old Ford.'

'Um. When did you decide to go to that pub for dinner?'

'Dad drove there straight from the races, for a drink, like, and then he phoned and said they could fit us all in for dinner, and we might as well celebrate my win.'

'Would he be likely,' I said, 'to be able to lay his hands on sixty packets of cheese slices?'

'Whatever are you on about?'

I sighed. 'They were in the van with me.'

'Well, I don't know, do I? I don't live with him any

more. I wouldn't reckon on him going to a supermarket, though. Women's work, see?'

'Yes. If you've decided to declare that cash, there are some legitimate expenses to set off against the profit.'

'Bloody tax,' he said. 'Sucks you dry. I'm not going to bother sweating my guts out on any more schemes. Not bloody worth it.'

He made an appointment for the following week and grumbled his way off the phone.

I sat and stared into space, thinking of Sticks Elroy and his violent father. Heavy taxation was always self-defeating, with the country losing progressively more for every tightening of the screw. Overtime and enterprise weren't worth it. Emigration was. The higher the tax rates, the less there was to tax. It was crazy. If I'd been Chancellor, I'd have made Britain a tax haven, and welcomed back all the rich who had taken their money and left. A fifty per cent tax on millions would be better for the country than a ninety-eight per cent on nothing. As it was, I had to interpret and advise in accordance with what I thought of as bad economics; uphold laws which I thought irrational. If the fury the Elroys felt against the system took the form of abuse of the accountant who forced them to face nasty facts, it wasn't unduly surprising. I did doubt though that even Elroy senior would make his abuse physical. Calling me a bastard was a long way from imprisonment.

Debbie came in with her arms full of files and her face full of fluster.

'There's a lady outside who insists on seeing you. She hasn't got an appointment and Mr King said you were definitely not to be worried today, but she won't go away. Oh!'

The lady in question was walking into the office in Debbie's wake. Tall, thin, assured, and middle-aged.

I stood up, smiling, and shook hands with Hilary Margaret Pinlock.

'It's all right, Debbie,' I said.

'Oh, very well.' She shrugged, put down the files, and went out.

'How are you?' I said. 'Sit down.'

Hilary Margaret Pinlock sat in the clients' chair and crossed her thin legs.

'You,' she said, 'look half-dead.'

'A half-empty bottle is also half-full.'

'And you're an optimist?'

'Usually,' I said.

She was wearing a brownish-grey flecked tweed coat, to which the sunless April day added nothing in the way of life. Behind the spectacles the eyes looked small and bright, and coral-pink lipstick lent warmth to her mouth.

'I've come to tell you something,' she said. 'Quite a lot of things, I suppose.'

'Good or bad?'

'Facts.'

'You're not pregnant?'

She was amused. 'I don't know yet.'

'Would you like some sherry?'

'Yes, please.'

I stood up and produced a bottle and two glasses from a filing cupboard. Poured. Handed her a generous slug of Harvey's Luncheon Dry.

'I came home yesterday,' she said. 'I read about you being kidnapped again, on the aeroplane coming back. They had newspapers. Then I heard on the news that you were found, and safe. I thought I would come and see you myself, instead of taking my information to the police.'

'What information?' I said. 'And I thought you were due back home last Saturday.'

She sipped her sherry sedately.

'Yes, I was. I stayed on, though. Because of you. It cost me a fortune.' She looked at me over her glass. 'I was sorry to read you had been recaptured after all. I had seen . . . your fear of it.'

'Mm,' I said ruefully.

'I found out about that boat for you,' she said.

I almost spilled the sherry.

She smiled. 'About the man, to be more exact. The man in the dinghy, who was chasing you.'

'How?' I said.

'After you'd gone, I hired a car and drove to all the places on Minorca where they said yachts could be moored. The nearest good harbour to Cala St Galdana was Ciudadela, and I should think that's where the boat went after they lost you, but it had gone by the time I started looking.' She drank some sherry. 'I asked some

English people on a yacht there, and they said there had been an English crew on a sixty-footer there the night before, and they'd overheard them talking about wind for a passage to Palma. I asked them to describe the captain, and they said there didn't seem to be a proper captain, only a tall young man who looked furious.' She stopped and considered, and explained further. 'All the yachts at Ciudadela were moored at right angles to the quayside, you see. Stern on. So that they were all close together, side by side, and you walked straight off the back of them on to dry land.'

'Yes,' I said. 'I see.'

'So I just walked along the whole row, asking. There were Spaniards, Germans, French, Swedes . . . all sorts. The English people had noticed the other English crew just because they *were* English, if you see what I mean.'

'I do,' I said.

'And also because it had been the biggest yacht that night in the harbour.' She paused. 'So instead of flying home on Saturday, I went to Palma.'

'It's a big place,' I said.

She nodded. 'It took me three days. But I found out that young man's name, and quite a lot about him.'

'Would you like some lunch?' I said.

# CHAPTER THIRTEEN

We walked along to La Riviera at the end of the High Street and ordered moussaka. The place was full as usual, and Hilary leaned forward across the table to make herself privately heard. Her strong plain face was full of the interest and vigour she had put into her search on my behalf, and it was typical of her self-confidence that she was concentrating only on the subject in hand and not the impression she was making as a woman. A headmistress, I thought: not a lover.

'His name,' she said, 'is Alastair Yardley. He is one of a whole host of young men who seem to wander around the Mediterranean looking after boats while the owners are home in England, Italy, France, and wherever. They live in the sun, on the water's edge, picking up jobs where they can, and leading an odd sort of drop-out existence which supplies a useful service to boat owners.'

'Sounds attractive.'

'It's bumming around,' she said succinctly.

'I wouldn't mind dropping out, right now,' I said.

'You're made of sterner stuff.'

Plasticine, I thought.

'Go on about Alastair Yardley,' I said.

'I asked around for two days without any success. My description of him seemed to fit half the population, and although I'd seen the boat, of course, I wasn't sure I would know it again, as I haven't an educated eye for that sort of thing. There are two big marinas at Palma, both of them packed with boats. Some boats are moored stern-on, like at Ciudadela, but dozens more were anchored away from the quays. I hired a boatman to take me round the whole harbour in his motorboat, but with no results. I'm sure he thought I was potty. I was pretty discouraged, actually, and was admitting defeat, when he – the boatman, that is – said there was another small harbour less than a day's sail away, and why didn't I look there. So on Wednesday I took a taxi to the port of Andraitx.'

She stopped to eat some moussaka, which had arrived and smelled magnificent.

'Eat,' she said, scooping up a third generous forkful and waving at my still full plate.

'Yes,' I said. It was the first proper meal I'd approached since the dinner with Jossie, and I should have been ravenous. Instead, the diet of processed cheese seemed to have played havoc with my appetite, and I found difficulty in eating much at all. I hadn't been able to face any supper, the evening before, when the journalists had finally gone, and not much breakfast either.

'Tell me about Andraitx,' I said.

'In a minute,' she said. 'I'm not letting this delicious food get cold.' She ate with enjoyment and disapproved of my unsuccessful efforts to do the same. I had to wait for the next instalment until she had finished the last morsel and lain down her fork.

'That was *good*,' she said. 'A great treat.'

'Andraitx,' I said.

She half laughed. 'All right, then. Andraitx. Small by Palma's standards, but bigger than Ciudadela. The small ports and harbours are the old parts of the islands. The buildings are old . . . there are no new ritzy hotels there, because there are no beaches. Deep water, rocky cliffs, and so on. I found out so much more about the islands this week than if I'd stopped in Cala St Galdana for my week and come home last Saturday. They have such a bloody history of battles and sieges and invasions. A horrible violent history. One may sneer now at the way they've been turned into a tourist paradise, but the brassy modern civilization must be better than the murderous past.'

'Dearest Hilary,' I said. 'Cut the lecture and come to the grit.'

'It was the biggest yacht in Andraitx,' she said. 'I was sure almost at once, and then I saw the young man on the quayside, not far from where I paid off the taxi. He came out of a shop and walked across the big open space that there is there, between the buildings and the water. He was carrying a heavy box of provisions. He dumped it on the edge of the quay, beside that black rubber dinghy which he brought ashore at Cala St Galdana. Then he went off again, up a street leading away from the quay. I didn't exactly follow him, I just watched. He went into a doorway a little way up the street, and soon came out again carrying a bundle wrapped in plastic. He went back to the dinghy, and loaded the box and the bundle and himself, and motored out to the yacht.'

The waiter came to take our plates and ask about puddings and coffee.

'Cheese,' Hilary decided.

'Just coffee,' I said. 'And do go on.'

'Well . . . I went into the shop he'd come out of, and asked about him, but they spoke only Spanish, and I don't. So then I walked up the street to the doorway I'd seen him go into, and that was where I hit the jackpot.'

She stopped to cut cheese from a selection on a board. I wondered how long it would be before I liked the stuff again.

'It was a laundry,' she said. 'All white and airy. And run by an English couple who'd gone to Majorca originally for a holiday and fallen in love with the place. A nice couple. Friendly, happy, busy, and very, very helpful. They knew the young man fairly well, they said, because he always took his washing in when he was in Andraitx. They do the boat people's laundry all the time. They reckon to have a bag of dirty clothes washed and ironed in half a day.'

She ate a biscuit and some cheese, and I waited.

'Alastair Yardley,' she said. 'The laundry people said he is a good sailor. Better than most of his kind. He often takes yachts from one place to another, so that they'll be wherever the owner wants. He can handle big boats, and is known for it. He sails into Andraitx four or five times a year, but three years ago he had a flat there, and used it as his base. The laundry people said they don't really know much about him, except that his father worked in a boat-building yard. He told them once that he'd learned to sail as soon as walk, and his first job was as a paid deck-hand in sea-trials for ocean-racing yachts. Apart from that, he hasn't said much about himself or who he's working for now, and the laundry people don't know because they aren't the prying sort, just chatty.'

'You're marvellous,' I said.

'Hm. I took some photographs of the boat, and I've had them processed at an overnight developers.' She opened her handbag, and drew out a yellow packet, which contained, among holiday scenes, three clear colour photographs of my first prison. Three different views, taken as the boat swung round with the tide.

'You can have them, if you like,' she said.

'I could kiss you.'

Her face lit with amusement. 'If you shuffle through that pack, you'll find a rather bad picture of Alastair Yardley. I didn't get the focus right. I was in a bit of a hurry, and he was walking towards me with his laundry, and I didn't want him to think I was taking a picture of him personally. I had to pretend to be taking a general view of the port, you see, and so I'm afraid it isn't very good.'

She had caught him from the waist up, and, as she said, slightly out of focus, but still recognizable to anyone who knew him. Looking ahead, not at the camera, with a white-wrapped bundle under his arm. Even in fuzzy outline, the uncompromising bones gave his face a powerful toughness, a look of aggressive determination. I thought that I might have liked him, if we'd met another way.

'Will you take the photos to the police?' Hilary asked.

'I don't know.' I considered it. 'Could you lend me the negatives, to have more prints made?'

'Sort them out and take them,' she said.

I did that, and we lingered over our coffee.

'I suppose,' she said, 'that you have thought once or twice about . . . the time we spent together?'

'Yes.'

She looked at me with a smile in the spectacled eyes. 'Do you regret it?'

'Of course not. Do you?'

She shook her head. 'It may be too soon to say, but I think it will have changed my entire life.'

'How could it?' I said.

'I think you have released in me an enormous amount of mental energy. I was being held back by feelings of ignorance and even inferiority. These feelings have entirely gone. I feel full of rocket fuel, ready for blast off.'

'Where to?' I said. 'What's higher than a head-mistress?'

'Nothing measurable. But my school will be better, and there are such things as power and influence, and the ear of policy makers.'

'Miss Pinlock will be a force in the land?'

'We'll have to see,' she said.

I thought back to the time I'd first slept with a girl, when I was eighteen. It had been a relief to find out what everyone had been going on about, but I couldn't remember any accompanying upsurge of power. Perhaps, for me, the knowledge had come too easily, and too young. More likely that I'd never had the Pinlock potential in the first place.

I paid the bill and went out into the street. The April air was cold, as it had been for the past entire week, and Hilary shivered slightly inside her coat.

'The trouble with warm rooms . . . life blasts you when you leave.'

'Speaking allegorically?' I said.

'Of course.'

We began to walk back towards the office, up the High Street, beside the shops. People scurried in and out of the doorways like bees at a hive mouth. The familiar street scene, after the last three weeks, seemed superficial and unreal.

We drew level with a bank: not, as it happened, the one where I kept my own money, nor that which we used as a firm, but one which dealt with the affairs of many of our clients.

'Would you wait a sec?' I said. 'I've had a thought or two this week . . . just want to check something.'

Hilary smiled and nodded cheerfully, and waited without comment while I went on my short errand.

'OK?' I said, rejoining her.

'Fine,' she said. 'Where did they keep you, in that van?'

'In a warehouse.' I looked at my watch. 'Do you want to see it? I want to go back for another look.'

'All right.'

'My car's behind the office.'

We walked on, past a small, pleasant-looking dress shop. I glanced idly into the window, and walked two strides past, and then stopped.

'Hilary . . .'

'Yes?'

'I want to give you a present.'

'Don't be ridiculous,' she said.

She protested her way into the shop and was reduced to silence only by the sight of what I wanted her to wear: the garment I'd seen in the window; a long bold scarlet cloak.

'Try it,' I said.

Shaking her head, she removed the dull tweed coat and let the girl assistant lower the bright swirling cape on to her shoulders. She stood immobile while the girl fastened the buttons and arranged the neat collar. Looked at herself in the glass.

Duck into swan, I thought. She looked imposing and magnificent, a plain woman transfigured, her height making dramatic folds in the drop of clear red wool.

'Rockets,' I said, 'are powered by flame.'

'You can't buy me this.'

'Why not?'

I wrote the girl a cheque, and Hilary for once seemed to be speechless.

'Keep it on,' I said. 'It looks marvellous.'

The girl packed the old coat into a carrier, and we continued our walk to the office. People looked at Miss Pinlock as they passed, as they had not done before.

'It takes courage,' she said, raising her chin.

'First flights always do.'

She thought instantly of the night in Cala St Galdana: I saw it in the movement of her eyes. She smiled to herself, and straightened a fraction to her full height. Nothing wrong with the Pinlock nerve, then or ever.

From the front the warehouse looked small and dilapidated, its paint peeling off like white scabs to leave uneven grey scars underneath. A weatherboard screwed to the wall offered 10,500 square feet to let, but judging from the aged dimness of the sign, the customers had hardly queued.

The building stood on its own at the end of a side road

which now had no destination, owing to the close-down of the branch railway and the subsequent massive re-organization of the landscape into motorways and roundabouts.

There was a small door let into a large one on rollers at the entrance, neither of them locked. The locks, in fact, appeared to have been smashed, but in time gone by. The splintered wood around them had weathered grey with age.

I pushed open the small door for Hilary, and we stepped in. The gloom as the door swung behind us was as blinding as too much light; I propped the door open with a stone, but even then there were enfolding shadows at every turn. It was clear why vandals had stopped at breaking down the doors. Everything inside was so thick with dust that to kick anything was to start a choking cloud.

Sounds were immediately deadened, as if the high, mouldering piles of junk were soaking up every echo before it could go a yard.

I shouted 'Hey' into the small central space, and it seemed to reach no further than my own throat.

'It's cold in here,' Hilary said. 'Colder than outside.'

'Something to do with ventilation bricks, I expect,' I said. 'A draught, bringing in dust and lowering the temperature.'

Our voices had no resonance. We walked the short distance to where the white van stood, with the dark tarpaulin sprawling in a huge heap beside it.

With eyes adjusting to the dim light, we looked inside. The police had taken the water carrier and the bag of cheese, and the van was empty.

It was a small space. Dirty, and hard.

'You spent nearly a week in there,' Hilary said, disbelievingly.

'Five nights and four and a half days,' I said. 'Let's not exaggerate.'

'Let's not,' she said dryly.

We stood looking at the van for a minute or two, and the deadness and chill of the place began to soak into our brains. I shuddered slightly and walked away, out through the door into the living air.

Hilary followed me, and kicked away the door-stop. The peeling door swung shut.

'Did you sleep well, last night?' she said bleakly.

'No.'

'Nightmares?'

I looked up to the grey sky, and breathed deep luxurious breaths.

'Well . . . dreams,' I said.

She swallowed. 'Why did you want to come back here?'

'To see the name of the estate agent who has this place on his books. It's on the board, on the wall. I wasn't noticing things much when the police took me out of here yesterday.'

She gave a small explosive laugh of escaping tension. 'So practical!'

'Whoever put the van in there knew the place existed,' I said. 'I didn't, and I've lived in Newbury for six years.'

'Leave it to the police,' she said seriously. 'After all, they did find you.'

I shook my head. 'Someone rang Scotland Yard to tell them where I was.'

'Leave it to them,' she urged. 'You're out of it now.'

'I don't know. To coin a cliché, there's a great big iceberg blundering around here, and that van's only the tip.'

We got into my car, and I drove her back to the park in town where she'd left her own. She stood beside it, tall in her scarlet cloak, and fished in her handbag for a pen and notebook.

'Here,' she said, writing. 'This is my address and telephone number. You can come at any time. You might need . . .' She paused an instant, ' . . . a safe place.'

'Can I come for advice?' I said.

'For anything.'

I smiled.

'No,' she said. 'Not for that. I want a memory, not a habit.'

'Take your glasses off,' I said.

'To see you better?' She took them off, humouring me quizzically.

'Why don't you wear contact lenses?' I said. 'Without glasses, your eyes are great.'

*

On the way back to the office I stopped to buy food, on the premise that if I didn't stock up with things I liked, I wouldn't get back to normal eating. I also left Hilary's negatives for a rush reprint, so that it was nearly five before I went through the door.

Debbie and Peter had both done their usual Friday afternoon bolt, for which dentists and classes were only sample reasons. The variety they had come up with over the years would have been valuable if applied to their work: but I knew from experience that if I forced them both to stay until five I got nothing productive done after a quarter past four. Bess, infected by them, had already covered her typewriter, and was busy applying thick new make-up on top of the old. Bess, eighteen and curvy, thought of work as a boring interruption of her sex life. She gave me a bright smile, ran her tongue round the fresh glistening lipstick, and swung her hips provocatively on her way to the weekend's sport.

There were voices in Trevor's room. Trevor's loud voice in short sentences, and a client's softer tones in long paragraphs.

I tidied my own desk, and carried the Glitberg, Ownslow and Connaught Powys files into the outer office on my way to the car.

The door to Trevor's room opened suddenly, and Trevor and his client were revealed there, warmly shaking hands.

The client was Denby Crest, solicitor, a short plump man with a stiff moustache and a mouth permanently twisted in irritation. Even when he smiled at you personally, he gave an impression of annoyance at the state of things in general. Many of his own clients saw that as sympathy for their troubles, which was their mistake.

'I'll make it worth your while, Trevor,' he was saying. 'I'm eternally grateful.'

Trevor suddenly saw me standing there and stared at me blankly.

'I thought you'd gone, Ro,' he said.

'Came back for some files,' I said, glancing down at them in my arms. 'Good afternoon, Denby.'

'Good afternoon, Roland.'

He gave me a brief nod and made a brisk dive for the outer door; a brusque departure, even by his standards. I watched his fast disappearing back and said to Trevor, 'Did you sign his certificate? He said he would wait until you got back.'

'Yes, I did,' Trevor said. He too showed no inclination for leisurely chat, and turned away from me towards his own desk.

'What was I doing wrong?' I said. 'I kept making him fifty thousand pounds short.'

'Decimal point in the wrong place,' he said shortly.

'Show me,' I said.

'Not now, Ro. It's time to go home.'

I put the files down on Bess's desk and walked into Trevor's office. It was larger than mine, and much tidier, with no wall of waiting cardboard boxes. There were three armchairs for clients, some Stubbs prints on the walls, and a bowl of flowering daffodils on his desk.

'Trevor . . .'

He was busy putting together what I recognized as Denby Crest's papers, and didn't look up. I stood in his room, waiting, until in the end he had to take notice. His face was bland, calm, uninformative, and if there had been any tension there a minute ago, it had now evaporated.

'Trevor,' I said. 'Please show me where I went wrong.'

'Leave it, Ro,' he said pleasantly. 'There's a good chap.'

'If you did sign his certificate, and he really is fifty thousand pounds short, then it concerns me too.'

'You're dead tired, Ro, and you look ill, and this is not a good time to discuss it.' He came round his desk and put his hand gently on my arm. 'My dear chap, you know how horrified and worried I am about what has been happening to you. I am most concerned that you should take things easy and recover your strength.'

It was a long speech for him, and confusing. When he saw me hesitate, he added. 'There's nothing wrong with Denby's affairs. We'll go through them, if you like, on Monday.'

'It had better be now,' I said.

'No.' He was stubbornly positive. 'We have friends coming for the evening, and I promised to be home early. Monday, Ro. It will keep perfectly well until Monday.'

I gave in, partly because I simply didn't want to face

what I guessed to be true, that Trevor had signed the certificate knowing the figures were false. I'd done the sums over and over on my cheese abacus, and the answer came monotonously the same, whichever method I used to work them out.

He shepherded me like an uncle to his door, and watched while I picked up the heap of files from Bess's desk.

'What are those?' he said. 'You really mustn't work this weekend.'

'They're not exactly work. They're back files. I just thought I'd take a look.'

He walked over and peered down at the labels, moving the top file to see what was underneath.

'Why these, for heaven's sake?' he said, frowning, coming across Connaught Powys.

'I don't know . . .' I sighed. 'I just thought they might possibly have some connection with my being abducted.'

He looked at me with compassion. 'My dear Ro, why don't you leave it all to the police?'

'I'm not hindering them.' I picked up the armful of files and smiled. 'I don't think I'm high on their urgency list, though. I wasn't robbed, ransomed, or held hostage, and a spot of unlawful imprisonment on its own probably ranks lower than parking on double yellow lines.'

'But,' he said doubtfully, 'don't you think they will ever discover who, or why?'

'It depends on where they look, I should think.' I shrugged a shoulder, walked to the door, and stopped to look back. He was standing by Bess's desk, clearly troubled. 'Trevor,' I said, 'I don't mind one way or the other whether the police come up with answers. I don't madly want public revenge, and I've had my fill of court-case publicity, as a witness. I certainly don't relish it as a victim. But for my own peace of mind, I would like to know. If I find out, I won't necessarily act on the knowledge. The police would have to. So there's the difference. It might be better – you never know – if it's I who did the digging, not the police.'

He shook his head, perturbed and unconvinced.

'See you Monday,' I said.

# CHAPTER FOURTEEN

Jossie met me on the doorstep, fizzing with life.

'Dad says please come in for a drink.' She held the door open for me and looked uncertainly at my face. 'Are you all right? I mean . . . I suppose I didn't realize . . .'

I kissed her mouth. Soft and sweet. It made me hungry.

'A drink would be fine,' I said.

William Finch was already pouring Scotch as we walked into his office-sitting-room. He greeted me with a smile and held out the glass.

'You look as if you could do with it,' he said. 'You've been having a rough time, by all accounts.'

'I've a fellow feeling for footballs.' I took the glass, lifted it in a token toast, and sipped the pale fine spirit.

Jossie said, 'Kicked around?'

I nodded, smiling. 'Somebody,' I said, 'is playing a strategic game.'

Finch looked at me curiously. 'Do you know who?'

'Not exactly. Not yet.'

Jossie stood beside her father, pouring grapefruit juice

out of a small bottle. One could see heredity clearly at work: they both had the same tall, well-proportioned frame, the same high carriage of head on long neck, the same air of bending the world to their ways, instead of being themselves bent. He looked at her fondly, a hint of civilized amusement in his fatherly pride. Even her habitual mockery, it seemed, stemmed from him.

He turned his greying head to me again, and said he expected the police would sort out all the troubles, in time.

'I expect so,' I said neutrally.

'And I hope the villains get shut up in small spaces for years and years,' Jossie said.

'Well,' I said, 'they may.'

Finch buried his nose in a large gin and tonic and surfaced with a return to the subject which interested him most. Kidnappings came a poor second to racing.

'My next ride?' I echoed. 'Tomorrow, as a matter of fact. Tapestry runs in the Oasthouse Cup.'

His astonishment scarcely boosted my non-existent confidence. 'Good heavens,' he said. 'I mean, to be frank, Ro, is it wise?'

'Totally not.'

'Then why?'

'I have awful difficulty in saying no.'

Jossie laughed. 'Spineless,' she said.

The door opened and a dark-haired woman came in, walking beautifully in a long black dress. She seemed to move in a glow of her own; and the joy died out of Jossie like an extinguished fire.

Finch went towards the newcomer with a welcoming smile, took her elbow proprietorially, and steered her in my direction. 'Lida, my dear, this is Roland Britten. Ro, Lida Swann.'

A tapeworm with hooks, Jossie had said. The tapeworm had a broad expanse of unlined forehead, dark blue eyes, and raven hair combed smoothly back. As we shook hands, she pressed my fingers warmly. Her heavy, sweet scent broadcast the same message as full breasts, tiny waist, narrow hips, and challenging smile: the sexual woman in full bloom. Diametrically opposite, I reflected, to my own preference for astringency and humour. Jossie watched our polite social exchanges with a scowl, and I wanted to walk over and hug her.

Why not, I thought. I disengaged myself from the sultry aura of Lida, took the necessary steps, and slid my arm firmly round Jossie's waist.

'We'll be off, then,' I said. 'To feed the starving.'

Jossie's scowl persisted across the hall, into the car, and five miles down the road.

'I hate her,' she said. 'That sexy throaty voice . . . it's all put on.'

'It's gin,' I said.

'What?'

'Too much gin alters the vocal chords.'

'You're having me on.'

'I think I love you,' I said.

'That's a damn silly thing to say.'

'Why?'

'You can't love someone just because she hates her father's girlfriend.'

'A better reason than many.'

She turned her big eyes searchingly my way. I kept my own looking straight ahead, dealing with night on the country road.

'Strong men fall for her like ninepins,' she said.

'But I'm weak.'

'Spineless.' She cheered up a good deal, and finally managed a smile. 'Do you want me to come to Kempton tomorrow and cheer you on?'

'Come and give Moira Longerman a double brandy when I fall off.'

Over dinner she said with some seriousness, 'I suppose it's occurred to you that the last twice you've raced, you've been whipped off into black holes straight after?'

'It has,' I said.

'So are you – uh – at all scared, about tomorrow?'

'I'd be surprised if it happened again.'

'Surprise wouldn't help you much.'

'True.'

'You're absolutely infuriating,' she said explosively. 'If you know why you were abducted, why not tell me?'

'I might be wrong, and I want to ask some questions first.'

'What questions?'

'What are you doing on Sunday?'

'That's not a question.'

'Yes, it is,' I said. 'Would you care for a day on the Isle of Wight?'

With guilty misgivings about riding Tapestry I did my best to eat, and later, after leaving Jossie on her doorstep, to go home and sleep. As my system seemed to be stubbornly resisting my intention that it should return to normal, both enterprises met with only partial success. The Saturday morning face in the shaving mirror would have inspired faith in no one, not even Moira herself.

'You're a bloody fool,' I said aloud, and my reflection agreed.

Coffee, boiled egg and toast to the good, I went down into the town to seek out owners of destitute warehouses. The estate agents, busy with hand-holding couples, told me impatiently that they had already given the information to the police.

'Give it to me, too, then,' I said. 'It's hardly a secret, is it?'

The bearded pale-faced man I'd asked looked harried and went off to consult. He came back with a slip of paper which he handed over as if contact with it had sullied his soul.

'We have ceased to act for these people,' he said earnestly. 'Our board should no longer be affixed to the wall.'

I'd never known anyone actually say the word 'affixed'

before. It wasn't all he could say, either. 'We wish to be considered as disassociated from the whole situation.'

I read the words written on the paper. 'I'm sure you do,' I said. 'Could you tell me when you last heard from these people? And has anyone been enquiring recently about hiring or using the warehouse?'

'Those people,' he said disapprovingly, 'appear to have let the warehouse several years ago to some army surplus suppliers, without informing us or paying fees due to us. We have received no instructions from them, then or since, regarding any further letting or sub-letting.'

'Ta ever so,' I said, and went grinning out to the street.

The words on the paper, which had so fussed the agents in retrospect, were 'National Construction (Wessex) Ltd', or in other words the mythical builders invented by Ownslow and Glitberg.

I picked up the rush reprint enlargements of Hilary's photographs, and walked along to the office. All quiet there, as usual on Saturdays, with undone work still sitting reproachfully in heaps.

Averting my eyes, I telephoned the police.

'Any news?' I said; and they said no there wasn't.

'Did you trace the owner of the van?' I asked. No, they hadn't.

'Did it have an engine number?' I said. Yes, they said, but it was not the original number for that particular vehicle, said vehicle having probably passed through many hands and rebuilding processes on its way to the warehouse.

'And have you asked Mr Glitberg and Mr Ownslow what I was doing in a van inside their warehouse?'

There was silence at the other end.

'Have you?' I repeated.

They wanted to know why I should ask.

'Oh come off it,' I said. 'I've been to the estate agents, same as you.'

Mr Glitberg and Mr Ownslow, it appeared, had been totally mystified as to why their warehouse should have been used in such a way. As far as they were concerned, it was let to an army surplus supply company, and the police should direct their enquiries to them.

'Can you find these army surplus people?' I asked. Not so far, they said. They cleared the police throat and cautiously added that Mr Glitberg and Mr Ownslow had categorically denied that they had imprisoned Mr Britten in a van in their warehouse, or anywhere else, for that matter, as revenge for the said Mr Britten having been instrumental in their custodial sentences for fraud.

'Their actual words?' I asked with interest. Not exactly. I had been given the gist.

I thanked them for the information, and disconnected. I thought they had probably not passed on everything they knew, but then neither had I, which made us quits.

The door of Trevor's private office was locked, as mine had been, but we both had keys for each other's rooms. I knew all the same that he wouldn't have been pleased to see me searching uninvited through the papers in his filing cupboard, but I reckoned that as I'd had access to them anyway while he was on holiday, another peep would be no real invasion. I spent a concentrated hour reading cash books and ledgers; and then with a mind functioning more or less as normal I checked through the Denby Crest figures yet again. I had made no mistake with them, even in a daze. Fifty thousand pounds of clients' trust funds were missing. I stared unseeingly at 'Lady and Gentleman in a Carriage' and thought bleakly about consequences.

There was a photocopier in the outer office, busily operated every weekday by Debbie and Peter. I spent another hour of that quiet Saturday morning methodically printing private copies for my own use. Then I put all the books and papers back where I'd found them, locked Trevor's office, and went down to the store in the basement.

The files I was looking for there were easy to find but were slim and uninformative, containing only copies of audits and not all the invoices, cash books and paying-in books from which the accounts had been drawn.

There was nothing odd in that. Under the Companies Act 1976, and also under the value added tax system, all such papers had to be kept available for three years and could legally be thrown away only after that, but most accountants returned the books to their clients for keeping, as like us they simply didn't have enough storage space for everyone.

I left the files where they were, locked all the office doors, sealed my folder of photocopies into a large envelope, and took it with me in some depression to Kempton Park.

The sight of Jossie in her swirly brown skirt brought the sun out considerably, and we despatched grapefruit juice in amicable understanding.

'Dad's brought the detestable Lida,' she said, 'so I came on my own.'

'Does she live with you?' I asked.

'No, thank God.' The idea alarmed her. 'Five miles away, and that's five thousand miles too close.'

'What does the ever-sick secretary have to say about her?'

'Sandy? It makes her even sicker.' She drank the remains of her juice, smiling over the glass. 'Actually Sandy wouldn't be so bad, if she weren't so wet. And you can cast out any slick theories about daughters being possessive of their footloose fathers, because actually I would have liked it rather a lot if he'd fallen for a peach.'

'Does he know you don't like Lida?'

'Oh sure,' she sighed. 'I told him she was a flesh-eating orchid and he said I didn't understand. End of conversation. The funny thing is,' she added, 'that it's only when I'm with you that I can think of her without spitting.'

'Appendicitis diverts the mind from toothache,' I said.

'What?'

'Thoughts from inside little white vans.'

'Half the time,' she said, 'I think you're crazy.'

She met some friends and went off with them, and I repaired to the weighing room to change into breeches, boots, and Moira Longerman's red and white colours. When I came out, with my jacket on over the bright shirt, Binny Tomkins was waiting. On his countenance, the reverse of warmth and light.

'I want to talk to you,' he said.

'Fine. Why not?'

He scowled. 'Not here. Too many people. Walk down this way.' He pointed to the path taken by the horses on their way from parade ring to track: a broad stretch of grass mostly unpopulated by racegoing crowds.

'What is it?' I said, as we emerged from the throng round the weighing room door, and started in the direction he wanted. 'Is there something wrong with Tapestry?'

He shook his head impatiently, as if the idea were silly.

'I want you to give the horse an easy race.'

I stopped walking. An easy race, in those terms, meant trying not to win.

'No,' I said.

'Come on, there's more . . .' He went on a pace or two, looking back and waiting for me to follow. 'I must talk to you. You must listen.'

There was more than usual scowling bad temper in his manner. Something like plain fear. Shaking my head, I went on with him, across the grass.

'How much would you want?' he said.

I stopped again. 'I'm not doing it,' I said.

'I know, but . . . How about two hundred, tax free?'

'You're stupid, Binny.'

'It's all right for you,' he said furiously. 'But if Tapestry wins today I'll lose everything. My yard, my livelihood – everything.'

'Why?'

He was trembling with tension. 'I owe a lot of money.'

'To bookmakers?' I said.

'Of course to bookmakers.'

'You're a fool,' I said flatly.

'Smug bastard,' he said furiously. 'I'd give anything to have you back inside that van, and not here today.'

I looked at him thoughtfully. 'Tapestry may not win anyway,' I said. 'Nothing's a certainty.'

'I've got to know in advance,' he said incautiously.

'And if you assure your bookmaker Tapestry won't win, he'll let you off the hook?'

'He'll let me off a bit,' he said. 'He won't press for the rest.'

'Until next time,' I said. 'Until you're in deeper still.'

Binny's eyes stared inwards to the hopeless future, and I guessed he would never take the first step back to firm ground, which was in his case to stop gambling altogether.

'There are easier ways for trainers to lose races,' I pointed out, 'than trying to bribe the jockey.'

His scowl reached Neanderthal proportions. 'She pays the lad who does her horse to watch him like a hawk and give her a report on everything that happens. I can't sack him or change him to another horse, because she says if I do she'll send Tapestry to another trainer.'

'I'm amazed she hasn't already,' I said: and she would have done, I thought, if she'd been able to hear that conversation.

'You've only got to ride a bad race,' he said. 'Get boxed in down the far side and swing wide coming into the straight.'

'No,' I said. 'Not on purpose.'

I seemed to be remarkably good at inspiring fury. Binny would happily have seen me fall dead at his feet.

'Look,' I said, 'I'm sorry about the fix you're in. I really am, whether you believe it or not. But I'm not going to try to get you out of it by cheating Moira or the horse or the punters or myself, and that's that.'

'You *bastard*,' he said.

Five minutes later, when I was back in the hub of the racecourse outside the weighing room, a hand touched me on the arm and a drawly voice spoke behind my ear.

'My dear Ro, what are your chances?'

I turned, smiling, to the intelligent face of Vivian Iverson. In the daylight on a racecourse, where I'd first met him, he wore his clothes with the same elegance and flair that he had extended to his Vivat Club. Dark green blazer over grey checked trousers; hair shining black in the April sun. Quiet amusement in the observant eyes.

'In love, war, or the three-thirty?' I said.

'Of remaining at liberty, my dear chap.'

I blinked. 'Um,' I said. 'What would you offer?'

'Five to four against?'

'I hope you're wrong,' I said.

Underneath the banter, he was detectably serious. 'It just so happens that last night in the club I heard our friend Connaught Powys talking on the telephone. To be frank, my dear Ro, after I'd heard your name mentioned, I more or less deliberately *listened*.'

'On an extension?'

'Tut tut,' he said reprovingly. 'Unfortunately not. I don't know who he was talking to. But he said – his exact words – "As far as Britten is concerned you must agree that precaution is better than cure," and a bit later he said "If dogs start sniffing around, the best thing to do is chain them up." '

'Charming,' I said blankly.

'Do you need a bodyguard?'

'Are you offering yourself?'

He shook his head, smiling. 'I could hire you one. Karate. Bulletproof glass. All the mod cons.'

'I think,' I said thoughtfully, 'that I'll just increase the insurance policies.'

'Against kidnapping? No one will take you on.'

'Checks and balances,' I said. 'No one'll push me off a spring-board if it means a rock falling on their own head.'

'Be sure to let them know the rock exists.'

'Your advice,' I said, smiling, 'is worth its weight in ocean-going sailing boats.'

*

Moira Longerman twinkled with her bright bird-eyes in the parade ring before Tapestry's race and stroked my arm repeatedly, her small thin hand sliding delicately over the shiny scarlet sleeve.

'Now, Roland, you'll do your best, I know you'll do your best.'

'Yes,' I said guiltily, flexing several flabby muscles and watching Tapestry's highly tuned ones ripple under his coat as he walked round the ring with his lad.

'I saw you talking to Binny just now, Roland.'

'Did you, Moira?' I switched my gaze to her face.

'Yes, I did.' She nodded brightly. 'I was up in the stands, up there in the bar, looking down to the paddock. I saw Binny take you away for a talk.'

She looked at me steadily, shrewdly, asking the vital question in total silence. Her hand went on stroking. She waited intently, expecting an answer.

'I promise you,' I said plainly, 'that if I make a hash of it, it'll be against my will.'

She stopped stroking, patted my arm instead, and smiled. 'That will do nicely, Roland.'

Binny stood ten feet away, unable to make even a show of the civility due from trainer to owner. His face was rigid, his eyes expressionless, and even the usual scowl had frozen into a more general and powerful gloom. I thought I had probably been wrong to think of Binny as a stupid fool. There was something about him at that moment which raised prickles on the skin and images of murder.

The bell rang for jockeys to mount, and it was the lad, not Binny, who gave me a leg-up into the saddle.

'I'm not going to take much more of this,' Moira said pleasantly to the world in general.

Binny ignored her as if he hadn't heard; and maybe he hadn't. He'd also given me no riding instructions, which I didn't mind in the least. He seemed wholly withdrawn and unresponsive, and when Moira waved briefly as I walked away on Tapestry, he did not accompany her across to the stands. Even for him, his behaviour was incredible.

Tapestry himself was in a great mood, tossing his head with excitement and bouncing along in tiny cantering strides as if he had April spring fever in all his veins. I remembered his plunging start in the Gold Cup and realized that this time I'd be lucky if he didn't bolt with me from the post. Far from being last from indecision, this time, in my weakened state, I could be forty lengths in front by the second fence, throwing away all chance of staying power at the end.

Tapestry bounced gently on his toes in the parade past the stands, while the other runners walked. Bounced playfully back at a canter to the start, which in three mile 'chases at Kempton Park was to the left of the stands and in full view of most of the crowd.

There were eleven other jockeys walking around there, making final adjustments to girths and goggles and answering to the starter's roll call. The starter's assistant, tightening the girths of the horse beside me, looked over his shoulder and asked me if mine were all right, or should he tighten those too.

If I hadn't recently been through so many wringers, I would simply have said yes, and he would have pulled the buckles up a notch or two, and I wouldn't have given it another thought. As it was, in my over-cautious state, I had a sudden sharp vision of Binny's dangerous detachment, and remembered the desperation behind his appeal to me to lose. The prickles returned in force.

I slid off Tapestry's back and looped his reins over my arm.

'Just want to check . . .' I said vaguely to the starter's assistant.

He nodded briefly, glancing at his watch. One minute to racetime, his face said, so hurry up.

It was my own saddle. I intimately knew its every flap, buckle, scratch and stain. I checked it thoroughly inch by inch with fingers and eyes, and could see nothing wrong. Girths, stirrups, leathers, buckles; everything as it should be. I pulled the girths tighter myself, and the starter told me to get mounted.

Looking over my shoulder, I thought, for the rest of my life. Seeing demons in shadows. But the feeling of danger wouldn't go away.

'Hurry up, Britten.'

'Yes, sir.'

I stood on the ground, looking at Tapestry tossing his head.

'*Britten!*'

Reins, I thought. Bridle. Bit Reins. If the bridle broke, I couldn't control the horse and he wouldn't win the race. Many races had been lost, from broken bridles.

It was not too difficult to see, if one looked really closely. The leather reins were stitched on to the rings at each side of the bit, and the stitches on the off-side rein had nearly all been severed.

Three miles and twenty fences at bucketing speed with just two strands of thread holding my right-hand rein.

'*Britten!*'

I gave a jerking tug, and the remaining stitches came apart in my hand. I pulled the rein off the ring and waved the free end in the air.

'Sorry, sir,' I said. 'I need another bridle.'

'What? Oh very well . . .' He used his telephone to call the weighing room to send a replacement out quickly. Tapestry's lad appeared, looking worried, to help change the headpiece, and I pointed out to him, as I gave him Binny's bridle, the parted stitching.

'I don't know how it could have got like that,' he said anxiously. 'I didn't know it was like that, honest. I cleaned it yesterday, and all.'

'Don't worry,' I said. 'It's not your fault.'

'Yes, but . . .'

'Give me a leg-up,' I said, 'and don't worry.'

He continued all the same to look upset. Good lads took it grievously to heart if anything was proved lacking in the way they turned out their horses, and Tapestry's lad was as good as the horse deserved. Binny, I thought not for the first time, was an all-out, one-man disaster area, a blight to himself and everyone around.

'Line up,' shouted the starter, with his hand on the lever. 'We're five minutes late.'

Tapestry did his best to put that right two seconds later with another arm-wrenching departure, but owing to one or two equally impetuous opponents I thankfully got him anchored in mid-field; and there we stayed for all of the first circuit. The pace, once we'd settled down, was nothing like as fast as the Gold Cup, and I had time to worry about the more usual things, like meeting the fences right, and not running out altogether, which was an added hazard at Kempton where the wings leading to the fences were smaller and lower than on other courses, and tended to give tricky horses bad ideas.

During the second circuit my state of unfitness raised its ugly head in no uncertain way, and it would be fair to say that for the last mile Tapestry's jockey did little except cling on. Tapestry truly was, however, a great performer, and in consequence of the cheers and acclaim in the unsaddling enclosure after the Gold Cup, he seemed, like many much-fêted horses, to have become conscious of his own star status. It was the extra dimension of his new pride which took us in a straight faultless run over the last three fences in the straight, and his own will to win which extended his neck and his stride on the run-in. Tapestry won the Oasthouse Cup by four lengths, and it was all the horse's doing, not mine.

Moira kissed her horse with tears running down her

cheeks, and kissed me as well, and everyone else within mouth-shot, indiscriminately. There was nothing uptight or inhibited about the Longerman joy, and the most notable person not there to share it was the horse's trainer. Binny Tomkins was nowhere to be seen.

'Drink,' Moira shrieked at me. 'Owners and trainers bar.'

I nodded, speechless from exertion and back-slapping, and struggled through the throng with my saddle to be weighed in. It was fabulous, I thought dazedly; fantastic, winning another big race. More than I'd ever reckoned possible. A bursting delight like no other on earth. Even knowing how little I'd contributed couldn't dampen the wild inner rejoicing. I'd never be able to give it up, I thought. I'd still be struggling round in the mud and the rain at fifty, chasing the marvellous dream. Addiction wasn't only a matter of needles in the arm.

Moira in the bar was dispensing champagne and bright laughs in copious quantities, and had taken Jossie closely in tow.

'Ro, darling Ro,' Moira said, 'have you seen Binny anywhere?'

'No, I haven't.'

'Wasn't it odd, the bridle breaking like that?' Her innocent-seeming eyes stared up into my own. 'I talked to the lad, you see.'

'These things do happen,' I said.

'You mean, no one can prove anything?'

'Roughly that.'

'But aren't you the teeniest bit angry?'

I smiled from the glowing inner pleasure. 'We won the race. What else matters?'

She shook her head. 'It was a wicked thing to do.'

Desperation, I thought, could spawn deeds the doers wouldn't sanely contemplate. Like cutting loose a rein. Like kidnapping the enemy. Like whatever else lay ahead before we were done. I shut out the shadowy devils and drank to life and the Oasthouse Cup.

Jossie, too, had a go at me when we wandered later out to the car park.

'Is Moira right?' she demanded. 'Did Binny rig it for you to come to grief?'

'I should think so.'

'She says you ought to report it.'

'There's no need.'

'Why not?'

'He's programmed to self-destruct before the end of the season.'

'Do you mean *suicide*?' she said.

'You're too literal. I mean he'll go bust to the bookies with a reverberating bang.'

'You're drunk.'

I shook my head, grinning. 'High. Quite different. Care to join me on my cloud?'

'A puff of wind,' she said, 'and you'd evaporate.'

# CHAPTER FIFTEEN

Jossie drove off to some party or other in London, and I, mindful of earlier unscheduled destinations after racing, took myself circumspectly down the road to the nearest public telephone box. No one followed, that I could see.

Hilary Margaret Pinlock answered at the twentieth ring, when I had all but given up, and said breathlessly that she had only that second reached home; she'd been out playing tennis.

'Are you busy this evening?' I said.

'Nothing special.'

'Can I come and see you?'

'Yes.' She hesitated a fraction. 'What do you want? Food? A bed?'

'An ear,' I said. 'And baked beans, perhaps. But no bed.'

'Right,' she said calmly. 'Where are you? Do you need directions?'

She told me clearly how to find her, and I drew up forty minutes later outside a large Edwardian house in a leafy road on the outskirts of a sprawling Surrey town.

Hilary, it transpired, owned the ground floor, a matter of two large, high-ceilinged rooms, modern kitchen, functional bathroom, and a pleasant old-fashioned conservatory with plants, cane armchairs, and steps down to an unkempt garden.

Inside, everything was orderly and organized, and comfortable in an uninspired sort of way. Well-built easy chairs in dim covers, heavy curtains in good velvet but of a deadening colour somewhere between brown and green, patterned carpet in olive and fawn. The home of a vigorous academic mind with no inborn response to refracted light. I wondered just how much she would wear the alien scarlet cloak.

The evening sun still shone into the conservatory, and there we sat, in the cane armchairs, drinking sherry, greenly surrounded by palms and rubber plants and *Monstera deliciosa*.

'I don't mind *watering*,' Hilary said. 'But I detest *gardening*. The people upstairs are supposed to do the garden, but they don't.' She waved disgustedly towards the view of straggly bushes, unpruned roses, weedy paths, and dried coffee-coloured stalks of last year's unmown grass.

'It's better than concrete,' I said.

'I'll use you as a parable for the children,' she said, smiling.

'Hm?'

'When things are bad, you endure what you must, and thank God it's not worse.'

I made a protesting sound in my throat, much taken aback. 'Well,' I said helplessly, 'what else is there to do?'

'Go screaming off to the Social Services.'

'For a gardener?'

'You know darned well what I mean.'

'Endurance is like tax,' I said. 'You're silly to pay more than you have to, but you can't always escape it.'

'And you can whine,' she said, nodding, 'or suffer with good grace.'

She drank her sherry collectedly and invited me to say why I'd come.

'To ask you to keep a parcel safe for me,' I said.

'But of course.'

'And to listen to a fairly long tale, so that . . .' I paused. 'I mean, I want someone to know . . .' I stopped once more.

'In case you disappear again?' she said matter-of-factly.

I was grateful for her calmness.

'Yes,' I said. I told her about meeting Vivian Iverson at the races, and our thoughts on insurance, springboards, and rocks. 'So you see,' I ended, 'you'll be the rock, if you will.'

'You can expect,' she said, 'rock-like behaviour.'

'Well,' I said, 'I've brought a sealed package of photocopied documents. It's in the car.'

'Fetch it,' she said.

I went out to the street and collected the thick envelope from the boot. Habit induced me to look into the back seat floor space, and to scan the harmless street. No one hiding, no one watching, that I could see. No one had followed me from the racecourse, I was sure.

Looking over my shoulder for the rest of my life.

I took the parcel indoors and gave it to Hilary, and also the negatives of her photographs, explaining that I already had the extra prints. She put everything on the table beside her and told me to sit down and get on with the tale.

'I'll tell you a bit about my job,' I said. 'And then you'll understand better.' I stretched out with luxurious weariness in the cane chair and looked at the intent interest on her strong plain face. A pity, I thought, about the glasses.

'An accountant working for a long time in one area, particularly in an area like a country town, tends to get an overall picture of the local life.'

'I follow you,' she said. 'Go on.'

'The transactions of one client tend to turn up in the accounts of others. For instance, a racehorse trainer buys horse food from the forage merchants. I check the invoice through the trainer's accounts, and then, because the forage merchant is also my client, I later check it again through his. I see that the forage merchant has paid a builder for an extension to his house, and later, in the builder's accounts, I see what *he* paid for the bricks and cement. I see that a jockey had paid *x* pounds on an air-taxi, and later, because the air-taxi firm is also my client, I see the receipt of *x* pounds from the jockey. I see the movement of money around the neighbourhood . . . the interlocking of interests . . . the pattern of commerce. I learn the names of suppliers, the size of businesses, and the kinds of services people use. My knowledge increases until I have a sort of mental map like a wide landscape, in which all the names are familiar and occur in the proper places.'

'Fascinating,' Hilary said.

'Well,' I said, 'if a totally strange name crops up, and you can't cross-reference it with anything else, you begin to ask questions. At first of yourself, and then of others. Discreetly. And that was how I ran into trouble in the shape of two master criminals called Glitberg and Ownslow.'

'They sound like a music-hall turn.'

'They're as funny as the Black Death.' I drank some sherry ruefully. 'They worked for the council, and the council's accounts and audits were done by a large firm in London, who naturally didn't have any intimate local knowledge. Ownslow and Glitberg had invented a construction firm called National Construction (Wessex) Limited, through which they had syphoned off more than a million pounds each of taxpayers' money. And I had a client, a builders' merchant, who had received several cheques from National Construction (Wessex). I'd never heard of National Construction (Wessex) in any other context, and I asked my client some searching questions, to which his reply was unmistakable panic. Glitberg and

Ownslow were prosecuted and went to jail swearing to be revenged.'

'On you?'

'On me.'

'Nasty.'

'A few weeks later,' I said, 'much the same thing happened. I turned up some odd payments made by a director of an electronics firm through the company's computer. His name was Connaught Powys. He'd taken his firm for over a quarter of a million, and he too went to jail swearing to get even. He's out again now, and so are Glitberg and Ownslow. Since then I've been the basic cause of the downfall of two more big-time embezzlers, both of whom descended to the cells swearing severally to tear my guts out and cut my throat.' I sighed. 'Luckily, they're both still inside.'

'And I thought accountants led dull lives!'

'Maybe some do.' I drained my sherry. 'There's another thing that those five embezzlers have in common besides me, and that is that not a penny of what they stole has been recovered.'

'Really?' She seemed not to find it greatly significant. 'I expect it's all sitting around in bank deposits, under different names.'

I shook my head. 'Not unless it is in literally thousands of tiny weeny deposits, which doesn't seem likely.'

'Why thousands?'

'Banks nowadays have to inform the Tax Inspectors of the existence of any deposit account for which the annual interest is £15 or more. That means the Inspectors know of all deposits of over three or four hundred quid.'

'I had no idea,' she said blankly.

'Anyway,' I said, 'I wanted to know if it could be Powys or Glitberg or Ownslow who had kidnapped me for revenge, so I asked them.'

'Good heavens.'

'Yeah. It wasn't a good idea. They wouldn't say yes or no.' I looked back to the night at the Vivat Club. 'They did tell me something else, though . . .' I said, and told Hilary what it was. Her eyes widened behind the glasses and she nodded once or twice.

'I see. Yes,' she said.

'So now,' I said. 'Here we are a few years later, and now I have not only my local area mental map but a broad view of most of the racing world, with uncountable interconnections. I do the accounts for so many racing people, their lives spread out like a carpet, touching, overlapping, each small transaction adding to my understanding of the whole. I'm part of it myself, as a jockey. I feel the fabric around me. I know how much saddles cost, and which saddler does most business, and which owners don't pay their bills, and who bets and who drinks, who saves, who gives to charity, who keeps a mistress. I know how much the woman whose horse I rode today paid to have him photographed for the Christmas cards she sent last year, and how much a bookmaker gave for his Rolls, and thousands and thousands of similar facts. All fitting, all harmless. It's when they don't fit . . . like a jockey suddenly spending more than he's earned, and I find he's running a whole new business and not declaring a penny of it . . . it's when the bits don't fit that I see the monster in the waves. Glimpsed, hidden . . . But definitely there.'

'Like now?' she said, frowning. 'Your iceberg?'

'Mm.' I hesitated. 'Another embezzler.'

'And this one – will he too go to jail swearing to cut your throat?'

I didn't answer at once, and she added dryly, 'Or is he likely to cut your throat before you get him there?'

I gave her half a grin. 'Not with a rock like you, he won't.'

'You be careful, Roland,' she said seriously. 'This doesn't feel to me like a joke.'

She stood up restlessly, towering among the palm fronds, as thin in her way as their stems.

'Come into the kitchen. What do you want to eat? I can do a Spanish omelette, if you like.'

I sat with my elbows on the kitchen table, and while she chopped onions and potatoes and green peppers I told her a good deal more, most of it highly unethical, as an accountant should never disclose the affairs of a client. She listened with increasing dismay, her cooking actions growing slower. Finally she laid down the knife and simply stood.

'Your partner,' she said.

'I don't know how much he's condoned,' I said, 'but on Monday . . . I have to find out.'

'Tell the police,' she said. 'Let them find out.'

'No. I've worked with Trevor for six years. We've always got on well together, and he seems fond of me, in his distant way. I can't shop him, just like that.'

'You'll warn him.'

'Yes,' I said. 'And I'll tell him of the existence of . . . the rock.'

She started cooking again, automatically, her thoughts busy behind her eyes.

'Do you think,' she said, 'that your partner knew about the other embezzlers, and tried to hush them up?'

I shook my head. 'Not Glitberg and Ownslow. Positively not. Not the last two, either. The firms they worked for were both my clients, and Trevor had no contact with them. But Connaught Powys . . .' I sighed. 'I really don't know. Trevor always used to spend about a week at that firm, doing the audit on the spot, as one nearly always does for big concerns, and I went one year only because he had an ulcer. It was Connaught Powys's bad luck that I cottoned on to what he was doing. Trevor might genuinely have missed the warning signs, because he doesn't always work the way I do.'

'How do you mean?'

'Well, a lot of an accountant's work is fairly mechanical. Vouching, for instance. That's checking that cheques written down in the cash book really were issued for the amount stated or, in other words, if the cashier writes down that cheque number 1234 was issued to Joe Bloggs in the sum of eighty pounds to pay for a load of sand, the auditor checks that the bank actually paid eighty pounds to Joe Bloggs on cheque no. 1234. It's routine work and takes a fairly long time on a big account, and it's often, or even usually, done, not by the accountant or auditor himself, but by an assistant. Assistants in our firm tend to come and go, and don't necessarily develop a sense of probability. The present ones wouldn't be likely to query, for instance, whether Joe Bloggs really existed, or sold sand, or sold eighty quid's worth, or delivered only fifty quid's worth, with Joe Bloggs and the cashier conspiring to pocket the thirty pounds profit.'

'Roland!'

I grinned. 'Small fiddles abound. It's the first violins that threaten to cut your throat.'

She broke four eggs into a bowl. 'Do you do all your own . . . er . . . vouching, then?'

'No, not all. It would take too long. But I do all of it for some accounts, and some of it for all accounts. To get the feel of things. To know where I am.'

'To fit into the landscape,' she said.

'Yes.'

'And Trevor doesn't?'

'He does a few himself, but on the whole not. Don't get me wrong. More accountants do as Trevor does, it's absolutely normal practice.'

'You want my advice?' she said.

'Yes, please.'

'Go straight to the police.'

'Thank you. Get on with the omelette.'

She sizzled it in the pan and divided it, succulent and

soft in the centre, onto the plates. It tasted like a testimonial to her own efficiency, the best I'd ever had. Over coffee, afterwards, I told her a great deal about Jossie.

She looked into her cup. 'Do you love her?' she said.

'I don't know. It's too soon to say.'

'You sound,' she said dryly, 'bewitched.'

'There have been other girls. But not the same.' I looked at her downturned face. My mouth twitched. 'In case you're wondering about Jossie,' I said, 'no, I haven't.'

She looked up, the spectacles flashing, her eyes suddenly laughing, and a blush starting on her neck. She uttered an unheadmistressly opinion.

'You're a sod,' she said.

It was an hour's drive home from Hilary's house. No one followed me, or took the slightest interest, that I could see.

I rolled quietly down the lane towards the cottage with the car lights switched off, and made a silent reconnoitre on foot for the last hundred yards.

Everything about my home was dark and peaceful. The lights of Mrs Morris's sitting-room, next door, shone dimly through the pattern of her curtains. The night sky was powdered with stars, and the air was cool.

I waited for a while, listening, and was slowly reassured. No horrors in the shadows. No shattering black prisons yawning like mantraps before my feet. No cut-throats with ready steel.

To be afraid, I thought, was no way to live; yet I couldn't help it.

I unlocked the cottage and switched on all the lights; and it was empty, welcoming and sane. I fetched the car from the lane, locked myself into the cottage, pulled shut the curtains, switched on the heaters, and hugged round myself the comforting illusion of being safe in the burrow.

After that I made a pot of coffee, fished out some brandy, and sprawled into an armchair with the ancient records of the misdeeds of Powys, Glitberg and Ownslow.

At one time I'd known every detail in those files with blinding clarity, but the years had blurred my memory. I found notes in my own handwriting about inferences I couldn't remember drawing, and conclusions as startling as acid. I was amazed, actually, at the quality of work I'd done, and it was weird to see it from an objective distance, as with a totally fresh eye. I supposed I could understand the comment there had been then, though at the time what I was doing had seemed a perfectly natural piece of work, done merely as best I could. I smiled to myself in pleased surprise. In that far-off time, I must have been hell to embezzlers. Not like nowadays, when it took me six shots to see Denby Crest.

I came across pages of notes about the workings of computers, details of which I had forgotten as fast as I'd learned them on a crash course in an electronics firm much like Powys's. It had pleased me at the time to be able to dissect and explain just what he'd done, and nothing had made him more furious. It had been vanity on my part, I thought: and I was still vain. Admiring your own work was one of the deadlier intellectual sins.

I sighed. I was never going to be perfect, so why worry.

There was no record anywhere in the Glitberg/Ownslow file of the buying of the warehouse, but it did seem possible, as I dug deeper in the search for clues, that it actually had been built by Glitberg and Ownslow, and was the sole concrete fabrication of National Construction (Wessex). Anyone who could invent whole streets of dwellings could put up a real warehouse without much trouble.

I wondered why they'd needed it, when everything else had been achieved on paper.

A tangible asset, uncashed, gone to seed, in which I had been dumped. The police had been told I was there, and the estate agent trail had led without difficulty straight to Ownslow and Glitberg.

Why?

I sat and thought about it for a good long time, and then I finished the coffee and brandy and went to bed.

I picked Jossie up at ten in the grey morning, and drove to Portsmouth for the hovercraft ferry to the Isle of Wight.

'The nostalgia kick?' Jossie said. 'Back to the boarding house?'

I nodded. 'The sunny isle of childhood.'

'Oh yeah?' She took me literally and looked up meaningfully at the cloudy sky.

'It heads the British sunshine league,' I said.

'Tell that to Torquay.'

A ten-minute zip in the hovercraft took us across the sea at Spithead, and when we stepped ashore at Ryde, the clouds were behind us, hovering like a grey sheet over the mainland.

'It's unfair,' Jossie said, smiling.

'It's often like that.'

The town was bright with new spring paint, the Regency buildings clean and graceful in the sun. Every year, before the holiday-makers came, there was the big brush-up and every winter, when they'd gone, the comfortable relapse into carpet slippers and salt-caked windows.

'Ryde pier,' I said, 'is two thousand, three hundred and five feet long, and was opened in 1814.'

'I don't want to know that.'

'There are approximately six hundred hotels, motels and boarding houses on this sunny island.'

'Nor that.'

'Nine towns, two castles, a lot of flamingoes and Parkhurst Prison.'

'Nor that, for God's sake.'

'My Uncle Rufus,' I said, 'was chief mucker-out at the local riding school.'

'Good grief.'

'As his assistant mucker-out,' I said, 'I scrambled under horses' bellies from the age of six.'

'That figures.'

'I used to exercise the horses and ponies all winter when the holiday people had gone home. And break in new ones. I can't really remember not being able to ride, but there's no racing here, of course. The first race I ever rode in was the Isle of Wight Foxhounds point-to-point over on the mainland, and I fell off.'

We walked along the Esplanade with the breeze blowing Jossie's long green scarf out like streamers. She waved an arm at the sparkling water and said, 'Why horses? Why not boats, for heaven's sake, when you had them on your doorstep.'

'They made me seasick.'

She laughed. 'Like going to heaven and being allergic to harps.'

I took her to a hotel I knew, where there was a sunny terrace sheltered from the breeze, with a stunning view of the Solent and the shipping tramping by to Southampton. We drank hot chocolate and read the lunch menu, and talked of this and that and nothing much, and the time slid away like a mill-stream.

After roast beef for both of us, and apple pie, ice-cream and cheese for Jossie, we whistled up a taxi. There weren't many operating on a Sunday afternoon in April, but there was no point in being a native if one didn't know where to find the pearls.

The driver knew me, and didn't approve of my having deserted to become a 'mainlander', but as he also knew I knew the roads backwards, we got a straight run over Blackgang Chine to the wild cliffs on the south-west coast, and no roundabout guff to add mileage. We dawdled along there for about an hour, stopping often to stand out of the car, on the windswept grass. Jossie took in great lungfuls of the soul-filling landscape and said whyever did I live in Newbury.

'Racing,' I said.

'So simple.'

'Do you mind if we call on a friend on the way back?' I said. 'Ten minutes or so?'

'Of course not.'

'Wootton Bridge, then,' I said to the driver. 'Frederick's boatyard.'

'They'll be shut. It's Sunday.'

'We'll try, anyway.'

He shrugged heavily, leaving me to the consequences of my own stupidity, and drove back across the island, through Newport and out on the Ryde road to the deep inlet which formed a natural harbour for hundreds of small yachts.

The white-painted façade of the boatyard showed closed doors and no sign of life.

'There you are,' said the driver. 'I told you so.'

I got out of the car and walked over to the door

marked 'Office', and knocked on it. Within a few moments it opened, and I grinned back to Jossie and jerked my head for her to join me.

'I got your message,' Johnny Frederick said. 'And Sunday afternoon, I sleep.'

'At your age?'

His age was the same as mine, almost to the day: we'd shared a desk at school and many a snigger in the lavatories. The round-faced, impish boy had grown into a muscular, salt-tanned man with craftsman's hands and a respectable hatred of paperwork. He occasionally telephoned me to find out if his own local accountant was doing things right, and bombarded the poor man with my advice.

'How's your father?' I said.

'Much the same.'

A balk of timber had fallen on Johnny's father's head in days gone by. There had been a lot of unkind jokes about thick as two planks before, three planks after, but the net result had been that an ailing family business had woken up in the hands of a bright new mind. With Johnny's designs and feeling for materials, Frederick Boats were a growing name.

I introduced Jossie, who got a shrewd once-over for aerodynamic lines and a shake from a hand like a piece of calloused teak.

'Pleased to meet you,' he said, which was about the nearest he ever got to social small-talk. He switched his gaze to me. 'You've been in the wars a bit, according to the papers.'

'You might say so.' I grinned. 'What are you building, these days?'

'Come and see.'

He walked across the functional little office and opened the far door, which led straight into the boatyard itself. We went through, and Jossie exclaimed aloud at the unexpected size of the huge shed which sloped away down to the water.

There were several smallish fibreglass hulls supported in building frames, and two large ones, side by side in the centre, with five-foot keels.

'What size are those?' Jossie said.

'Thirty-seven feet overall.'

'They look bigger.'

'They won't on the water. It's the largest size we do, at present.' Johnny walked us round one of them, pointing out subtleties of hull design with pride. 'It handles well in heavy seas. It's stable, and not too difficult to sail, which is what most people want.'

'Not a racer?' I said.

He shook his head. 'Those dinghies are. But the big ocean-racers are specialist jobs. This yard isn't large enough; not geared to that class. And anyway, I like cruisers. A bit of carpet in the saloon and lockers that slide like silk.'

Jossie wandered off down the concrete slope, peering into the half-fitted dinghies and looking contentedly interested. I pulled the envelope of enlarged photographs from my inner pocket and showed them to Johnny. Three views of a sailing boat, one of an out-of-focus man.

'That's the boat I was abducted on. Can you tell anything about it from these photos?'

He peered at them, his head on one side. 'If you leave them with me, maybe. I'll look through the catalogues, and ask the boys over at Cowes. Was there anything special about it, that you remember?'

I explained that I hadn't seen much except the sail locker. 'The boat was pretty new, I think. Or at any rate well maintained. And it sailed from England on Thursday, March 17th, some time in the evening.'

He shuffled the prints to look at the man.

'His name is Alastair Yardley,' I said. 'I've written it on the back. He came from Bristol, and worked from there as a deck-hand on sea-trials for ocean-going yachts. He skippered the boat. He's about our age.'

'Are you in a hurry for all this info?'

'Quicker the better.'

'OK. I'll ring a few guys. Let you know tomorrow, if I come up with anything.'

'That's great.'

He tucked the prints into their envelope and let his gaze wander to Jossie.

'A racing filly,' he said. 'Good lines.'

'Eyes off.'

'I like earthier ones, mate. Big boobs and not too bright.'

'Boring.'

'When I get home, I want a hot tea, and a cuddle when I feel like it, and no backchat about women's lib.'

When I got home, I thought, I wouldn't mind Jossie.

She walked up the concrete with big strides of her long legs, and came to a stop at our side. 'I had a friend whose boyfriend insisted on taking her sailing,' she said. 'She said she didn't terribly mind being wet, or cold, or hungry, or seasick, or frightened. She just didn't like them all at once.'

Johnny's eyes slid my way. 'With this boyfriend she'd be all right. He gets sick in harbour.'

Jossie nodded. 'Feeble.'

'Thanks,' I said.

'Be my guest.'

We went back through the office and into the taxi, and Johnny waved us goodbye.

'Any more chums?' Jossie said.

'Not this trip. If I start on the aunts, we'll be here for ever. Visit one, visit all, or there's a dust-up.'

We drove, however, at Jossie's request, past the guest house where I'd lived with my mother. There was a new glass sun lounge across the whole of the front, and a car park where there had been garden. Tubs of flowers, bright sun-awnings, and a swinging sign saying 'Vacancies'.

'Brave,' Jossie said, clearly moved. 'Don't you think?'

I paid off the taxi there and we walked down to the sea, with seagulls squawking overhead and the white little town sleeping to tea-time on its sunny hillside.

'It's pretty,' Jossie said. 'And I see why you left.'

She seemed as content as I to dawdle away the rest of the day. We crossed again in the hovercraft, and made our way slowly northwards, stopping at a pub at dusk for a drink and rubbery pork pie, and arriving finally outside the sprawling pile of Axwood House more than twelve hours after we'd left.

'That car,' Jossie said, pointing with disfavour at an inoffensive Volvo parked ahead, 'belongs to the detestable Lida.'

The light over the front door shone on her disgruntled face. I smiled, and she transferred the disfavour to me.

'It's all right for you. You aren't threatened with her moving into your home.'

'You could move out,' I said mildly.

'Just like that?'

'To my cottage, perhaps.'

'Good grief!'

'You could inspect it,' I said, 'for cleanliness, dry rot and spiders.'

She gave me her most intolerant stare. 'Butler, cook, and housemaids?'

'Six footmen and a lady's maid.'

'I'll come to tea and cucumber sandwiches. I suppose you do have cucumber sandwiches?'

'Of course.'

'Thin, and without crusts?'

'Naturally.'

I had really surprised her, I saw. She didn't know what to answer. It was quite clear, though, that she was not going to fall swooning into my arms. There was a good deal I would have liked to say, but I didn't know how to. Things about caring, and reassurance, and looking ahead.

'Next Sunday,' she said. 'At half past three. For tea.'

'I'll line up the staff.'

She decided to get out of the car, and I went round to open the door for her. Her eyes looked huge.

'Are you serious?' she said.

'Oh yes. It'll be up to you . . . to decide.'

'After tea?'

I shook my head. 'At any time.'

Her expression slowly softened to unaccustomed gentleness. I kissed her, and then kissed her again with conviction.

'I think I'll go in,' she said waveringly, turning away.

'Jossie . . .'

'What?'

I swallowed. Shook my head. 'Come to tea,' I said helplessly. 'Come to tea.'

# CHAPTER SIXTEEN

Monday morning, after another night free of alarms and excursions, I went back to the office with good intentions of actually doing some work. Peter was sulking with Monday morning glooms, Bess had menstrual pains, and Debbie was tearful from a row with the screw-selling fiancé: par for office life as I knew it.

Trevor came into my room looking fatherly and anxious, and seemed reassured to find my appearance less deathly than on Friday.

'You did rest, then, Ro,' he said relievedly.

'I rode in a race and took a girl to the seaside.'

'Good heavens. At any rate, it seems to have done you good. Better than spending your time working.'

'Yes . . .' I said. 'Trevor, I did come into the office on Saturday morning, for a couple of hours.'

His air of worry crept subtly back. He waited for me to go on with the manner of a patient expecting bad news from his doctor: and I felt the most tremendous regret in having to give it to him.

'Denby Crest,' I said.

'Ro . . .' He spread out his hands, palms downwards, in a gesture that spoke of paternal distress at a rebellious son who wouldn't take his senior's word for things.

'I can't help it,' I said. 'I know he's a client, and a friend of yours, but if he's misappropriated fifty thousand pounds and you've condoned it, it concerns us both. It concerns this office, this partnership, and our future. You must see that. We can't just ignore the whole thing and pretend it hasn't happened.'

'Ro, believe me, everything will be all right.'

I shook my head. 'Trevor, you telephone Denby Crest and tell him to come over here today, to discuss what we're going to do.'

'No.'

'Yes,' I said positively. 'I'm not having it, Trevor. I'm half of this firm, and it's not going to do anything illegal.'

'You're uncompromising.' The mixture of sorrow and irritation had intensified. The two emotions, I thought fleetingly, that gave you regrets while you shot the rabbit.

'Get him here at four o'clock,' I said.

'You can't bully him like that.'

'There are worse consequences,' I said. I spoke without emphasis, but he knew quite well that it was a threat.

Irritation won hands down over sorrow. 'Very well, Ro,' he said sourly. 'Very well.'

He went out of my room with none of the sympathetic concern for me with which he had come in, and I felt a lonely sense of loss. I could forgive him anything myself,

I thought in depression, but the law wouldn't. I lived by the law, both by inclination and choice. If my friend broke the law, should I abandon it for his sake: or should I abandon my friend for the sake of the law? In the abstract, there was no difficulty in my mind. In the flesh, I shrank. There was nothing frightfully jolly in being the instrument of distress, ruin, and prosecution. How much easier if the miscreant would confess of his own free will, instead of compelling his friend to denounce him: a sentimental solution, I thought sardonically, which happened only in weepy films. I was afraid that for myself there would be no such easy way out.

Those pessimistic musings were interrupted by a telephone call from Hilary, whose voice, when I answered, sounded full of relief.

'What's the matter?' I said.

'Nothing. I just . . .' She stopped.

'Just what?'

'Just wanted to know you were there, as a matter of fact.'

'Hilary!'

'Sounds stupid, I suppose, now that we both know you *are* there. But I just wanted to be sure. After all, you wouldn't have cast me in the role of rock if you thought you were in no danger at all.'

'Um,' I said, smiling down the telephone. 'Sermons in stones.'

She laughed. 'You just take care of yourself, Ro.'

'Yes, ma'am.'

I put down the receiver, marvelling at her kindness; and almost immediately the bell rang again.

'Roland?'

'Yes, Moira?'

Her sigh came audibly down the wire. 'Thank goodness! I tried all day yesterday to reach you, and there was no reply.'

'I was out all day.'

'Yes, but I didn't know that. I mean, I was imagining all sorts of things, like you being kidnapped again, and all because of me.'

'I'm so sorry.'

'Oh, I don't mind, now that I know you're safe. I've had this terrible picture of you shut up again, and needing someone to rescue you. I've been so worried, because of Binny.'

'What about Binny?'

'I think he's gone really *mad*,' she said. 'Insane. I went over to his stables yesterday morning to see if Tapestry was all right after his race, and he wouldn't let me into the yard. Binny, I mean. All the gates were shut and locked with padlocks and chains. It's insane. He came and stood on the inside of the gate to the yard where Tapestry is, and waved his arms about, and told me to go away. I mean, it's *insane*.'

'It certainly is.'

'I told him he could have caused a terrible accident, tampering with that rein, and he screamed that he hadn't done it, and I couldn't prove it, and anything that happened to you was my fault for insisting that you rode the horse.' She paused for breath. 'He looked so . . . well, so *dangerous.* And I'd never thought of him being dangerous, but just a fool. You'll think I'm silly, but I was quite frightened.'

'I don't think you were silly,' I said truthfully.

'And then it came to me, like a revelation,' she said, 'that it had been Binny who had kidnapped you before, both times, and that he'd done it again, or something even worse . . .'

'Moira . . .'

'Yes, but you didn't *see* him. And then there was no answer to your telephone. I know you'll think I'm silly, but I was so worried.'

'I'm very grateful . . .' I started to say.

'You see, Binny never thought you'd win the Gold Cup,' she said, rushing on. 'And the very second you had, I told him you'd ride Tapestry always from then on, and he was *furious*, absolutely furious. You wouldn't believe. So of course he had you kidnapped at once, so that you'd be out of the way, and I'd *have* to have someone else, and then you escaped, and you were going to ride at Ascot, so he kidnapped you *again*, and he went absolutely berserk when I wouldn't let Tapestry go at Ascot with another jockey. And I made such a fuss in the press that he had to let you out, and so he had to try something else, like cutting the rein, and now I think he's so insane that he doesn't really know what he's doing. I mean, I think he thinks that if he kidnaps you, or kills you even, that I'll *have* to get another jockey for the Whitbread Gold Cup a week next Saturday, and honestly I think he's out of his *senses*, and really awfully dangerous because of that *obsession*, and so you see I really was terribly worried.'

'I do see,' I said. 'And I'm incredibly grateful for your concern.'

'But what are you going to *do*?' she wailed.

'About Binny? Listen, Moira, please listen.'

'Yes,' she said, her voice calming down. 'I'm listening.'

'Do absolutely nothing.'

'But *Roland*,' she protested.

'Listen. I'm sure you are quite right that Binny is in a dangerous mental state, but anything you or I could do would make him worse. Let him cool down. Give him several days. Then send a horsebox with if possible a police escort – and you can get policemen for private jobs like that, you just apply to the local nick, and offer to pay for their time – collect Tapestry, and send him to another trainer.'

'Roland!'

'You can carry loyalty too far,' I said. 'Binny's done marvels with training the horse, I agree, but you owe him nothing. If it weren't for your own strength of mind he'd have manipulated the horse to make money only for himself, as well you know, and your enjoyment would have come nowhere.'

'But about kidnapping you . . .' she began.

'No, Moira,' I said. 'He didn't; it wasn't Binny. I don't doubt he was delighted it was done, but he didn't do it.'

She was astonished. 'He must have.'

'No.'

'But why not?'

'Lots of complicated reasons. But for one thing, he wouldn't have kidnapped me straight after the Gold Cup. He wouldn't have had any need to. If he'd wanted to abduct me to stop me riding Tapestry, he wouldn't have done it until just before the horse's next race, nearly three weeks later.'

'Oh,' she said doubtfully.

'The first abduction was quite elaborate,' I said. 'Binny couldn't possibly have had time to organize it between the Gold Cup and the time I was taken, which was only an hour or so later.'

'Are you sure?'

'Yes, Moira, quite sure. And when he really did try to stop me winning, he did very direct and simple things, not difficult like kidnapping. He offered me a bribe, and cut the rein. Much more in character. He always was a fool, and now he's a dangerous fool, but he isn't a kidnapper.'

'Oh dear,' she said, sounding disappointed. 'And I was so *sure*.'

She cheered up a bit and asked me to ride Tapestry in the Whitbread. I said I'd be delighted, and she deflated my ego by passing on the opinion of a press friend of hers to the effect that Tapestry was one of those horses who liked to be in charge, and an amateur who just sat there doing nothing very much was exactly what suited him best.

Grinning to myself I put down the receiver. The press friend was right; but who cared.

For the rest of the morning I tried to make inroads into the backlog of correspondence, but found it impossible to concentrate. The final fruit of two hours of reading letters and shuffling them around was three heaps marked 'overdue', 'urgent', and 'if you don't get these off today there will be trouble'.

Debbie looked down her pious nose at my inability to apply myself, and primly remarked that I was under-utilizing her capability. Under-utilizing . . . Ye Gods! Where did the gobbledegook jargon come from?

'You mean I'm not giving you enough to do.'

'That's what I said.'

At luncheon I stayed alone in the office and stared into space: and my telephone rang again.

Johnny Frederick, full of news.

'Do you mind if I send you a bill for 'phone calls?' he said. 'I must have spent thirty quid. I've been talking all morning.'

'I'll send you a cheque.'

'OK. Well, mate, pin back your lugholes. That boat you were on was built at Lymington, and she sailed from there after dark on March 17th. She was brand spanking new, and she hadn't completed her trials, and she wasn't registered or named. She was built by a top-notch shipyard called Goldenwave Marine, for a client called Arthur Robinson.'

'Who?'

'Arthur Robinson. That's what he said his name was, anyway. And there was only one slightly unusual thing about Mr Robinson, and that was that he paid for the boat in cash.'

He waited expectantly.

'How much cash?' I said.

'Two hundred thousand pounds.'

'Crikey.'

'Mind you,' Johnny said, 'that's bargain basement stuff for Goldenwave. They do a nice job in mini-liners at upwards of a million, with gold taps, for Arabs.'

'In cash?'

'Near enough, I dare say. Anyway, Arthur Robinson always paid on the nail, in instalments as they came due during the boat-building, but always in your actual folding. Goldenwave Marine wouldn't be interested in knowing whether the cash had had tax paid on it. None of their business.'

'Quite,' I said. 'Go on.'

'That Thursday – March 17th – in the morning, some time, Arthur Robinson rang Goldenwave and said he wanted to take some friends aboard for a party that evening, and would they please see that the water and fuel tanks were topped up, and everything shipshape. Which Goldenwave did.'

'Without question.'

'Of course. You don't argue with two hundred thousand quid. Anyway, the boat was out on a mooring in the deep water passage, so they left her fit for the owner's visit and brought her tender ashore, for him to use when he got there.'

'A black rubber dinghy?'

'I didn't ask. The nightwatchman had been told to expect the party, so he let them in, and helped generally, and saw them off. I got him out of bed this morning to talk to him, and he was none too pleased, but he remembers the evening quite well, because of course the boat sailed off that night and never came back.'

'What did he say?'

'There were two lots of people, he said. One lot came in an old white van, which he didn't think much of for an owner of such a boat. You'd expect a Rolls, he said.' Johnny chuckled. 'The first arrivals, three people, were the crew. They unloaded stores from an estate car and made two trips out to the boat. Then the white van arrived with several more men, and one of those was lying down. They told the nightwatchman he was dead drunk, and that was you, I reckon. Then the first three men and the drunk man went out to the boat, and the other men drove away in the old van and the estate car, and that was that. The nightwatchman thought it a very boring sort of party, and noted the embarkation in his log, and paid no more attention. Next morning, no boat.'

'And no report to the police?'

'The owner had taken his own property, which he'd fully paid for. Goldenwave had expected him to take command of her a week later, anyway, so they made no fuss.'

'You've done absolute marvels,' I said.

'Do you want to hear about Alastair Yardley?'

'There's more?'

'There sure is. He seems to be quite well-known. Several of the bigger shipyards have recommended him to people who want their boats sailed from England, say, to Bermuda, or the Caribbean, and so on, and don't have a regular crew, and also don't want to cross oceans themselves. He signs on his own crew, and pays them himself. He's no crook. Got a good reputation. Tough, though. And he's not cheap. If he agreed to help shanghai you, you can bet Mr Arthur Robinson paid through the nose for the service. But you can ask him yourself, if you like.'

'What do you mean?'

Johnny was justifiably triumphant. 'I struck dead lucky, mate. Mind you, I chased him round six shipyards, but he's in England now to fetch another yacht, and he'll talk to you if you ring him more or less at once.'

'I don't believe it!'

'Here's the number.' He read out the numbers, and I wrote them down. 'Ring him before two o'clock. You can also talk to the chap in charge of Goldenwave, if you like. This is his number. He said he'd help in any way he could.'

'You're fantastic,' I said, stunned to breathlessness by his success.

'We got a real lucky break, mate, because when I took those photographs to Cowes first thing this morning, I asked around everybody, and there was a feller in the third yard I tried who'd worked at Goldenwave last year, and he said it looked like their Golden Sixty Five, so I rang them, and it was the departure date that clinched it.'

'I can't begin to thank you.'

'To tell you the truth, mate, it's been a bit of excitement, and there isn't all that much about, these days. I've enjoyed this morning, and that's a fact.'

'I'll give you a ring. Tell you how things turn out.'

'Great. Can't wait. And see you.'

He disconnected, and with an odd sinking feeling in my stomach I rang the first of the numbers he'd given me. A shipyard. Could I speak to Alastair Yardley? Hang on, said the switchboard. I hung.

'Hullo?'

The familiar voice. Bold, self-assertive, challenging the world.

'It's Roland Britten,' I said.

There was a silence, then he said, 'Yeah,' slowly.

'You said you'd talk to me.'

'Yeah.' He paused. 'Your friend this morning, John Frederick, the boat-builder, he tells me I was sold a pup about you.'

'How do you mean?'

'I was told you were a blackmailer.'

'A *what*?'

'Yeah.' He sighed. 'Well, this guy Arthur Robinson, he said you'd set up his wife in some compromising photographs and were trying to blackmail her, and he wanted you taught a lesson.'

'Oh,' I said blankly. It explained a great deal, I thought.

'Your friend Frederick told me that was all crap. He said I'd been conned. I reckon I was. All the other guys in the yard here know all about you winning that race and going missing. They just told me. Seems it was in all the papers. But I didn't see them, of course.'

'How long,' I said, 'were you supposed to keep me on board?'

'He said to ring him Monday evening, April 4th, and he'd tell me when and where and how to set you loose. But of course, you jumped ship the Tuesday before, and how you got that lever off is a bloody mystery . . . I rang him that night, and he was so bloody angry he couldn't get the words out. So then he said he wouldn't pay me for the job on you, and I said if he didn't he could whistle for his boat, I'd just sail it into some port somewhere and walk away, and he'd have God's own job finding it. So I said he could send me the money to Palma, where I bank, and when I got it I'd do what he wanted, which was to take his boat to Antibes and deliver it to the ship brokers there.'

'Brokers?'

'Yeah. Funny, that. He'd only just bought it. What did he want to sell it for?'

'Well . . .' I said. 'Do you remember his telephone number?'

'No. Threw it away, didn't I, as soon as I was shot of his boat.'

'At Antibes?'

'That's right.'

'Did you meet him?' I asked.

'Yeah. That night at Lymington. He told me not to talk to you, and not to listen, because you'd tell me lies, and not to let you know where we were, and not to leave a mark on you, and to watch out because you were as slippery as an eel.' He paused a second. 'He was right about that, come to think.'

'Do you remember what he looked like?'

'Yeah,' he said, 'what I saw of him; but it was mostly in the dark, out on the quay.' He described Arthur Robinson as I'd expected, and well enough to be conclusive.

'I wasn't intending to go for another week,' he said. 'The weather forecasts were all bad for Biscay, and I'd only been out in her once, in light air, not enough to know how she'd handle in a gale, but he rang Goldenwave that morning and spoke to me, and told me about you, and said gale or no gale he'd make it worth my while if I'd go that evening and take you with me.'

'I hope it was worth it,' I said.

'Yeah,' he said frankly. 'I got paid double.'

I laughed in my throat. 'Er . . .' I said, 'is it possible for a boat just to sail off from England and wander round Mediterranean ports, when it hasn't even got a name? I mean, do you have to pass Customs, and things like that?'

'You can pass Customs if you want to waste a bloody lot of time. Otherwise, unless you tell them, a port doesn't know whether you've come from two miles down the coast, or two thousand. The big ports collect mooring fees, that's all they're interested in. If you drop anchor at somewhere like Formentor, which we did one night with you, no one takes a blind bit of notice. Easy come, easy go, that's what it's like on the sea. Best way to live, I reckon.'

'It sounds marvellous,' I sighed enviously.

'Yeah. Look . . .' he paused a second, 'are you going to set the police on me, or anything? Because I'm off today, on the afternoon tide, and I'm not telling where.'

'No,' I said. 'No police.'

He let his breath out audibly in relief. 'I reckon . . .' He paused. 'Thanks, then. And well, sorry, like.'

I remembered the paperback, and the socks, and the soap and I had no quarrel with him.

From Goldenwave Marine, ten minutes later, I learned a good many background facts about big boats in general and Arthur Robinson in particular.

Goldenwave had four more Golden Sixty Fives on the stocks at the moment, all commissioned by private customers, and Arthur Robinson had been one of a stream. Their Golden Sixty Five had been a successful design, they were pleased and proud to say, and their standard of ship-building was respected the world over.

End of commercial.

I replaced the receiver gratefully. Sat, thinking, chewing bits off my fingernails. Decided, without joy, to take a slightly imprudent course.

Debbie, Peter, Bess and Trevor came back, and the place filled up with tap-tap and bustle. Mr Wells arrived for his appointment twenty minutes before the due time, reminding me of the psychiatrists'-eye-view of patients: if they're early, they're anxious, if they're late, they're aggressive, and if they're on time, they're pathological. I often thought the psychiatrists didn't understand about trains, buses and traffic flow, but in this case there wasn't much doubt about the anxiety. Mr Wells' hair, manner and eyes were all out of control.

'I rang the people you sent the rubber cheque to,' I said. 'They were a bit sticky, but they've agreed not to prosecute if you take care of them after the inevitable Receiving Order.'

'I what?'

'Pay them later,' I said. Jargon . . . I did it myself.

'Oh.'

'The order of paying,' I said, 'will be first the Inland Revenue, who will collect tax in full, and will also charge interest for every day overdue.'

'But I haven't anything to pay them with.'

'Did you sell your car, as we agreed you should?'

He nodded, but wouldn't meet my eyes.

'What have you done with the money?' I said.

'Nothing.'

'Pay it to the Revenue, then, on account.'

He looked away evasively, and I sighed at his folly. 'What have you done with the money?' I repeated.

He wouldn't tell me, and I concluded that he had been following the illegal path of many an imminent bankrupt, selling off his goods and banking the proceeds distantly under a false name, so that when the bailiffs came there wouldn't be much left. I gave him some good advice which I knew he wouldn't take. The suicidal hysterics of his earlier visit had settled into resentment against everyone pressing him, including me. He listened with a mulish stubbornness which I'd seen often enough before, and all he would positively agree to was not to write any more cheques.

By three-thirty I'd had enough of Mr Wells, and he of me.

'You need a good solicitor,' I said. 'He'll tell you the same as me, but maybe you'll listen.'

'It was a solicitor who gave me your name,' he said glumly.

'Who's your solicitor?'

'Fellow called Denby Crest.'

It was a small community, I thought. Touching, overlapping, a patchwork fabric. When the familiar names kept turning up, things were normal.

As it happened, Trevor was in the outer office when I showed Mr Wells to the door. I introduced them, explaining that Denby had sent him to see us. Trevor cast a benign eye, which would have been jaundiced had he known the Wells state of dickiness, and made affable small talk. Mr Wells took in Trevor's substantial air, seniority, and general impression of worldliness, and I practically saw the thought cross his mind that perhaps he had consulted the wrong partner.

And perhaps, I thought cynically, he had.

When he'd gone, Trevor looked at me sombrely.

'Come into my office,' he sighed.

# CHAPTER SEVENTEEN

I sat in one of the clients' chairs, with Trevor magisterially behind his desk. His manner was somewhere between unease and cajoling, as if he were not quite sure of his ground.

'Denby said he'd be here by four.'

'Good.'

'But Ro . . . he'll explain. He'll satisfy you, I'm sure. I think I'll leave it to him to explain, and then you'll see . . . that there's nothing for us to worry about.'

He raised an unconvincing smile and rippled his fingertips on his blotter. I looked at the familiar, friendly figure, and wished with all my heart that things were not as they were.

Denby came ten minutes early, which would have gratified the psychiatrists, and he was wound up like a tight spring, as well he might be. His backbone was ramrod stiff inside the short plump frame, the moustache bristling on the forward jutting mouth, the irritated air plainer than ever.

He didn't shake hands with me: merely nodded.

Trevor came round his desk to offer a chair, a politeness I thought excessive.

'Well, Ro,' Denby said crossly. 'I hear you have reservations about my certificate.'

'That's so.'

'What, exactly?'

'Well,' I said. 'To be exact . . . fifty thousand pounds missing from the clients' deposit account.'

'Rubbish.'

I sighed. 'You transferred money belonging to three separate clients from the clients' deposit to the clients' current account,' I said. 'You then drew five cheques from the current account, made out to yourself, in varying sums, over a period of six weeks, three to four months ago. Those cheques add up to fifty thousand pounds exactly.'

'But I've repaid the money. If you'd've looked more carefully you'd have seen the counter credits on the bank statement.' He was irritated. Impatient.

'I couldn't make out where those credits had come from,' I said, 'so I asked the bank to send a duplicate statement. It came this morning.'

Denby sat as if turned to stone.

'The duplicate statement,' I said regretfully, 'shows no record of the money having been repaid. The bank statement you gave us was . . . well . . . a forgery.'

Time ticked by.

Trevor looked unhappy. Denby revised his position.

'I've only *borrowed* the money,' he said. There was

still no regret, and no real fear. 'It's perfectly safe. It will be repaid very shortly. You have my word for it.'

'Um . . .' I said. 'Your word isn't enough.'

'Really, Ro, this is ridiculous. If I say it will be repaid, it will be repaid. Surely you know me well enough for that?'

'If you mean,' I said, 'would I have thought you a thief, then no, I wouldn't.'

'I'm not a thief,' he said angrily. 'I told you, I borrowed the money. A temporary expediency. It's unfortunate that . . . as things turned out . . . I was not able to repay it before the certificate became due. But as I explained to Trevor, it is only a matter of a few weeks, at the most.'

'The clients' money,' I said reasonably, 'is not entrusted to you so that you can use it for a private loan to yourself.'

'We all know that,' Denby said snappily, in a teaching-grandmother-to-suck-eggs manner. My grandmother, I reflected fleetingly, had never sucked an egg in her life.

'You're fifty thousand short,' I said, 'and Trevor's condoned it, and neither of you seems to realize you'll be out of business if it comes to light.'

They both looked at me as if I were a child.

'But there's no need for it to come to light, Ro,' Trevor said. 'Denby will repay the money soon, and all will be well. Like I told you.'

'It isn't ethical,' I said.

'Don't be so pompous, Ro,' Trevor said, at his most fatherly, shaking his head with sorrow.

'Why did you take the money?' I asked Denby. 'What for?'

Denby looked across enquiringly at Trevor, who nodded.

'You'll have to tell him everything, Denby. He's very persistent. Better tell him, then he'll understand, and we can clear the whole thing up.'

Denby complied with bad grace. 'I had a chance,' he said, 'of buying a small block of flats. Brand new. Not finished. Builder in difficulties, wanted a quick sale, that sort of thing. Flats were going cheap, of course. So I bought them. Too good to miss. Done that sort of deal before, of course. Not a fool, you know. Knew what I was doing, and all that.'

'Your own conveyancer?' I said.

'What? Oh yes.' He nodded. 'Well, then, I needed a bit more extra capital to finance the deal. Perfectly safe. Good flats. Nothing wrong with them.'

'But they haven't sold?' I said.

'Takes time. Market's sluggish in the winter. But they're all sold now, subject to contracts. Formalities, mortgages, all that. Takes time.'

'Mm.' I said. 'How many flats in the block, and where is it?'

'Eight flats, small, of course. At Newquay, Cornwall.'

'Have you seen them?' I said.

'Of course.'

'Do you mind if I do?' I said. 'And will you give me the

addresses of all the people who are buying the flats, and tell me how much each is paying?'

Denby bristled. 'Are you saying you don't believe me?'

'I'm an auditor,' I said. 'I don't believe. I check.'

'You can take my word for it.'

I shook my head. 'You sent us a forged bank statement. I can't take your word for anything.'

There was a silence.

'If those flats exist, and if you repay that money this week, I'll keep quiet,' I said. 'I'll want confirmation by letter from the bank. The money must be there by Friday, and the letter here by Saturday. Otherwise, no deal.'

'I can't get the money this week,' Denby said peevishly.

'Borrow it from a loan shark.'

'But that's ridiculous. The interest I would have to pay would wipe out all my profit.'

Serve you right, I thought unfeelingly. I said, 'Unless the clients' money is back in the bank by Friday, the Law Society will have to be told.'

'Ro!' Trevor protested.

'However much you try to wrap it up as "unfortunate" and "expedient",' I said, 'the fact remains that all three of us know that what Denby has done is a criminal offence. I'm not putting my name to it as a partner of this firm. If the money is not repaid by Friday, I'll write a letter explaining that in the light of fresh knowledge we wish to cancel the certificate just issued.'

'But Denby would be struck off!' Trevor said.

They both looked as if the stark realities of life were something that only happened to other people.

'Unfriendly,' Denby said angrily. 'Unnecessarily aggressive, that's what you are, Ro. Righteous. Unbending.'

'All those, I dare say,' I said.

'It's no good, I suppose, suggesting I . . . er . . . cut you in?'

Trevor made a quick horrified gesture, trying to stop him.

'Denby, Denby,' he said, distressed. 'You'll never bribe him. For God's sake have some sense. If you really want to antagonize Ro, you offer him a bribe.'

Denby scowled at me and got explosively to his feet.

'All right,' he said bitterly. 'I'll get the money by Friday. And don't ever expect any favours from me for the rest of your life.'

He strode furiously out of the office leaving eddies of disturbed air and longer trails of disturbed friendship. Turbulent wake, I thought. Churning and destructive, overturning everything it touched.

'Are you satisfied, Ro?' Trevor said gently, in sorrow.

I sat without answering.

I felt like a man on a high diving board, awaiting the moment of strength. Ahead, the plunge. Behind, the quiet way down. The choice, within me.

I could walk away, I thought. Pretend I didn't know what I knew. Settle for silence, friendship and peace.

Refrain from bringing distress and disgrace and dreary unhappiness.

My friend or the law. To which did I belong? To the law or my own pleasure . . .

O great God almighty.

I swallowed with a dry mouth.

'Trevor,' I said, 'do you know Arthur Robinson?'

There was no fun, no fun at all, in looking into the face of ultimate disaster.

The blood slowly drained from Trevor's skin, leaving his eyes like great dark smudges.

'I'll get you some brandy,' I said.

'Ro . . .'

'Wait.'

I fetched him a tumbler, from his entertaining cupboard, heavy with alcohol, light on soda.

'Drink it,' I said with compassion. 'I'm afraid I've given you a shock.'

'How . . .' His mouth quivered suddenly, and he put the glass to his lips to hide it. He drank slowly, and took the glass a few inches away: a present help in trouble. 'How much . . . do you know?' he said.

'Why I was abducted. Who did it. Who owns the boat. Who sailed her. Where she is now. How much she cost. And where the money comes from.'

'My God . . . My God . . .' His hands shook.

'I want to talk to him,' I said. 'To Arthur Robinson.'

A faint flash of something like hope shone in his eyes.

'Do you know . . . his other name?'

I told him what it was. The spark of light died to a pebble-like dullness. He clattered the glass against his teeth.

'I want you to telephone,' I said. 'Tell him I know. Tell him I want to talk. Tell him, if he has any ideas of doing anything but what I ask, I'll go straight from this office to the police. I want to talk to him tonight.'

'But Ro, knowing you . . .' He sounded despairing. 'You'll go to the police anyway.'

'Tomorrow morning,' I said.

He stared at me for a long, long time. Then with a heavy half-groaning sigh, he stretched out his hand to the telephone.

We went to Trevor's house. Better for talking, he suggested, than the office.

'Your wife?' I said.

'She's staying with her sister, tonight. She often does.'

We drove in two cars, and judging by the daze of his expression Trevor saw nothing consciously of the road for the whole four miles.

His big house sat opulently in the late afternoon sunshine, nineteen-twenties respectability in every brick. Acres of diamond-shaped leaded window panes, black paint, a wide portico with corkscrew pillars, wisteria creeping here and there, lots of gables with beams stuck on for effect.

Trevor unlocked the front door and led the way into dead inside air which smelled of old coffee and furniture polish. Parquet flooring in the roomy hall, and rugs.

'Come into the snug,' he said, walking ahead.

The snug was a longish room which lay between the more formal sitting and dining rooms, looking outwards to the pillared loggia, with the lawn beyond it. To Trevor the snug was psychologically as well as geographically the heart of the house, the place where he most felt a host to his businessmen friends.

There was the bar, built in, where he liked to stand, genially pouring drinks. Several dark red leather armchairs. A small, sturdy dining table, with four leather-seated dining chairs. A large television. Bookshelves. An open brick fireplace, with a leather screen. A palm in a brass pot. More Stubbs prints. Several small chair-side tables. A leaf-patterned carpet. Heavy red velvet curtains. Red lampshades. On winter evenings, with the fire lit, curtains drawn, and lights glowing warmly, snug, in spite of its size, described it.

Trevor switched on the lights, and although it was full daylight, drew the curtains. Then he made straight for the bar.

'Do you want a drink?' he said.

I shook my head. He fixed himself a brandy of twice the size I'd given him in the office.

'I can't believe any of this is happening,' he said.

He took his filled glass and slumped down in one of the red leather armchairs, staring into space. I hitched a hip on to the table, which like so much in that house was protected by a sheet of plate glass. We both waited, neither of us enjoying our thoughts. We waited nearly an hour.

Nothing violent, I told myself numbly, would happen in that genteel house. Violence occurred in back alleys and dark corners. Not in a well-to-do sitting-room on a Monday evening. I felt the flutter of apprehension in every nerve and thought about eyes black with the lust for revenge.

A car drew up outside. A door slammed. There were footsteps outside on the gravel. Footsteps crossing the threshold, coming through the open front door, treading across the parquet, coming to the door of the snug. Stopping there.

'Trevor?' he said.

Trevor looked up dully. He waved a hand towards me, where I sat to one side, masked by the open door.

He pushed the door wider. Stepped into the room.

He held a shotgun; balanced over his forearm, butt under the armpit, twin barrels pointing to the floor.

I took a deep steadying breath, and looked into his firm, familiar face.

Jossie's father. William Finch.

*

'Shooting me,' I said, 'won't solve anything. I've left photostats and all facts with a friend.'

'If I shoot your foot off, you'll ride no more races.'

His voice already vibrated with the smashing hate: and this time I saw it not from across a courtroom thick with policemen, but from ten feet at the wrong end of a gun.

Trevor made jerky calming gestures with his hands.

'William . . . surely you see. Shooting Ro would be disastrous. Irretrievably disastrous.'

'The situation is already irretrievable.' His voice was thick, roughened and deepened by the tension in throat and neck. 'This little creep has seen to that.'

'Well,' I said, and heard the tension in my own voice, 'I didn't make you steal.'

It wasn't the best of remarks. Did nothing to reduce the critical mass: and William Finch was like a nuclear reactor with the rods too far out already. The barrels of the gun swung up into his hands and pointed at my loins.

'William, for God's sake,' Trevor said urgently, climbing ponderously out of his armchair. 'Use your reason. If he says killing him would do no good, you must believe him. He'd never have risked coming here if it wasn't true.'

Finch vibrated with fury through all his elegant height. The conflict between hatred and common sense was plain in the bunching muscles along his jaw and the claw-like curve of his fingers. There was a fearful moment when I was certain that the blood-lust urge to avenge himself would blot out all fear of consequences, and I thought disconnectedly that I wouldn't feel it . . . you never felt the worst of wounds in the first few seconds. It was only after, if you lived, that the tide came in. I wouldn't know . . . I wouldn't feel it, and I might not even know . . .

He swung violently away from me and thrust the shotgun into Trevor's arms.

'Take it. Take it,' he said through his teeth. 'I don't trust myself.'

I could feel the tremors down my legs, and the prickling of sweat over half my body. He hadn't killed me at the very start, when it would have been effective, and it was all very well risking he wouldn't do it now when he'd nothing to gain. It had come a good deal too close.

I leaned my behind weakly against the table, and worked some saliva into my mouth. Tried to set things out in a dry-as-dust manner, as if we were discussing a small point of policy.

'Look . . .' It came out half-strangled. I cleared my throat and tried again. 'Tomorrow I will have to telephone to New York, to talk to the Nantucket family. Specifically, to talk to one of the directors on the board of their family empire; the director to whom Trevor sends the annual Axwood audited accounts.'

Trevor took the shotgun and stowed it away out of sight behind the ornate bar. William Finch stood in the centre of the room with unreleased energy quivering through all his frame. I watched his hands clench and unclench, and his legs move inside his trousers, as if wanting to stride about.

'What will you tell them, then?' he said fiercely. 'What?'

'That you've been . . . er . . . defrauding the Nantucket family business during the past financial year.'

For the first time some of the heat went out of him.

'During the past . . .' He stopped.

'I can't tell,' I said, 'about earlier years. I didn't do the audits. I've never seen the books, and they are not in our office. They have to be kept for three years, of course, so I expect you have them.'

There was a lengthy silence.

'I'm afraid,' I said, 'that the Nantucket director will tell me to go at once to the police. If it was old Naylor Nantucket who was involved, it might be different. He might just have hushed everything up, for your sake. But this new generation, they don't know you. They're hard-nosed businessmen who disapprove of the stable anyway. They never come near the place. They do look upon it as a business proposition, though, and they pay you a good salary to manage it, and they undoubtedly regard any profits as being theirs. However mildly I put it, and I'm not looking forward to it at all, they are going to have to know that for this financial year their profits have gone to you.'

My deadpan approach began to have its results. Trevor poured two drinks and thrust one into William

Finch's hand. He looked at it unseeingly and after a few moments put it down on the bar.

'And Trevor?' he said.

'I'll have to tell the Nantucket director,' I said regretfully, 'that the auditor they appointed has helped to rip them off.'

'Ro,' Trevor said, protesting, I gathered, at the slang expression more than the truth of it.

'Those Axwood books are a work of fiction,' I said to him. 'Cash books, ledgers, invoices . . . all ingenious lies. William would never have got away with such a wholesale fraud without your help. Without, anyway . . .' I said, modifying it slightly, 'without you knowing, and turning a blind eye.'

'And raking off a bloody big cut,' Finch said violently, making sure he took his friend down with him.

Trevor made a gesture of distaste, but it had to be right. Trevor had a hearty appetite for money, and would never have taken such a risk without the gain.

'These books look all right at first sight,' I said. 'They would have satisfied an outside auditor, if the Nantuckets had wanted a check from a London firm, or one in New York. But as for Trevor, and as for me, living here . . .' I shook my head. 'Axwood Stables have paid thousands to forage merchants who didn't receive the money, to saddlers who don't exist, to maintenance men, electricians and plumbers who did no work. The invoices are there, all nicely printed, but the transactions they refer to are thin air. The cash went straight to William Finch.'

Some of the slowly evaporating heat returned fast to Finch's manner, and I thought it wiser not to catalogue aloud all the rest of the list of frauds.

He'd charged the Nantuckets wages for several more lads than he'd employed: a dodge hard to pin down, as the stable-lad population floated from yard to yard.

He'd charged the Nantucket company more than nine thousand pounds for the rent of extra loose boxes and keep for horses by a local farmer, when I knew he had paid only a fraction of that, as the farmer was one of my clients.

He'd charged much more for shares in jockeys' retainers than the jockeys had received; and had invented travelling expenses to the races for horses which according to the form books had never left the yard.

He had pocketed staggering sums from a bloodstock agent in the form of commission on the sales of Nantucket horses to outside owners: fifty thousand or so in the past year, the agent had confirmed casually on the telephone, not knowing that Finch had no right to it.

I imagined Finch had also been sending enlarged bills to all the non-Nantucket owners, getting them to make out their cheques to him personally rather than to the company, and then diverting a slice to himself before paying a reasonable sum into the business.

The Nantuckets were far away, and uninterested. All I guessed they'd wanted had been a profit on the bottom line, and he'd given them just enough to keep them quiet.

As a final irony, he'd charged the Nantuckets six thousand pounds for auditors' fees, and nowhere in our books was there a trace of six thousand pounds from Axwood Stables. Trevor might have had his half, though, on the quiet: it was enough to make you laugh.

A long list of varied frauds. Much harder to detect than one large one. Adding up, though, to an average rake-off for Finch of over two thousand pounds a week. Untaxed.

Year in, year out.

Assisted by his auditor.

Assisted also, it was certain, by the ever-sick secretary, Sandy, though with or without her knowledge I didn't know. If she was ill as often as all that, and away from her post, maybe she didn't know. Or maybe the knowledge made her ill. But as in most big frauds, the paperwork had to be done well, and in the Axwood Stables case, there had been a great deal of it done well.

Ninety to a hundred horses. Well trained, well raced. A big stable with a huge weekly turnover. A top trainer. A trainer, I thought, who didn't own his own stable, who was paid only a salary, and a highly taxed one at that, and who faced having no capital to live on in old age, in a time of inflation. A man in his fifties, an employee, seeing into a future without enough money. An enforced retirement. No house of his own. No power. A man with money at present passing daily through his hands like a river in flood.

All racehorse trainers were entrepreneurs, with

organizing minds. Most were in business on their own account, and had no absent company to defraud. If William Finch had been his own master, I doubted that he would ever have thought of embezzlement. With his abilities, in the normal course of things, he would have had no need.

Need. Ability. Opportunity. I wondered how big a step it had been to dishonesty. To crime.

Probably not very big. A pay-packet for a non-existent stable lad, for a little extra regular cash. The cost of an unordered ton of hay.

Small steps, ingenious swindles, multiplying and swelling, leading to a huge swathing highway.

'Trevor,' I said mildly, 'how long ago did you spot William's . . . irregularities?'

Trevor looked at me sorrowfully, and I half-smiled.

'You saw them . . . some of the first ones . . . in the books,' I said, 'and you told him it wouldn't do.'

'Of course.'

'You suggested,' I said, 'that if he really put his mind to it you would both be a great deal better off.'

Finch reacted strongly with a violent gesture of his whole arm, but Trevor's air of sorrow merely intensified.

'Just like Connaught Powys,' I said. 'I tried hard to believe that you genuinely hadn't seen how he was rigging that computer, but I reckon . . . I have to face it that you were doing it together.'

'Ro . . .' he said sadly.

'Anyway,' I said to Finch, 'you sent the books in for

the annual audit, and after all this time neither you nor Trevor are particularly nervous. Trevor and I have been chronically behind with our work for ages, so I guess he just locked them in his cupboard, to see to as soon as he could. He would know I wouldn't look at your books. I never had, in six years; and I had too many clients of my own. And then, when Trevor was away on his holidays, the unforeseen happened. On Gold Cup day, through your letterbox, and mine, came the summons for you to appear before the Tax Commissioners a fortnight later.'

He stared at me with furious dark eyes, his strong, elegant figure tall and straight like a great stag at bay against an impudent hound. Round the edges of the curtains the daylight was fading to dark. Inside, electric lights shone smoothly on civilized man.

I smiled twistedly. 'I sent you a message. Don't worry, I said, Trevor's on holiday, but I'll apply for a postponement, and make a start on the books myself. I went straight off to ride in the Gold Cup and never gave it another thought. But you, to you, that message meant ruin. Degradation, prosecution, probably prison.'

A quiver ran through him. Muscles moved along his jaw.

'I imagine,' I said, 'that you thought the simplest thing would be to get the books back; but they were locked in Trevor's cupboard, and only he and I have keys. And in any case I would have thought it very suspicious, if, with the Commissioners breathing down our necks, you refused to let me see the books. Especially suspicious if the office had been broken into and those papers stolen. Anything along those lines would have led to investigation, and disaster. So as you couldn't keep the books from *me*, you decided to keep *me* from the books. You had the means to hand. A new boat, nearly ready to sail. You simply arranged for it to go early, and take me with it. If you could keep me away from the office until Trevor returned, all would be well.'

'This is all nonsense,' he said stiffly.

'Don't be silly. It's past denying. Trevor was due back in the office on Monday, April 4th, which would give him three days to apply for a postponement to the Commissioners. A perfectly safe margin. Trevor would then do the Axwood books as usual, and I would be set free, never knowing why I'd been abducted.'

Trevor buried his face in his brandy, which made me thirsty.

'If you've any mineral water, or tonic, Trevor, I'd like some,' I said.

'Give him nothing,' Finch said, the pent-up violence still thick in his voice.

Trevor made fluttery motions with his hands, but after a moment, with apologetic glances at Finch's tightened mouth, he fetched a tumbler and poured into it a bottle of tonic water.

'Ro . . .' he said, giving me the glass. 'My dear chap . . .'

'My dear *shit*,' Finch said.

I drank the fizzy quinine water gratefully.

'I bust things up by getting home a few days early,' I

said. 'I suppose you were frantic. Enough, anyway, to send the kidnapping squads to my cottage to pick me up again. And when they didn't manage it, you sent someone else.' I drank bubbles and tasted gall. 'Next day, you sent your daughter Jossie.'

'She knows nothing, Ro,' Trevor said.

'Shut up,' Finch said. 'She strung him along by the nose.'

'Maybe she did,' I said. 'It was supposed to be only for a day or two. Trevor was due back that Sunday. But I told you, while you were busy filling my time by showing me round your yard, that Trevor's car had broken down in France, and he wouldn't be back until Wednesday or Thursday. And I assured you again that you didn't have to worry, I had already applied for the postponement, and I would start the audit myself. The whole situation was back to square one, and the outlook was as deadly as ever.'

Finch glared, denying nothing.

'You offered me a day at the races with Jossie,' I said. 'And a ride in the novice hurdle. I'm a fool about accepting rides. Never know when to say no. You must have known that Notebook was unable to jump properly. You must have hoped when you flew off to the Grand National, that I'd fall with him and break a leg.'

'Your neck,' he said vindictively, with no vestige of a joke.

Trevor glanced at his face and away again, as if embarrassed by so much raw emotion.

'Your men must have been standing by in case I survived undamaged, which of course I did,' I said. 'They followed us to the pub where I had dinner with Jossie, and then to the motel where I planned to stay. Your second attempt at abduction was more successful, in that I couldn't get out. And when Trevor was safely back, you rang Scotland Yard, and the police set me free. From one point of view all your efforts had produced precisely the desired result, because I had not in fact by then seen one page or one entry of the Axwood books.'

I thought back, and amended that statement. 'I hadn't seen any except the petty cash book, which you gave me yourself. And that, I imagine, was your own private accurate record, and not the one re-written and padded for the sake of the audit. It was left in my car with all my other belongings, and I took it to the office when I went back last Friday. It was still there on Saturday. It was Saturday morning that I got out the Axwood books and studied them, and made the photocopies.'

'But why, Ro?' Trevor asked frustratedly. 'What made you think . . . Why did you think of William?'

'The urgency,' I said. 'The ruthless haste, and the time factors. I believed, you see, when I was on the boat, that I'd been kidnapped for revenge. Any auditor who's been the downfall of embezzlers would think that, if he'd found himself in such a position. Especially if he's been directly threatened, face to face, as I had, by Connaught Powys, and earlier by Ownslow and Glitberg, and later also by others. But when I escaped and came home, there was hardly any interval before I was in danger again. Hunted, really. And caught. So the second time, last week, in the van, I began to think . . . that perhaps it wasn't revenge, but *prevention*, and after that, it was a matter of deduction, elimination, boring things, on the whole. But I had hours . . .' I swallowed involuntarily, remembering. 'I had hours in which to think of all the possible people, and work it out. So then, on Saturday morning, I went to the office, when I had the place to myself, and checked.'

Finch turned on Trevor, looking for a whipping boy. 'Why the hell did you keep those books where he could see them? Why didn't you lock them in the bloody safe?'

'I've a key to the safe,' I said dryly.

'Christ!' He raised his hands in a violent, exploding, useless gesture. 'Why didn't you take them home?'

'I never take books home,' Trevor said. 'And you told me that Ro was going to the races Saturday, and out with Jossie Sunday, so we'd nothing to worry about. And anyway, neither of us dreamt that he knew . . . or guessed.'

Finch swung his desperate face in my direction.

'What's your price?' he said. 'How much?'

I didn't answer. Trevor said protestingly, 'William . . .'

'He must want something,' Finch said. 'Why is he telling us all this instead of going straight to the police? Because he wants a deal, that's why.'

'Not money,' I said.

Finch continued to look like a bolt of lightning

trapped in bones and flesh, but he didn't pursue the subject. He knew, as he'd always known, that it wasn't a question of money.

'Where did you get the men who abducted me?' I said.

'You know so much. You can bloody well find out.'

Rent-a-thug, I thought cynically. Someone, somewhere, knew how to hire some bully boys. The police could find out, I thought, if they wanted to. I wouldn't bother.

'The second time,' I said. 'Did you tell them not to leave a mark on me?'

'So what?'

'Did you?' I said.

'I didn't want the police taking any serious interest,' he said. 'No marks. No stealing. Made you a minor case.'

So the fists and boots, I thought, had been a spot of private enterprise. Payment for the general run-around I'd given the troops. Not orders from above. I supposed I was glad, in a sour sort of way.

He'd chosen the warehouse, I guessed, because it couldn't have been easy to find a safer place in a hurry: and because he thought it would divert my attention even more strongly towards Ownslow and Glitberg, and away from any thought of himself.

Trevor said, 'Well . . . What . . . what are we going to do now?' but no one answered, because there were wheels outside on the gravel. Car doors slammed.

'Did you leave the front door open?' Trevor said.

Finch didn't need to answer. He had. Several feet

tramped straight in, crossed the hall, and made unerringly for the snug.

'Here we are then,' said a powerful voice. 'Let's get on with it.'

The light of triumph shone in Finch's face, and he smiled with grateful welcome at the newcomers crowding into the room.

Glitberg. Ownslow. Connaught Powys.

'Got the rat cornered, then?' Powys said.

# CHAPTER EIGHTEEN

I had an everlasting picture of the five of them, in that freezing moment. I straightened to my feet, and my heart thumped, and I looked at them one by one.

Connaught Powys in his city suit, as Establishment as a pillar of the government. Coffee-coloured tan on his fleshy face. Smooth hair; pale hands. A large man aiming to throw his weight about, and enjoying it.

Glitberg with his mean eyes and the repulsive four-inch frill of white whiskers, which stood out sideways from his cheeks like a ruff. Little pink lips, and a smirk.

Ownslow the bull, with his bald crown and long straggling blond hair. He'd shut the door of the snug and leaned against it, and folded his arms with massive satisfaction.

William Finch, tall and distinguished, vibrating in the centre of the room in a tangle of fear, and anger, and unpleasant pleasure.

Trevor, silver-haired, worldly, come to dust. Sitting apprehensively in his armchair, facing his future with more sorrow than horror. The only one of them who showed the slightest sign of realizing that it was they who had got themselves into trouble, not I.

Embezzlers were not normally men of violence. They robbed on paper, not with their fists. They might hate and threaten, but actual physical assault wasn't natural to them. I looked bleakly at the five faces and thought again of the nuclear effect of critical mass. Small separate amounts of radio-active matter could release harnessable energy. If small amounts got together into a larger mass, they exploded.

'Why did you come?' Trevor said.

'Finchy rang and told us he'd be here,' Powys said, jerking his head in my direction. 'Never get another opportunity like it, will we? Seeing as you and Finchy will be out of circulation, for a bit.'

Finch shook his head fiercely: but I reckoned there were different sorts of circulation, and it would be a very long time before he was back on a racetrack. I wouldn't have wanted to face the ruin before him: the crash from such a height.

Glitberg said, 'Four years locked in a cell. Four sodding years, because of him.'

'Don't bellyache,' I said. 'Four years in jail for a million pounds is a damned good bargain. You offer it around, you'd get a lot of takers.'

'Prison is dehumanizing,' Powys said. 'They treat you worse than animals.'

'Don't make me cry,' I said. 'You chose the way that led there. And all of you have got what you wanted.

Money, money, money. So run away and play with it.' Maybe I spoke with too much heat, but nothing was going to defuse the developing bomb.

Anger that I'd let myself in for such a mess was a stab in the mind. I simply hadn't thought of Finch summoning reinforcements. He'd had no need of it: it had been merely spite. I'd believed I could manage Finch and Trevor with reasonable safety, and here all of a sudden was a whole new battle.

'Trevor,' I said, flatly, 'don't forget the photostats I left with a friend.'

'What friend?' Finch said, gaining belligerence from his supporters.

'Barclays Bank,' I said.

Finch was furious, but he couldn't prove it wasn't true, and even he must have seen that any serious attempt at wringing out a different answer might cost them more time in the clink.

I had hoped originally to make a bargain with Finch, but it was no longer possible. I thought merely, at that point, of getting through whatever was going to happen with some semblance of grace. A doubtful proposition, it seemed to me.

'How much does he know?' Ownslow demanded of Trevor.

'Enough . . .' Trevor said. 'Everything.'

'Bloody hell.'

'How did he find out?' Glitberg demanded.

'Because William took him on his boat,' Trevor said.

'A mistake,' Powys said. 'That was a mistake, Finchy. He came sniffing round us in London, asking about boats. Like I told you.'

'You chain dogs up,' Finch said.

'But not in a floating kennel, Finchy. Not this bastard here with his bloody quick eyes. You should have kept him away from your boat.'

'I don't see that it matters,' Trevor said. 'Like he said, we've all got our money.'

'And what if he tells?' Ownslow demanded.

'Oh, he'll tell,' Trevor said with certainty. 'And of course there will be trouble. Questions and enquiries and a lot of fuss. But in the end, if we're careful, we should keep the cash.'

'Should isn't enough,' Powys said fiercely.

'Nothing's certain,' Trevor said.

'One thing's certain,' Ownslow said. 'This creep's going to get his come-uppance.'

All five of the faces turned my way together, and in each one, even in Trevor's, I read the same intent.

'That's what we came for,' Powys said.

'Four bloody years,' Ownslow said. 'And the sneers my kids suffered.' He pushed off the door and uncrossed his arms.

Glitberg said, 'Judges looking down their bloody noses.'

They all, quite slowly, came nearer.

It was uncanny, and frightening. The forming of a pack.

Behind me there was the table, and behind that, solid wall. They were between me and the windows, and between me and the door.

'Don't leave any marks,' Powys said. 'If he goes to the police it'll be his word against ours, and if he's nothing to show that can't do much.' To me, directly, he said, 'We'll have a bloody good alibi, I'll tell you that.'

The odds looked appalling. I made a sudden thrusting jump to one side, to dodge the menacing advance, outflank the cohorts, scramble for the door.

I got precisely nowhere. Two strides, no more. Their hands clutched me from every direction, dragging me back, their bodies pushing against me with their collective weight. It was as if my attempt to escape had triggered them off. They were determined, heavy, and grunting. I struggled with flooding fury to disentangle myself, and I might as well have wrestled with an octopus.

They lifted me up bodily and sat me on the end of the table. Three of them held me there with hands like clamps.

Finch pulled open a drawer in the side of the table, and threw out a checked red and white table cloth, which floated across the room and fell on a chair. Under the cloth, several big square napkins. Red and white checks. Tapestry's racing colours. Ridiculous thought at such a moment.

Finch and Connaught Powys each rolled a napkin into a shape like a bandage and knotted it round one of my ankles. They tied my ankles to the legs of the table. They pulled my jacket off. They rolled and tied a red and white napkin round each of my wrists, pulling the knots tight and leaving cheerful bright loose ends like streamers.

They did it fast.

All of the faces were flushed, and the eyes fuzzy, in the fulfilment of lust. Glitberg and Ownslow, one on each side, pushed me down flat on my back. Finch and Connaught Powys pulled my arms over my head and tied the napkins on my wrists to the other two legs of the table. My resistance made them rougher.

The table was, I supposed, about two feet by four. Long enough to reach from my knees to the top of my head. Hard, covered with glass, uncomfortable.

They stood back to admire their handiwork. All breathing heavily from my useless fight. All overweight, out of condition, ripe to drop dead from coronaries at any moment. They went on living.

'Now what?' said Ownslow, considering. He went down on his knees and took off my shoes.

'Nothing,' Trevor said. 'That's enough.'

The pack instinct had died out of him fastest. He turned away, refusing to meet my eyes.

'Enough!' Glitberg said. 'We've done nothing yet.'

Powys eyed me assessingly from head to foot, and maybe he saw just what they had done.

'Yes,' he said slowly. 'That's enough.'

Ownslow said 'Here!' furiously, and Glitberg said,

'Not on your life.' Powys ignored them and turned to Finch.

'He's yours,' he said. 'But if I were you I'd just leave him here.'

'*Leave* him?'

'You've got better things to do than fool around with him. You don't want to leave marks on him, and I'm telling you, the way we've tied him will be enough.'

William Finch thought about it, and nodded, and came half way back to cold sense. He stepped closer until he stood near my ribs. He stared down, eyes full of the familiar hate.

'I hope you're satisfied,' he said.

He spat in my face.

Powys, Glitberg and Ownslow thought it a marvellous idea. They did it in turn, as disgustingly as they could.

Not Trevor. He looked on uncomfortably and made small useless gestures of protest with his hands.

I could hardly see for slime. It felt horrible, and I couldn't get it off.

'All right,' Powys said. 'That's it, then. You push off now, Finchy, and you get packed, Trevor, and then we'll all leave.'

'Here!' Ownslow said again, protestingly.

'Do you want an alibi, or don't you?' Powys said. 'You got to make some effort. Be seen by a few squares. Help the lies along.'

Ownslow gave in with a bad grace, and contented

himself with making sure that none of the table napkins had worked loose. Which they hadn't.

Finch had gone from my diminished sight and also, it appeared, from my life. A car started in the drive, crunched on the gravel, and faded away.

Trevor went out of the room and presently returned carrying a suitcase. In the interval Ownslow sniggered, Glitberg jeered, and Powys tested the amount that I could move my arms. Half an inch, at the most.

'You won't get out of that,' he said. He shook my elbow and watched the results. 'I reckon this'll make us even.' He turned as Trevor came back. 'Are all doors locked?'

'All except the front one,' Trevor said.

'Right. Then let's be off.'

'But what about *him?*' Trevor said. 'We can't just leave him like that.'

'Can't we? Why not?'

'But . . .' Trevor said: and fell silent.

'Someone will find him tomorrow,' Powys said. 'A cleaner, or something. Do you have a cleaner?'

'Yes,' Trevor said doubtfully. 'But she doesn't come in on Tuesdays. My wife will be back though.'

'There you are, then.'

'All right.' He hesitated. 'My wife keeps some money in the kitchen. I'll just fetch it.'

'Right.'

Trevor went on his errand and came back. He stood near me, looking worried.

'Ro . . .'

'Come on,' said Powys impatiently. 'He's ruined you, like he ruined us. You owe him bloody nothing.'

He shepherded them out of the door; Trevor unhappy, Glitberg sneering, Ownslow unassuaged. Powys looked back from the doorway, his own face, what I could see of it, full of smug satisfaction.

'I'll think of you,' he said. 'All night.'

He pulled the door towards him, to shut it, and switched off the light.

Human bodies were not designed to remain for hours in one position. Even in sleep, they regularly shifted. Joints bent and unbent, muscles contracted and relaxed.

No human body was designed to lie as I was lying, with constant strain already running up through legs, stomach, chest, shoulders and arms. Within five minutes, while they were still there, it had become in any normal way intolerable. One would not have stayed in that attitude from choice.

When they had gone, I simply could not visualize the time ahead. My imagination short-circuited. Blanked out. What did one do if one couldn't bear something, and had to?

The worst of the spit slid slowly off my face, but the rest remained, sticky and itching. I blinked my eyes wide open in the dark and thought of being at home in my own quiet bed, as I'd hoped to be that night.

I realized that I was having a surprising amount of difficulty in breathing. One took breathing so much for granted; but the mechanics weren't all that simple. The muscles between the ribs pulled the ribcage out and upwards, allowing air to rush down to the lungs. It wasn't, so to speak, the air going in which expanded the chest, but the expansion of the chest which drew in the air. With the ribcage pulled continuously up, the normal amount of muscle movement was much curtailed.

I still wore a collar and tie. I would choke, I thought.

The other bit that breathed for you was the diaphragm, a nice hefty floor of muscle between the heart-lung cavity and the lower lot of guts. Thank God for diaphragms, I thought. Long may they reign. Mine chugged away, doing its best.

If I passed the night in delirium, I thought, it would be a good idea. If I'd studied Yoga . . . mind out of body. Too late for that. I was always too late. Never prepared.

Stabs of strain afflicted both my shoulders. Needles. Swords.

Think of something else.

Boats. Think of boats. Big expensive boats, built to high standards in top British boat yards, sailing away out of Britain to ship-brokers in Antibes and Antigua.

Huge floating assets in negotiable form. None of the usual bureaucratic trouble about transferring money abroad in huge amounts. No dollar premiums to worry about, or other such hurdles set up by grasping governments. Just put your money in fibreglass and ropes and sails, and float away on it on the tide.

The man at Goldenwave had told me they never lacked for orders. Boats, he said, didn't deteriorate like aeroplanes or cars. Put a quarter of a million into a boat, and it would most likely increase in value, as years went by. Sell the boat, bank the money, and hey presto, all nicely, tidily, and legally done.

There were frightful protests from my arms and legs. I couldn't move them in any way more than an inch: could give them no respite. It really was, I thought, an absolutely bloody revenge.

No use reflecting that it was I who had stirred up Powys and Ownslow and Glitberg. Poke a rattlesnake with a stick, don't be surprised if he bites you. I'd gone to find out if it was they who'd abducted me, and found out instead what they'd done with all the missing money.

Paid for boats. The mention of boats had produced the menace, not the mention of abduction. Boats paid for by the taxpayers, the electronics firm, and the Nantuckets of New York. Gone with the four winds. Exchanged for a pile of nice strong currency, lying somewhere in a foreign bank, waiting for the owners to stroll along and collect.

Trevor linked them all. Maybe the boats had originally been his idea. I hadn't thought of William Finch knowing Connaught Powys: certainly not as well as he clearly did. But through Trevor, along the track from embezzlement to ship building . . . along the way, they had met.

The pains in my arms and legs intensified, and there was a great shaft of soreness up my chest.

I thought: I don't know how to face this. I don't know how. It isn't possible.

Trevor, I thought. Surely Trevor wouldn't have left me like this . . . not like this . . . if he had realized. Trevor, who had been so distressed at my dishevelled appearance in the police station, who as far as I could see had really cared about my health.

Ye Gods, I thought, I'd go gladly back to the sail locker . . . to the van . . . to almost anywhere one could think of.

Some of my muscles were trembling. Would the fibres simply collapse? I wondered. Would the muscles just tear apart; the ligaments disconnect from the bones? Oh for God's sake, I told myself, you've got enough to worry about, without that. Think of something cheerful.

I couldn't, off-hand. Even cheerful subjects like Tapestry were no good. I couldn't see me being able to ride in the Whitbread Gold Cup.

Minutes dragged and telescoped, stretching to hours. The various separate pains gradually coalesced into an all pervading fire. Thought became fragmentary, and then, I reckon, more or less stopped.

The unbearable was there, inside, savage and consuming. Unbearable . . . there was no such word.

By morning I'd gone a long way into an extreme land I hadn't known existed. A different dimension, where the memory of ordinary pain was a laugh.

An internal place; a heavy core. The external world had retreated. I no longer felt as if I were any particular shape: had no picture of hands or feet, or where they were. Everything was crimson and dark.

I existed as a mass. Unified. A single lump of matter, of a weight and fire like the centre of the earth.

There was nothing else. No thought. Just feeling, and eternity.

A noise dragged me back.

People talking. Voices in the house.

I saw that daylight had returned and was trickling in round the edge of the curtains. I tried to call out, and could not.

Footsteps crossed and recrossed the hall, and at last, at last, someone opened the door, and switched on the light.

Two women came in. I stared at them, and they stared at me: on both sides with disbelief.

They were Hilary Pinlock, and Jossie.

Hilary cut through the red checked table napkins with a small pair of scissors from her handbag.

I tried to sit up and behave with sangfroid, but my stretched muscles wouldn't respond to directions. I ended somehow with my face against her chest and my throat heaving with unstoppable half-stifled groans.

'It's all right, Ro. It's all right, my dear, my dear.'

Her thin arms held me close and tight, rocking me

gently, taking into herself the impossible pain, suffering for me like a mother. Mother, sister, lover, child . . . a woman who crossed the categories and left them blurred.

I had a mouthful of blouse button and was comforted to my soul.

She put an arm round my waist and more or less carried me to the nearest chair. Jossie stood looking on, her face filled with a greater shock than finding me there.

'Do you realize,' she said, 'that Dad's gone?'

I didn't feel like saying much.

'Did you hear?' Jossie said. Her voice was tight, unfriendly. 'Dad's gone. Walked out. Left all the horses. Do you hear? He's cleared half the papers out of the office and burned them in the incinerator, and this lady says it is because my father is an embezzler, and you . . . you are going to give him away to the Nantuckets, and the police.'

The big eyes were hard. 'And Trevor, too. Trevor. I've known him all my life. How could you? And you *knew* . . . you knew on Sunday . . . all day . . . what you were going to do. You took me out, and you knew you were going to ruin all our lives. I think you're hateful.'

Hilary took two strides, gripped her by the shoulders, and positively shook her.

'Stop it, you silly girl. Open your silly eyes. He did all this for you.'

Jossie tore herself free. 'What do you mean?' she demanded.

'He didn't want your father to go to prison. Because he's your father. He's sent others there, but he didn't want it to happen to your father, or to Trevor King. So he warned them, and gave them time to destroy things. Evidence. Paper and records.' She glanced back at me. 'He told me on Saturday what he planned . . . to tell your father how much he knew, and to offer him a bargain. Time, enough time, if he would destroy his tracks and go, in a way which would cause you least pain. Time to go before the police arrived to confiscate his passport. Time to arrange his life as best he could. And they made him pay for the time he gave them. He paid for every second of it . . .' She gestured in frustrated disgust towards the table and the cut pieces of cloth, ' . . . in *agony.*'

'Hilary,' I protested.

There never had been any stopping Hilary Pinlock in full flight. She said fiercely to Jossie, 'He can put up with a lot, but I reckon it's too much to have you reviling him for what he's suffered for your sake. So you just get some sense into your little bird-brain, and beg his pardon.'

I helplessly shook my head. Jossie stood with her mouth open in shattered shock, and then she looked at the table, and discarded the thought.

'Dad would never have done that,' she said.

'There were five of them,' I said wearily. 'People do

things in gangs which they would never have done on their own.'

She looked at me with shadowed eyes. Then she turned abruptly on her heel and walked out of the room.

'She's terribly upset,' Hilary said, making allowances.

'Yes.'

'Are you all right?'

'No.'

She made a face. 'I'll get you something. They must at least have aspirins in this house.'

'Tell me first,' I said, 'how you got here.'

'Oh. I was worried. I rang your cottage all evening. Late into the night. And again this morning, early. I had a feeling . . . I didn't think it would hurt if I came over to check, so I drove to your cottage . . . but of course you weren't there. I saw your neighbour, Mrs Morris, and she said you hadn't been home all night. So then I went to your office. They were in a tizzy because some time between last night and this morning your partner had taken away a great many papers, and neither of you had turned up for work.'

'What time . . .' I said.

'About half past nine, when I went to the office.' She looked at her watch. 'It's a quarter to eleven, now.'

Fourteen hours, I thought numbly. It must have been at least fourteen hours, that I'd been lying there.

'Well, I drove to Finch's house,' she said. 'I had a bit of

trouble finding the way, and when I got there, everything was in a shambles. There was a girl secretary weeping all over the place. People asking what was going on . . . and your girl Jossie in a dumbstruck state. I asked her if she'd seen you. I said I thought you could be in real trouble. I asked her where Trevor King lived. I made her come with me, to show me the way. I tried to tell her what her father had been doing, and how he'd abducted you, but she didn't want to believe it.'

'No.'

'So then we arrived here, and found you.'

'How did you get in?'

'The back door was wide open.'

'Wide . . .?'

I had a sudden picture of Trevor going out to the kitchen, saying it was to fetch some money. To open the door. To give me a tiny chance. Poor Trevor.

'That package I gave you,' I said. 'With all the photostats. When you get home, will you burn it?'

'If that's what you want.'

'Mm.'

Jossie came back and sprawled in a red armchair, all angular legs.

'Sorry,' she said abruptly.

'So am I.'

'You did help him,' she said.

Hilary said, 'Do good to those who despitefully use you.'

I slid my eyes her way. 'That's enough of that.'

'What are you talking about?' Jossie demanded.

Hilary shook her head with a smile and went on an aspirin hunt. Butazolidin, I imagined, would do more good. Things were better now I was sitting in a chair, but a long old way from right.

'He left me a letter,' Jossie said. 'More or less the same as yours.'

'How do you mean?'

'Dear Jossie, Sorry, Love, Dad.'

'Oh.'

'He said he was going to France . . .' She broke off, and stared ahead of her, her face full of misery. 'Life's going to be unutterably bloody, isn't it,' she said, 'for a long time to come?'

'Mm.'

'What am I going to do?' The question was a rhetorical wail, but I answered it.

'I did want to warn you,' I said. 'But I couldn't . . . before I'd talked to your father. I meant it, though, about you coming to live in the cottage. If you thought . . . that you could.'

'Ro . . .' Her voice was little more than a breath.

I sat and ached, and thought in depression about telephoning the Nantuckets, and the chaos I'd have to deal with in the office.

Jossie turned her head towards me and gave me a long inspection.

'You look spineless,' she said. Her voice was halfway back in spirit to the old healthy mockery; shaky, but doing its best. 'And I'll tell you something else.' She paused and swallowed.

'When Dad went, he left *me* behind, but he took the detestable Lida with him.'

There was enough, in that, for the future.

## PRAISE FOR HÅKAN NESSER

### THE INSPECTOR AND SILENCE

'The atmosphere of the small town, the mysterious fringes of the forest full of aspens and blueberries, are evocatively drawn . . . The clarity of Nesser's vision, the inner problems of good and evil with which Van Veeteren struggles, recall the films of Bergman'

*Independent*

'Satisfying novel from a rising Swedish star . . . Van Veeteren [the detective], disengaged, thinking of retirement and wonderfully enigmatic, makes an enjoyable change from all those fictional policemen who persist in taking their work home with disastrous consequences . . . an intense read'

*Guardian Review*

'Nesser works the slow pace skilfully and Van Veeteren is an appealing companion'

*Metro* Crime Books of the Year

## WOMAN WITH A BIRTHMARK

'Håkan Nesser is in the front rank of Swedish crime writers . . . A novel with superior plot and characters'
*The Times*

'It's set to become Nesser's breakthrough novel in this country, and he is being favourably compared with Henning Mankell and Stieg Larsson'
*Sunday Times*

'Nesser is one of the best of the Swedish crime writers . . . a literate writing style, a brooding atmosphere and a plot that never wallows in the purely salacious . . . what might have been a routine serial-killer novel becomes a tense and subtle morality tale'
*Mail on Sunday*

## THE MIND'S EYE

'Van Veeteren is a terrific character, and the courtroom scenes that begin this novel are cracking'
*Daily Telegraph*

'Håkan Nesser's Chief Inspector Van Veeteren has earned his place among the great Swedish detectives with a series of intriguing investigations . . . This is Van Veeteren at his quirkiest and most engaging'
*Seven* magazine, *Sunday Telegraph*

'A psychological thriller in a class of its own . . . This stunning novel by one of Sweden's foremost crime writers might have been written as a script for Alfred Hitchcock'
*Sunday Times*

## THE RETURN

'Nesser made a strong impression with *Borkmann's Point*, the first of his novels published into English. *The Return* is just as tense and clever'

Marcel Berlins, *The Times*

'Nesser's insight into his main characters and gently humorous narrative raise his otherwise conventional police procedural to a higher level'

*Sunday Telegraph*

'This is splendid stuff: Scandinavian crime writing that is so rivetingly written it makes most contemporary crime fare – Nordic or otherwise – seem rather thin gruel'

Barry Forshaw, *Waterstone's Books Quarterly*

## BORKMANN'S POINT

'An absorbing tale with an unexpected ending'
***Sunday Telegraph***

'The novel's prime asset is the mordant clarity of Nesser's voice. Its understatement is a pleasure in itself, as investigations pause for Van Veeteren to finish his beer'
***Times Literary Supplement***

'Van Veeteren is destined for a place amongst the great European detectives'
**Colin Dexter**